THE TIME OF THE STRANGERS

Claire's head flew back. She gripped the arms of the chair.

She saw the future.

Michael! He was standing still. His hazel eyes stared at her, but his face was otherwise utterly expressionless, a blank.

Her son-in-law, this Michael-in-the-future, said nothing. Then, the crinkles around his eyes deepened and he smiled.

Then Michael changed. His face, the face of the son-in-law she loved as dearly as a son, was gone. She was no longer seeing Michael. She was looking at . . .

I am Death!

Death was not a skeleton brandishing a scythe. He rode no ghostly steed. Death occupied Michael Louden's body, but Death's head . . .

Death's head was hellfire, a lunatic pinwheel of pulsing red. It was the writhing, black-scarlet flame of a great infernal candle. It was an evil blazing ruby, the color of the blood of victims, martyrs, innocents.

Though he had no eyes, Death's gaze fell upon her. Though he had no mouth, Death spoke to her:

Soon! My time is soon!

THE
STRANGERS

MORT CASTLE

LEISURE BOOKS ∞ **NEW YORK CITY**

For Jane, my wife, with gratitude and love

A LEISURE BOOK

Published by

Dorchester Publishing Co., Inc.
6 East 39th Street
New York, NY 10016

Printed in the United States of America

Every two seconds a serious crime is committed somewhere in America, yet only one criminal in five is arrested, and, of those, fewer than half are punished.

"America's Battle With Crime"
WGN Television, Chicago, Illinois
March 15, 1982

Once I talked to the head of a great institution in America for the education of criminal children, and was told about a very interesting experience. They have two categories of children. The majority of them, when they come to the institution, feel ever so much better, they develop very nicely and normally and they eventually grow out of whatever their original evil was. The other category, the minority . . . are the born criminals whom you cannot change. They are normal when they do wrong.

Dr. Carl G. Jung
Analytical Psychology, Its Theory and Practice

PROLOGUE

It was a quarter to one in the morning. The Buick Regal's headlights picked out the beachball-sized puffs of summer fog that hovered over the winding road skirting the forest preserve. After a sweltering day, the temperature had descended to the mid-70s, but because of the humidity, the automobile's air-conditioning was running on high, the steady *whoosh* masking the sound of the engine.

Without turning his head to look at his companion, the middle-aged man behind the wheel said, "Did you find the day splendidly dull?"

"Dull? A new products exhibition?" The younger man's words were flat, polished smooth by sarcasm. "Please, we got to see the latest, up-to-the-minute advances in janitorial supplies. Floor finishes, deodorant blocks for urinals, corn brooms . . . That's what I call exciting."

The driver laughed metallically, precise snippets of sound. "You have marvelous enthusiasm."

"Well gee, Boss, golly! I'm a guy who's got so damned much to be enthused about. I have my slice of the American pie. A wonderful wife, two adorable kids, and a tract home. Then to add to my abundant good fortune, there's what *you've* done for me, the raise

7

and promotion. National sales manager, that always was my goal, and I guarantee you, I'll give 110 percent to Superior Chemical. I sincerely mean that sincerely."

The driver nodded. The light of the dashboard's instruments turned his silver hair green and seemed to define a flesh-masked angularity beneath his round, good-natured face. He said, "It's people like you who make this country what it is."

"No. . . It's people like *us.*"

Both men laughed quietly, and then the younger slipped down a bit in the seat, stretching his legs. He loosened his tie and leaned back his head. The man's sandy hair had begun the receding trek upward on his brow and there were suggestions of crows-feet-to-come at the corners of his eyes, but he looked no older than his thirty-five years. His face was blandly American, hinting at no identifiable ethnic background. He was not quite handsome and nowhere near homely. If you'd met him once, twice, you were more likely to recall his name than his appearance.

With no trace of humor, he said, "Does the waiting ever get to you?"

"Of course," the driver answered. "Often— and I have been waiting considerably longer than you."

"Sure, I know, but sometimes I get so my nerves are sticking out a half-inch. You wait and you wait and you think there'll never be an end to it . . ."

"There will be."

" . . . And you want to rip off the mask, let them all see the *real* smile behind the fake

8

one . . ."

"And become a newspaper headline for three days?" interrupted the driver. "And then a jail cell? One of their mental asylums? Death?"

The younger man sighed. "Yes, that's what happens."

"No." The correction was quiet but forceful. "That's what happens to those who are not clever or cunning—*and* to those who can no longer be patient."

"So we wait."

"Indeed, and we ease our tensions and frustrations as best we can." The driver's full lips twitched in a smile. "You might spend more time performing the conjugal act with your wonderful wife, perhaps create still another adorable child."

" 'No more Adorables,' says the Wonderful. She has an itch to develop a new identity. She's tuning to the liberated woman concept a mere ten years after the rest of the nation."

"We do have companionship," the driver said. "And of course we're always ready to take advantage of whatever amusements fate and circumstance send our way . . ." His voice trailed off as he lifted his foot from the gas. The Buick slowed and the younger man sat up, alert. The driver said, "Seems to be a problem."

Ahead, just before a sharp curve, a Ford with a raised hood was on the left hand shoulder, a man peering at the engine, turning his head when the Buick's headlights spotlighted him.

The Buick stopped on the opposite

shoulder. The driver did not switch off the motor. He searched under the front seat with his hands, bringing out a heavy, rubber-insulated, night watchman's flashlight. "If you'll open the glove compartment . . ."

The younger man did. He took out the skinning knife, the handle wrapped with black tape, the five inch blade double-edged and needle-pointed. "Very nice," he said.

"You hold onto it," the driver said. "You seem in need of this sort of activity to lessen your present boredom."

"Yes." The word hissed, mingling with the invasion of night sounds, the hushings and tickings and tiny whistles from the surrounding woods that came when the older man opened the door. He said, "Let's see what we can do to help a stranded traveler on the road of life."

Fred Harley considered himself a lucky guy. Okay, the Ford decided to pull a no-go, but here he was, stuck for no more than three minutes and someone was stopping. A lonely road, this hour, yeah, it was a lucky break. He wouldn't have to go tromping off, trying to find a telephone or to flag down a passing car. No, you could tell the mosquitoes to forget it; Fred Harley would keep all his blood tonight.

He watched the two men get out of the Buick. Simultaneously, he noted that they were white and well dressed. Fred didn't think he was what you'd call a prejudiced person, but the US of A wasn't exactly a paradise of racial harmony. Had the two men been black, Fred would have been uneasy.

And had Fred Harley been a man with a particular psychic gift, he would have been more than uneasy. He would have been dry-mouthed, adrenalin-quaking, clammy-necked terrified.

A clairvoyant with the ability to see auras —see in a way that is only marginally related to the perceptive powers of the human eye— and who understood what those auras signified might have bolted and gone frantically running into the forest, praying to get away, to hide, to find safety.

There was a fire-red nimbus about the head of each man, a halo invisible to those who did not possess psychic sight. The aura was a scarlet pulsing, expanding, contracting as though it breathed, like a specimen seen under a microscope in high school biology, its scientific name forgotten but its image remembered forever in nightmares. The auras of the younger man and the older man marked them for what they were and who they were, identified them to those who could see and understand.

They were Strangers.

But the only light that Fred Harley saw came from Mallory heavy-duty batteries. The beam that linked him to the two men lessened in length.

The Strangers drew closer.

Just as Fred Harley was saying, "Thanks, guys," the flashlight blinded him. Blinking, he saw only the after-image, an oozing, yellow circle.

The barrel of the heavy flashlight smashed

into his face. He heard the dry snap and wet rush. The sound came from inside his own skull and he knew he'd lost teeth, that his nose was broken.

Reeling, he tried to say something that came out, "Gwuff!" and then he was struck again, a blow to the side of the head that dropped him to his hands and knees.

He thought, *Hey, this doesn't make sense!*

The younger man straddled Fred Harley's shoulders, squatting like a child mounting for piggyback. He entwined his fingers in Fred's hair and yanked his head up and back.

Fred Harley thought, *They are killing me and there's no reason, no reason . . .*

At that moment of complete understanding, the younger man cut Fred Harley's throat.

ONE

"WHAT SAY to a cold brew?" Brad Zeller shouted over to the roar of lawnmower.

It was late afternoon, Sunday. Michael Louden was on the final strip of lawn near the house. He nodded, signalled thumb-up. "Be with you in a couple of minutes," he called to his neighbor on the other side of the four-foot high redwood fence.

Finishing up, Michael was chafed by the perspiration-clammy waistband of his khaki shorts; his T shirt was sopping. Flecks of grass were sweat-stuck to his forearms and calves, annoying little itches.

He switched off the engine, wiped his brow with the back of his hand, and pushed the mower toward the garage. With summer nearing an end, the five-year-old lawnmower was still holding up, though it was one nasty bastard to start. He hoped it would make it through the season and he wouldn't have to buy another until next year. More sensible to get a new one, though, than to try to repair something really on its way out and—uh-huh! he was a sensible guy.

Or maybe he wouldn't be concerned about the lawn at all next year. Michael Louden permitted himself a small smile at the thought.

In the garden that lay alongside the garage, Beth was on her hands and knees. She'd long ago triumphed in the war against weeds and insects and animal pests, but she remained vigilant, guarding against a guerilla invasion by so much as a bold dandelion. She loved her zinnias and marigolds, her phlox and white campion, *her* flowers. The garden was special to her. It made her not merely a housewife and mother but a gardener.

At the corner of the flower plot, Michael stood with the heels of his hands pressed to the steel of the mower's handle. He watched the small woman in the cut-off jeans and yellow terrycloth halter. He could see it happen: *One strong yank on the rope and this time the cranky sonofabitch kicks right over. Beth's arm-waving panic—the sheer unbelief—the knife-sharp cry of "No!" The flowers destroyed, a rushing spray of multicolored confetti . . .*

"That looks real good," Michael said approvingly.

"Thanks," Beth said. "Next year, I'll have irises right up against the garage. You have to be careful, they can take over the place, but they're so hardy nothing can kill them."

Michael laughed teasingly. "Oh, you thought I was talking about the flowers. Sure, they look fine, but I meant that cute little butt you've got stuck up in the air."

Over her shoulder, Beth grinned at him. Curled tendrils of brown hair, cut short at the start of summer, had escaped from the blue kerchief tied Aunt Jemima style on her head. There was a Charlie Chaplin dirt smudge mustache beneath her sparingly freckled nose. "You are silly!" she said.

"Yuh-yuh-yup," he stammered; his Porky-Pig-Happy-Happy-Imbecile impersonation. He stepped away from the mower and held out his arms. "I'm a wild and crazy guy. I can't come trekking in there without trampling your daffydillies, so get over and kiss me, kiddo!"

"I'm all dirty!"

"I'm dirtier, so get over here before I get mad and don't let you."

He thought there was something of both happiness and desperation in her rush to him; she might have been a toddler welcoming Daddy home after a week's business trip. He swooped her up, kissed her solidly, and pinched a handful of her rump. As he so often did, he complimented himself on choosing her, this miniature he had decided on for "wife" in the collection of people and things he'd acquired to disguise himself. Beth Louden, *nee* Wynkoop, 102 pounds distributed pleasingly over a shade less than five feet of height, the ultra-compact version of the standard model that one selects as wife and mother. Beth was perfect for his needs. And she'd given him two perfect children, completing the image of the middle class, nose-to-the-grindstone, more-or-less contented surburban husband he had to appear to be.

Beth's words came as though a plea for understanding. "I *do* love you."

"Jeez, that works out! I love you, too!"

She pushed away from him, tiny hands on his chest. He wondered if she thought those hands could hold him back, if there were any way on earth or in hell she figured she could do that if he decided he would *not* be held back, not any longer.

"Michael, I . . ." Beth's brown eyes, so round they made Michael think of paintings of waifs in the alleged "Art" sections of department stores, were troubled. "I've wanted . . . For awhile, I've really needed to talk with you. Sometimes it's not easy to talk, I guess."

"What is it?" he said, resting his hands on her bare shoulders. "This is me, remember? You can say anything at all."

Beth looked down. She licked her lips. "Michael, I'm worried about us."

"Us?" he said. Then he let amazement drift out of his tone to be replaced by a note of concern. "I'm not following, honey . . ."

Beth shrugged and he put his arms at his sides. He shaped his face—eyebrows, drawn-in upper lip—into a silent message that read: *I do want to understand.*

Beth said, "There's a distance, Michael, a distance between us. It's there, I feel it, and it worries me."

"I . . ." He praised himself for the pause. He considered tossing in a bit of head-scratching and rejected it—too hayseed. Robert DeNiro an actor? Shit, he could sign up for lessons from Michael Louden!

Michael said seriously, "I guess I do know what you mean. I've felt that, too, in the times I slow down enough to realize what the heck is going on." He made his shoulders sag. "A lot of it's probably me, you know. Ever since Vern gave me the promotion, I've had

16

nothing but business on my mind. That's yanked me out of the real world, the world we've made together."

Beth said, "I know there are pressures on you."

Pressures? he thought. What the hell could she know about the daily pressures of a Stranger? He said, "I guess, but I'm sorry I've been so out of it, so far away from you. I don't mean to be, okay?"

"Sure," Beth said, with "not-so-sure" tentativeness.

"Honest to God, Beth," he went on, "you're the one person in my life I always want to feel close to."

He tried a hopeful-mischievous smile. "I have an idea about how we can maybe bridge that distance between us. With Marcy and Kim not coming home from camp until tomorrow, we've got the house empty all tonight yet, just you and me. We can . . . get close anywhere we please. The kitchen even, or the rec room or"—he made the smile grow —"right on the living room carpet. We'll be romatic! I'll build a fire . . ."

He had her laughing now. No problem, no problem at all, he thought.

"A fire? You goof! It's so hot . . ."

"So we'll have the fire and turn the air-conditioning all the way up!"

Beth's laughter ended abruptly. She said softly, "Oh, I do want to be with you, Michael, really *with* you."

"And that's what tonight is all about," he said. "Now, I'll tell you, I've promised Zeller

I'd come over for a beer . . ."

"He does get lonely," Beth said, implying that Zeller wasn't the only one who did.

" . . . And as soon as I get back," Michael continued, "I'll bicycle over to Kentucky Fried. We'll gobble up chicken, then we can take a shower—you and me." He leered. "How 'bout it, kiddo? You soap mine and I'll soap yours, huh? Then we've got the whole night ahead, and . . ."

"All right," Beth said. She smiled. "Yes, that sounds fine."

"Then that's what we do."

Okay, he thought, as he wheeled the lawnmower to the garage, she was mollified for the time being. He knew, though, it wouldn't last. He understood the humdrum rhythms and monotonous cadences, the mundane dialogues and typical scenes of his all-too-usual marriage. Tonight, he would give her a royal screwing—maybe a couple—and she'd interpret sex as a re-establishing of temporarily lost intimacy. And that would make her want to talk—a "serious discussion" about "where we are and where we're going" as individuals, as a man and wife, as a family. And she'd probably belabor him with her typically indecisive jibber-jabber about whether she ought to go back to college. Maybe he'd be able to hold her off, though, if he really gave her a pounding tonight, wore her down and out so that sleeping was all she had on her excuse for a mind.

Beth called to him as he stepped into the garage. She wanted the hedge clipper so she could get the shrubs lining the driveway.

The two and a half car garage sheltered his Ford LTD and Beth's Chevette Scooter, his tools and work bench, her gardening supplies, the family's bicycles, all the "should haves" of the suburbs. Michael was certain *his* garage was no different than any of the other garages in Park Estates. It was the garage of a model citizen in a model community.

Leaving the garage, he handed Beth the wooden handled clippers. He teasingly pinched the outlined nipple of a small firm breast. "Back *real* soon," he promised, and went next door.

Sitting in the lawnchair, Michael didn't even have time to cross his legs before Zeller was in and back out of the sliding glass door to the kitchen with two cans of Old Milwaukee. At the corner of the patio, Dusty lay in the shade of the gas grill. The black and white, fuzzy, terrier - and - God - knows - what opened his eyes and peered at Michael. The dog apparently decided it wasn't worth the effort to struggle up on his arthritic legs to welcome him with the customary sniff.

"Hell of a hot one," Brad said, raising his beer can in a toast to whatever. He sat on a chair on the other side of a TV snack tray on which was a muttering portable radio, the volume low, tuned to WBBM, Chicago's all-news station.

Zeller was, Michael saw, already two sheets to the wind. Brad spent his afternoons drinking beer; the evenings, harder stuff. "Yeah," Michael said, "it's a hot one for certain.''

Zeller said, ''Course it's not so much the heat, it's the humidity.''

''That's right,'' Michael said. He raised an eyebrow as though struck by an important thought. ''I bet some people never think about that, but you hit the nail right on the head. You can handle the heat okay, but the humidity . . . When it's muggy-like, it seems hotter than it is, you know what I mean, and when you've got that, it's not really so much the heat as it is the humidity.''

Brad Zeller gave him a slow, alcoholic blink. ''I guess,'' he said, his voice questioning.

Careful, Michael cautioned himself. Boozy Brad was no moron. Oh, he was no smarter than the rest of them, the ''normals'' who had lengthy discussions about gas mileage, prostate operations, and overpaid sports stars, but drunkard or no, if you dumped enough shit at old Zeller's feet, eventually he'd notice the stink.

''So how's it going, pal?'' Micheal asked.

''What's there to say?'' Zeller replied, and then he began saying it, the familiar litany of complaint, laments, and regrets. Dusty's adenoidal snore provided the sound track for Brad Zeller's life story. Michael inserted ''uh-huh'' and ''That's right'' and ''I know what you mean'' when appropriate.

Brad had retired from office products sales four years ago at age sixty-two—and no, he didn't want to get out but the bastards made it clear they wanted him out. Eight months later, his wife of forty years was dead of cancer, at which point Brad Zeller retired from life. Joanie, the Zellers' only child, was a goddamned mess, a member of a wacko cult in California, living on natural foods and cosmic bliss. She didn't even come home for her mother's funeral—"the snot nose"—and for sure she didn't give a rat's fuzzy ass about her old man; she was a forty-two year old, self-centered, spoiled brat.

"You're a lucky guy, Michael," Zeller said. "Your kids are little sweethearts. Marcy and Kim might be the only kids in the country who know how to say 'Please' and 'Thank you.'"

Michael's smile was fittingly modest and proud. "They are pretty good girls," he admitted, "but they're no angels. They do goof sometimes but, all in all, I'm not griping."

Michael raised his beer and sipped. "Ready for a fresh?" Zeller said. Zeller was; he was rising to get another. Michael said he didn't need another beer yet.

No, too much alcohol and you could lose control. The act always had to be perfect— always—never giving them the least scent of suspicion. And that's why it was so damnably difficult, the unending pretense that was a minute by infinite minute denial of yourself as you were!

Zeller returned from his beer run, plopped down, snapping the top of the Old Milwaukee. Dusty slowly got up. Stiff-legged, he lurched over to Brad, sitting by his chair, pink tongue lolling.

Brad scratched the dog's head. Dusty shut

his eyes with pleasure and burped.

Suddenly, Brad turned his head to squint at the portable radio. He quickly thumbed up the volume. "You hear about this?" he asked.

" . . . Glenvale Road. Police are investigating . . . We'll be back with coverage of the . . ."

Zeller dialed the radio down to a ticking chatter. He shook his head. "Glenvale Road, that's only eight, ten miles from here."

"I know," Michael said, "but what happened? I didn't catch it."

"Guy got killed last night. Just awful. Murdered him, cut his throat. Didn't even steal anything is what the cops say."

"Jeez," Michael said. "You don't figure stuff like that can happen out here in the south suburbs. Maybe it was a mob thing. Drugs, maybe."

"Cops don't think so, is what I hear," Zeller said. "It was just a guy. Here or anywhere else, it's getting so no one's safe. World's not what it used to be, everything is nuts . . ."

Brad Zeller began his editorial on the problems of modern society. Straining, Dusty hoisted his hindquarters, waddled over to Michael, a nose on the shin demanding attention. Michael petted him.

Zeller's monologue came to a sheepishly grinned conclusion. "Damn it, I'm boring you. You get old, that's your hobby. You bore people."

"No way, Brad," Michael insisted. "I always enjoy talking with you. You know that."

"Ah," Zeller waved a hand, "I get a little batty, no one to talk to, so I unload on you,

Michael. Tell you, I've thought about selling, moving to a retirement condo, but this house, I've got memories here. I don't want to wait to die surrounded by a bunch of strangers."

Michael covered his smile with his hand. "Sure," he said.

Zeller pointed to Dusty. "I talk to that little guy a lot."

"Dusty is a good dog," Michael said. "I like dogs, always have. They have sense. A dog likes a guy, that's someone you know you can trust."

"Dogs have that kind of instinct," Zeller said.

Michael tickled behind Dusty's ear. He *did* like dogs. A friendly dog's eyes held a look of stupidly blissful trust until the very instant you killed it.

"You know, maybe sometime soon I'll go to the humane society and pick up a surprise pooch for the kids," Michael said. He chuckled. "Be a better pet for 'em than those ugly guinea pigs they have."

"Kids ought to have a dog," Zeller said.

"Thing is," Michael said, "if we get one, I don't want to give him a typical name. I'd like something unusual—imaginative, you know. Maybe King or Rex."

Zeller hesitated, then said, "Those are okay names."

"What about Sport? Maybe Prince? What do you think of Duke?"

Zeller was staring—then he grinned. "Ah, you're kidding me, Michael."

Turn it off, Michael ordered himself. "Yes," he said, "that's me. Always kidding around." He drained the final mouthful of beer; it was as warm as it was flat. He clicked the can down on the snack tray and rose.

"How about you drop over for dinner some night this week, Brad? Afterward, you and I can do some serious drinking and come up with solutions of all the world's problems."

"Thanks, I'd like that," Brad said, his voice rough with appreciation.

"See you soon, then," Michael said. "You, too, Dusty, old fella," he added.

The dog wagged his tail at the sound of his name.

Beth had reached the end of the driveway shrubbery. From the nape of her neck an aching tiredness radiated down through her shoulders and arms. Her fingers were stiff and sore from squeezing the hedge clipper to snapl off any twig that failed to conform to her vision of what the bushes should look like.

Standing on the sidewalk for a better view, she was pleased with her efforts. Nice job with the out-of-doors—and, come to think of it, she wasn't any too bad with the indoors, either. She had an eye for color and composition; she liked the way she'd decorated their home and felt comfortable in it. And if finances were okay next month, then those antique crystal lamps would be perfect in the living room . . .

Is that all there is? The remembered lyric from an old Peggy Lee song floated through her head, souring the pleasure she'd felt. Was that all there was for her? *Yardwork and housework,* prettifying this and that, raising kids and clipping coupons, traditional woman's work in a time when women were throwing away tradition. Good God! She knew and was friendly with every woman on the block, and was a real friend to none of them; comparing cures for childhood diseases or chatting about soap operas was hardly a basis for a true friendship.

She just had to find something that would stimulate her mind, get her intellectually excited as once she'd been—assuming her mind wasn't ten years past its shelf life with disuse!

With a wave, Michael bicycled past her. She turned her head to watch him ride down Walnut, the sun ahead of him. For a moment, it was as though he had merged with the sunlight, the outline of the leap-hipped man melting in golden-silver, his shoulders and head seeming transfigured as though by an internal radiance.

The thought surprised her, though it was a thought she'd had before. She watched the receding silhouette of the man on the bicycle and in her mind she said, *I do not know who he is.* She had a feeling not unlike the one of leaving the house and then, an hour later, not being sure—only *somewhat* sure—that she'd unplugged the coffeepot.

Oh, it was ridiculous, she thought. They'd been married twelve years. She knew the jokes Michael would tell at parties, knew he liked his eggs over easy and could not tolerate them scrambled, knew exactly what type of sweetly sentimental card he'd give her on her birthday, Mother's Day, anniversary, even Sweetest Day, he never forgot—knew the mole on his behind, the way his little toes curled under, the faded white scar on his knee.

But with all her knowing, the myriad of bits of information that are supposed to make up the totality of a human being, she still sometimes had the fleeting idea that there was a secret inner self in Michael Louden, a self she had never had more than the merest glimpse of, as though there were someone else residing in Michael's familiar body.

A stranger.

She was being stupid. With nothing of real importance to fill her brain, she was constructing fluff-brained fantasies spun off from the 3 PM movies on television: *Beth Louden* in *The Invasion of The Body Snatchers!*

She returned the clippers to the garage and went into the refreshing chill of the air-conditioned house. With keen anticipation, she awaited Michael's return. They *would* have a special time, a time with each other, for each other. She would regain the feeling of closeness with the man she knew so well, her husband, Michael Louden.

He was a "people" dog. He liked people, the way they smelled and how they scratched his head or patted his flanks and fed him food from their plates.

The dog liked this man. When the man squatted, called the dog's name in a whisper

26

and softly snapped his fingers, the dog lifted himself up, first his rear end and then his front, and came to the man.

The man said, "Good dog, what a nice old crippled-up fart."

The dog knew the words "good dog," and so he wagged his tail. He didn't know the other words, but he knew the sound of the voice that spoke them and that meant everything was good.

The man petted him. The dog's hindquarters swung in tail-wagging happiness. The man said, "You are a miserable old piece of shit, aren't you? Sure you are, you useless old fucker."

Still stroking the dog's back, the man turned the animal around, talking softly and reassuringly. Then the man clamped his hand around the dog's muzzle.

The dog didn't like that. He tried to open his mouth and could not; tried to squirm free and could not. Then the man was twisting the dog's head, hurting, pressing down on his neck, hurting.

In the dog's throat was a growl and a yipe of pain that couldn't get out.

When the dog's neck broke, the sound was muffled by fur and flesh.

TWO

STEAM ROSE from the tub and their bodies. The enclosure's fiberglass doors were clouded. In these few square feet of wet and heat, Beth felt sealed away from the starkness of a sometimes too-real world; this was better, a wispy, ethereal softness enveloping her like a good dream.

Smiling, Michael said, "I'll get your back for you." She turned, dipping her head into the full force of the shower spray, rinsing out the lathered shampoo.

Washcloth covering his fingers, Michael massaged her neck, kneading away the muscular stiffness. He rubbed her shoulders, then moved down the center of her back, tracing the ridges of her spine.

"That's nice," Beth sighed, feeling as though she understood why cats purr. Then she nearly hiccuped, but managed to catch herself, changing it to a giggle.

She was drunk—not *drunk* drunk but happily buoyant and wonderfully relaxed. Along with the chicken, Michael had brought home a bottle of Blue Nun. Lounging on throw pillows on the carpet in the basement rec room, they'd had an air conditioned picnic with paper plates and plastic glasses. *And all right, I ordinarily don't drink that much but it was so good!* They'd had the stereo on, violin-heavy "beautiful music," the type she generally ignored in elevators or doctors' waiting rooms, but that tonight had seemed sweet and lushly romantic. And when the meal was concluded, the wine bottle nearer empty than full, Michael said, "I do love you, Beth, really love you." The way he'd said it, his hazel eyes, touched her as a spontaneous overflow of his truest feelings and her own eyes misted.

Michael's washcloth-gloved hand was now on her left buttock. Playfully, she smacked his wrist. "I'm not a baby. I can wash my own bottom."

"And deny me the pleasure?" Michael laughed.

"Well, if you insist," Beth felt a warm shiveriness at his touch as though there were goosebumps just beneath the surface of her skin.

"Definitely a lovely ass, my dear," Michael said. Beth shifted her feet apart and rose up on tip-toe, bracing herself with her palms on the tile wall. She pushed her hips back, buttocks tightening, arched toward him.

Michael smoothed the washcloth over the outer swell of her hip. "Rub-a-dub-dub," he said, and then he was stroking her inner thighs, his fingers a so definite touch beneath the heat-holding wetness of the cloth, moving up, touching her, higher between her legs, rubbing.

Beth shuddered with pleasure. She floated into the totality of Now: Michael's caresses. The water, its feel, the hissing ring of it the only sound in all the universe. The simple and magical *niceness* of hereandnow, being clean and naked and steamy with this clean and naked man, who touched her, who loved her, *her husband, Michael* . . .

She lurched away from the wall, turning, to throw her arms around him. She wanted him—wanted him with an achingly intense desire that she'd not known for too long—and she knew he wanted her, felt his want, the rigidity of him that was now between them but that would unite them, make them one, BethandMichael, MichaelandBeth, a completion, much more than the sum of the parts.

They could not make love in the shower.

They did not delay by leaving the washroom, going across the hall to their bedroom.

Naked and wet, the hair on his chest gleaming with water droplets, Michael lay on his back on the large brown oval rug on the tile floor. His arms were out to her. "Come on, honey, yes."

She lowered herself upon him, guiding his smooth maleness into flesh that was moist with readiness to receive him.

So good, she thought . . . *Magic!* The fullness within her was exciting, yet was also somehow sentimentally nostalgic, like a trip home after years of wandering. This was a joining together. This was connection.

Pressing the heels of her hands on his hipbones, her fingers spread on his lean belly, Beth rocked and felt rooted to him. *We are One*, she thought, *no way to tell where his flesh leaves off and mine begins*.

She moved slowly at first, and then, as thinking became unnecessary, then impossible, with an increasing speed. Her heart-beat quickened. Her body found a rhythm of up-and-down and side-to-side that suited it, encouraged and guided by Michael's hands cupping her buttocks.

Beth neared the peak moment, felt its promise warm within her. A rising pressure in her throat became a moan.

And then she was *there*, the blissful convulsion, the whirling rush into release. It was not a falling into the nothingness of dissolution but a blending—of their selves: *HeandI, BethandMichael* . . .

Michael bucked up hard, his body bridging, lifting her. His climactic pulse—*inside her*—made him groan, his mouth set in a rictus. Then his face lost all expression, became death-mask placid as his hips fell and he hissed like a tea kettle.

Beth slumped, resting on him. She liked the flesh-covered line of his collarbone where her cheek lay. She liked his hairy chest tickling her buzzingly sensitive nipples. His breath was a soft breeze around her eyes—*a life breeze from inside him, love him* . . .

Michael said, "I love you, honey."

She thought, *I am so very happy now and everything is so fine and everything will always be fine* . . .

The cold ring of the bedroom telephone seemed to drill into the center of her forehead. She felt Michael start.

She held her breath. She hoped for a wrong number discovered after a single ring, but no such luck.

Michael swatted her, his palm a damp *spat*

on her backside. "I do believe you're closer to the phone."

"I . . . Damn!"

"Uh-huh, always rings just when you don't want it to."

The flesh parting from flesh was too hurried, making them both say, "Oh." Snatching a tissue from the plastic dispenser on the toilet's flush tank, Beth hurried across the hall.

The call? Michael thought as he sat up. He realized how unlikely that was. There'd been so many calls since he'd begun the waiting time. Calls from aluminum siding salesmen and newspaper subscription hustlers and insurance agents. Calls from Beth's mother, Claire, who insisted on remaining alive and annoying despite astronomically high blood pressure that should have given her at least one major coronary by now. The pestering, piping-voiced calls: "Can I talk to Marcy?" "Can I talk to Kim?" The wrong numbers. The calls from the damned dentist, reminding him his teeth needed cleaning. A call from the Red Cross asking him to be a blood donor . . .

Never *the* call! The Call of The Strangers— for The Stranger.

He stood up. He splashed water from the vanity basin—*too cold, damn it!*—to clean his flaccid penis and pubic hair, dried himself thoroughly with the big brown towel monogrammed "Dad," and wrapped it around his waist.

Smoothing back his hair, he studied his reflection in the mirrored doors of the medicine chest. Even after all these years of knowing, it came with the faintest tick of surprise that he was unable to see the aura—*his* aura. His special glow. The inner light of the Stranger.

He knew all human beings had auras, variously hued, blue, yellow, green, sometimes utterly clear, sometimes—*so rare*—a deep red, a red that seemed suffused with the thickness of arterial blood, but only a few people possessed a form of sixth sense, the psychic sight, that enabled them to perceive auras. And of those who had that gift, there were not too many with knowledge beyond the rational logic of accepted science to interpret what an aura revealed about a person. Certainly—Michael sneered—most of the so-called clairvoyants who set up card-tables at shopping center "psychic fairs" were frauds or even fools who couldn't read the "E" on an optometrist's chart if they'd written it themselves.

Yes, he knew that about his head was a writhing red nimbus, and he'd had moments when he'd thought he could literally *feel* it, a force that was his life essence, but he had never seen his aura. Nor had he seen the aura of Vern Engelking, his boss and ally, or that of Eddie Markell . . .

When he was very young, though, he had imagined he'd seen the corona around the head of Jan Pretre. Jan . . . whom he had not seen for so many years. Jan Pretre, his teacher, who'd guided him through his rite of initiation. Jan Pretre who wore the invisible red light crown of the Stranger *and who could see the shining brand on other Strangers.*

Others . . . Michael thought. John Wayne Gracy? A community leader, a friendly neighbor, the kind of guy who helped young people, lining them up with summer construction jobs, killing them, entombing their corpses beneath the floor of his modest suburban house in Des Plaines. It was possible.

No, the bathroom mirror reflected no aura. Michael Louden saw only the unremarkable features of an "average guy," the falsehood as the world saw it.

"Michael?"

He turned. Beth had put on her gold terry-cloth robe. She stood at the bathroom door. She might have seen him as he was intently studying what was—and wasn't—in the mirror . . .

"I can't understand it," he said quickly. "I'm no teenager, so why do I still get blackheads?" He traced a line across his unblemished forehead.

"Brad Zeller's on the phone," Beth said. "Dusty got lost. Brad sounds just heartsick."

"Dusty?" Michael said. "Jeez . . ."

"I told Brad you'd talk to him, Michael. I know Brad. He's old fashioned and he feels uncomfortable letting a woman know he's so upset. I think he needs to talk to you."

"Sure," Michael said. "Of course."

Standing by the night table on Beth's side of the bed, the telephone to his ear, Michael heard it clearly: Zeller was in a bad way.

He let Brad go on for a minute, savouring

34

the hurt and worry that shaped the words, and then Michael said, "Brad, you take it easy, okay? I'm just out of the shower so give me a couple minutes and then we'll go on a Dusty hunt together."

"Michael . . . Thank you. I need . . ."

"No sweat, my friend," Michael said. "It's not likely Dusty booked himself a flight to Rome. We'll find him."

Michael put down the receiver. In case Beth walked in, he turned his back to the door.

He grinned.

Michael put on a pair of jeans and a brown and yellow plaid sport shirt. He went next door. When Zeller let him in, Brad's face was the color of sooty snow except for the red streaks of broken capillaries on his nose.

Zeller's words came at Michael in a flurry, repeating only that Dusty was gone and adding little to that. *Just the facts, asshole,* Michael thought.

He quietly interrupted Zeller's monologue. "When did you discover he was missing, Brad?"

"See I went out," Brad replied. "I wasn't gone fifteen minutes. I just drove over to the White Eagle so I'd have some coffee in the morning. Dusty didn't want to come in the house, so I let him stay out back. What could it hurt? And he wasn't there when I came back."

Michael nodded. "I see," he said. Then he asked, "Are you sure, Brad? Maybe you did bring him in . . ."

"I'm old, Michael," Zeller snapped, "and sometimes I drink more than I should. But I'm not senile and I'm not a drunk. I know I left Dusty out back."

Michael raised a placating hand. "Brad," he said smoothly, "All I'm saying is, well, sometimes I'm so damned sure I left my keys on the table or the dresser, okay? It's like I can actually see myself putting them down, but they wind up right in my pants pocket."

"Sure," Zeller said.

"It won't be a big deal for us to check the house, Brad. Hell, Dusty might be snoring under your bed right now, playing a joke on us. Let's look around, just to satisfy me."

"All right," Zeller sighed.

Zeller wasn't hoping, not yet—Michael saw that—but it was possible the old shithead was starting to feel he had a chance for hope. Good; that would make it better. Let him think everything just might work out okay. There was probably a stupid bastard on the *Titanic* who thought that way three seconds before he was treading ice water.

They searched the house the dog and man shared. Dusty was not in it.

At Michael's suggestion, they went to the backyard. Michael said he was looking for a place where Dusty might have burrowed under the fence.

"Uh-uh," Zeller said, an edge to his voice. "He's not a roamer. Never has been."

"Brad," Michael said softly, "I'm only trying to help."

"Yeah, I know," Brad said pinching the bridge of his nose, rubbing his eyes with thumb and forefinger. "You're helping me and I'm spitting at you like a fighting tomcat."

"Forget it," Michael said. He clapped Brad on the shoulder. *Want to play the "Getting warmer-colder game," Brad, old buddy, old pal?* he thought. "Let's drive around the neighborhood, maybe we'll spot him," he said.

In the silvery dusk, Brad slowly drove his eight-year-old Dodge Dart down Walnut. He stopped at the corner where a group of junior high school age—perhaps younger—boys and girls stood in the artificially casual attitudes of young people striving to maintain their images within the clique. They all had cigarettes in their mouths or hands.

Michael leaned his head out the window and asked them. No, they hadn't seen a black and white dog.

Brad pulled away, muttering, "Brats smoking like that right out in the open."

Michael knew Brad was talking to hear himself talk and to keep himself from thinking about his "lost" dog. Michael said, "I catch *my* kids with a cigarette, I'll set the seat of their pants smoking."

Zeller shook his head. "Kids acting like that, that's modern times. It was different when I was a kid, you know? Hell, I bet you didn't act that way either."

"No," Michael said, "people used to think I was a pretty good kid." The ironic honesty tightened the corners of his mouth.

Yes, you're a good boy, aren't you? That's what you want them to think. It was Jan

Pretre who spoke to him across all the years, Jan's voice reverberating in the echo chamber of memory.

They drove around the neighborhood until dusk had changed to dark. Disconsolately, Zeller said, "We're not going to find him, Michael. Not now."

"We'll keep looking if you want, Brad."

"No, no use. Let's head back."

Turning into his drive, Zeller switched off the headlamps and braked the car. He twisted the ignition key. The Dart dieseled a sputtering instant before it died.

Zeller didn't move. Staring straight ahead, he said, "You know, I really don't believe this. Dusty's gone and I don't know what happened."

Want some food for thought? Michael mused. *Good, tough gristle and sinew you can chew on?* He said, "I don't know either, but maybe someone . . ." He paused, as though he'd had an idea but dismissed it, or decided it was nothing he wanted to say after all.

"Go on," Brad said tonelessly.

"Okay," Michael sighed. "You do hear about dognappers grabbing animals for scientific labs so they can do experiments, dissect them . . ." He stopped there as though the idea were too ghastly to contemplate.

"Yeah," Zeller said. "I don't want to believe that. I *don't* believe it."

"Nah, me either," Michael said, making sure his voice was loud and emphatic—*too* loud and *too* emphatic. "It's a stupid idea and I don't know why I even said it. Just forget it, okay?"

"It's young dogs they want for stuff like that. Dusty's old. He's no good for them. He's . . ."

"Like I said, Brad, a stupid idea. Don't even think about it," Michael said.

Zeller said nothing. He pushed open the car door, the dome light a sudden, sickly yellow glow. He turned his head and said, "I'm going to have a drink. Want to have one with me?"

"Sure, Brad," Michael said. "A beer."

Zeller had a shot of Seagram's Imperial and chased it with another and then he poured a third. Sitting at the kitchen table, Michael said, "You give the police a call, Brad. There's no real crime in Park Estates so they have plenty of time to look for lost pets. I'll bet they find him."

Zeller nodded. "I will call the cops." He lifted the shot glass with leprous white fingers. "But they won't find my dog. Dusty's gone and that's all. That's what I feel."

"Don't you think that way, Brad," Michael said. He finished the Old Milwaukee. "You can't give up hope."

Michael rose. Zeller gazed at him, eyes anguished under the bright alcoholic sheen. Michael put a hand on Zeller's shoulder. "You'll see, it'll be okay," he said.

Then he added something he truly believed. "You'll see Dusty again," he said. "I'm sure of that."

THREE

BETH WAS upset to hear there was no sign of Dusty. She wished there was something they could do for Brad, something more . . .

Michael assured her he, too, was concerned. "Brad's so attached to that dog, it would just destroy him if anything happened."

There'd been two calls while Michael was out, Beth informed him: her mother and Vern Engelking. Beth had said, "yes" to the invitation to the cookout Vern and Laura were having on Saturday, Labor Day weekend. Oh, and while Vern said it was nothing important, there was something about business, so if Michael wanted to call back, that would be okay.

"Guess I will get back to Vern," Michael said with a realistic sigh. "If I don't, I'll be wondering what it could be, and"—he smiled at Beth—"I don't want anything on my mind now except us."

Michael went upstairs to the room he'd made his office. He turned on the overhead light and closed the door. He looked at the file cabinets and the magazine rack with its copies of *Fortune, Time, Newsweek* and *US News and World Report,* the bland seascape hanging on the wall, the desk with its digital calendar-clock pen holder, the adding machine, the portable manual typewriter.

No question about it, he thought, he had the ordinary at-home office of a white collar nonentity. From the desk, he took the ordinary photo. There they were, he and Beth and the kids, pressed under no-glare glass, a picture taken last year at the lake. The sky was blue, the water more so; they all wore the lop-sided smiles of "family togetherness time," preserved in the orange tone of Kodachrome. People said Kim resembled Beth and that Marcy was "100 percent *his* girl," but he couldn't see it. The children looked like children, period—like small nothings who might someday grow up to be big nothings—if he let them.

Michael sat in the swivel desk chair, not reaching for the telephone. He relaxed. Here, with only himself, he *was* himself and no one else.

I am a Stranger, he thought, relishing the affirmation of his power and guile. Then he telephoned the Stranger who was the president of Superior Chemical Company.

"Michael," Vern Engelking boomed cheerfully, "I'm so pleased you and your lovely family will be attending our little get-together. We'll drink beer—lemonade for the wee ones, of course—eat hamburgers charred to carbon on the Weber kettle, and have a marvelous time."

"Right," Michael laughed dryly. "There was business you wanted to discuss?"

"A trifling matter," Vern said, "but it seems our suspicions regarding Herb Cantlon have sadly proven correct. That's the basic gist of the report Eddie Markell's provided me. Herb is utterly unethical, a viper at the bosom of Superior Chemical."

"He's ripping us off," Michael said.

"Indeed," Vern agreed. "We'll have to terminate him."

"Yes." Michael's grin was wide.

"We'll arrange the details with Eddie in the near future. I'm afraid we'll have to punish Herb Cantlon rather severely."

Michael laughed. "A man's got to do what a man's got to do."

Vern Engelking chuckled, too. "Well, now you have *two* festive occasions to look forward to, our party and Herb Cantlon. I hope this brightens your evening. Goodnight, Michael, and see you tomorrow."

"Goodnight," Michael said, and hung up the phone.

Not *the* call, he reflected, but *a* call, promising a new chance to again know the exquisite pleasure, the thrill of near-omnipotence that came from killing.

In the living room, Beth sat at the end of the sofa encircled by the light of the end table lamp. While Michael had been with Zeller, she'd put on her pastel green baby-doll pajamas.

"Nothing urgent?" she asked, as Michael sat down. Her small foot spanned the distance between them to press against the side of his thigh.

"Vern? No, no big deal. A price change on paper towels, that's all."

"Oh," Beth said.

"You said your mom called," Michael said.

"How's she doing?"

Mom was all right, Beth told him, but her pressure was still too high. The doctor had her on new medication and wanted her to take it easier. At age sixty-eight, Claire Wynkoop still put in a forty plus hour week as the librarian in Belford, the small town sixty miles to the south where Beth had been raised. "Mom refuses to slow down," Beth said, "or even to *sit* down long enough to consider slowing down."

Michael patted Beth's calf. "Don't worry, honey," he assured her, "your mom's one tough lady. She'll outlive us all." Then with an amused smile, he asked, "Mom have any earthshaking predictions?"

Beth laughed, but she did not really find the question funny. Unlike Michael, she did not think ridiculous her mother's modest claims to have occasional psychic intuitions of the future. No, Mom had never foretold a political assassination, air disaster, or erupting volcano, but . . . Two years ago, Kim, then a first-grader, had broken her wrist in a schoolyard tumble and the call from Mom came only seconds after the one from the school nurse: "Kim is hurt. I know that. How bad is it?"

Or what about *the* story, the one told frequently enough over the years to have the *feel* of truth? Hank Wynkoop, Beth's father, had died of a sudden heart attack when Beth was a high school freshman, and Claire related: "I watched him get in the car that morning. He waved to me. I thought: 'This is the last time I'll see him alive'—and it was."

43

Beth felt a cold tingle at the nape of her neck. So people had hunches. Okay, she could accept that; it was normal. But she didn't like the disquieting feeling that stemmed from thinking about the "not quite normal," the "cannot happen" that *does* happen.

"I asked if your mom gave us any revealing glimpses of the future," Michael said, drawing Beth out of her uneasy contemplation.

"No," Beth said. She chided herself for worrying about nothing that required worry. Mom *was* good old normal Mom, the same way she herself was normal Beth or Michael was Mr. Normal Louden.

And that is that, she decided, and, in order to maintain her certainty, she told Michael she wanted to watch "Trapper John, MD," when they went down to the rec room instead of going along with his TV suggestion: a re-run of Rod Serling's classic "Twilight Zone."

They went to bed at 11. Beth felt a fresh stirring of desire and expressed it with her hands and lips. Michael responded, his arms around her, tongue in her mouth, and she felt his growing tumesence.

His pajama bottoms down, hers off and dropped to the carpet, Michael carefully moved over her. He braced himself on his elbows and she guided him to her core. His "There!" was a satisfied puff of complete immersion inside her.

For Beth their earlier lovemaking had been a wildly reckless attempt at reunification. It had—thankfully—been a success. Now, Michael moving, she with him, a mutually established, pleasure-giving pace, was a *confirmation*, the final tearing down of any barrier that might yet remain between them.

Beth wanted no barriers. She wanted to talk with him. And she was certain she could do that after this meaningful ritual of the senses in that mellow time that would follow when they lay in this cool and dark room together, satisfied and fulfilled.

Michael's thrusting grew more rapid and forceful. She thought she was not ready, but scurrying messages traveling the maze of her nerve endings signalled yes, she was. Her hips churned. Her thighs gripped him and she clutched his shoulders.

She had a flash of remembered feelings. She was a child, racing up the ladder of the playground slide, eager to reach the top for that thrilling fright-hesitant instant befor the world-blurring descent. And now . . . *Oh, oh yes!* . . . She was there, as head spinning, a pinwheeling heat in her belly, she zoomed down, each bump of rippled steel a tremor of excitement that tossed her and made her gasp.

Beth sighed just as Michael convulsed in orgasm. He grunted, pressing down on her. His weight was not oppressive, not now. Beth stroked his hair, the back of his neck. How helpless, how weak Michael seemed, she thought, his penis dwindling inside her, and she felt a special tenderness toward him.

Michael rolled away with, "I love you, Beth." She moved close to him, her head on his chest. He put an arm around her shoulder.

"Are you sleep, Michael?"

45

"No, not really."

"Do you feel like talking?"

"Sure, honey."

"I'm glad," Beth said. "It's been a while since we've talked."

"I know that, honey, and I told you, I let the damned work pressure turn me into a zombie. I haven't been spending enough time with you, or for that matter, with the kids. That's going to change."

"That's probably part of our problem, Michael," Beth said, "but not all of it. I'm to blame, too."

Slowly, Michael said, "What do you mean?"

"I mean . . . " Oh, the feeling she *could* talk freely was there, but knowing *what* to say—*how*—was suddenly a tongue-twisting challenge. She stammered something about intellect and self-realization, knew it was a cliche borrowed from a woman's magazine article, and said, "Let me think a minute."

It wasn't until her first year of college that Beth had discovered she was truly bright. Grade school and high school had been easy and therefore dull; she'd been an under-achiever. But at Illinois Central University, she'd met teachers who praised her analytical questions, complimented her inquiring explorations of complex issues, and she'd found out just how exciting it was to really use her mind. She'd thought of a career in social work or clinical psychology.

Then she met Michael, a senior, majoring in business. She fell in love with him. He graduated. She married him.

And that was that!

"Penny for your thoughts," Michael prompted.

"That's more than they're worth," Beth said, a weak joke that she thought too true to be funny. "It's . . . Sometimes I feel so out of it, Michael, like I'm a stereotype of a feather-brained little housewife who calls it a national catastrophe if the supermarket happens to run out of tomato-rice soup or Stove-Top Stuffing. That's why it's sometimes hard for me to feel we have enough in common. You're out in the *real* world, accomplishing *real* things, and I'm home matching the socks and getting dumber by the day."

Michael squeezed her. "No way are you dumb, honey! I've never once thought that."

"*I've* thought it," Beth said, "and that's what counts. I think it's one of the reasons *I* probably drift away from *you.*"

"I see," Michael said quietly. "I understand."

Bless him, she thought, he *did* understand —he always understood if she gave him half a chance.

Even as the decision she'd been pondering for so long was being made, she announced it: "Michael, I'm going to go back to school. I'll sign up for a course at Lincoln Junior College. I'll take it slow, just to see if I can revitalize my brain cells, then"—she took a deep breath, somewhat fearful of her boldness—"maybe go right on to finish up my degree and get a real job."

Michael said, "All right, that makes good

sense to me."

"You are serious?" Beth moved away from him, propping herself up on an elbow. If he were humoring her, giving her a patronizing pat on the head . . . She was ashamed to even be thinking this way, but . . .

Michael said, "So I'll watch the kids a few nights a week. Did you expect me to get all bent out of shape because you have a fine mind and want to use it? Come on, Beth, I'm probably a whole bunch of things, but not a male chauvinist."

"No," Beth said sincerely, "you're a wonderful man, that's what you are."

"True," Michael laughed, "and I'm pleased you noticed it. Now how about we get some sleep?"

Beth cuddled as close to him as she could. Happy, excited about college, their marriage, *everything!* She was not sleepy. The words poured out of her: "There's so much I've wanted to say, and now feels so right for saying it, saying it all . . ."

"Shh!" Michael hissed sharply. She felt him tense. "Sit up," he whispered.

She did. Michael was alongside her.

"What is it?"

"Downstairs," he said. "I thought I heard something." He paused for a long moment that brought a pinch of nervousness to her throat.

Michael whispered, "Yeah, I know I did. I'm going to have a look."

In his pajamas, Michael slowly walked down the hall. He needed no light. This was his house. He passed the room Marcy and

Kim shared, catching a whiff of the pinewood chips that littered the aquarium in which their guinea pigs lived. He passed his office, then, hand light on the bannister, he made his way downstairs.

That's the nice thing about a modern house, he thought. *The steps do not creak. You can move quietly, so quietly, no warning, no sound to mark your coming.*

In the dark living room, his hand moved unerringly to the cord and the drapes hissed along the rod. He gazed out the picture window at Park Estates, his neighborhood, his neighbors, the houses dark, most of them, except for the glow of 20th century night-lights, the television sets, black and white bedroom portables, the color consoles in nightowls' living rooms. A night in a good suburb, safe . . . Yet Michael knew there was a fear in Park Estates, the coast-to-coast fear that blanketed all of America. It was "The Age of Paranoia." And what genius had come up with the insightful "Just because you're paranoid doesn't mean they aren't out to get you"?

They were, the Strangers—and he was.

The woman upstairs was afraid, too, Michael thought, remembering how she'd squeezed his arm, urging him to "be careful." He'd given her general fear a focal point with the intruding noise of "something down-stairs."

Michael listened. He heard the chill exhalation of the air-conditioning—that and his own breathing. And that was all there was to hear.

He'd had to get away from Beth's babble. He'd felt the impulse come to him, so strong, the wanting to shut her up forever, his hand on her throat, allowing her only enough air so that her mind functioned for the instant it would take her to realize he was not the patient and understanding husband, not a real life Dagwood Bumstead-Ozzie Nelson-Dad "Leave It To Beaver" Cleaver—*that he was a Stranger who was killing her, killing her* . . .

To get away, he'd made up the noise downstairs.

"Michael?" Beth's voice thin and worried, drifted down to him.

Good, Michael thought. Her fear of the unknown was becoming a greater fear of the imagined. Her loving husband—*yours truly*—might have met a prowler with a tire iron, a wrench, a knife—might have met Death.

"Michael! Are you all right?"

He smiled.

The dumb bitch did not have to worry, he thought. He was not the one fated to die in the night.

Quickly and silently, he walked back upstairs. He stopped just before their bedroom door and waited.

"Michael! Answer me!"

He knew Beth was no more than a dozen heartbeats away from explosive panic, a shrieking, lights-on, dial-the-police, "Oh, help!" frenzy. He counted his own pulsing heart beat four times . . . six . . .

He stepped into the bedroom. "Guess it was nothing after all . . ."

Beth screamed.

He raced to her, held her. "Honey, hey, it's okay . . ."

"God, you scared me! I was so . . ." Beth sobbed. "Oh, God, Michael, I didn't know what to think, and then suddenly, there you were and . . ."

"I'm sorry," Michael crooned. "I didn't mean to frighten you. There's nothing to be afraid of." *And*, he thought, *I'll bet there's nothing you feel like talking about now, is there?*

Beth choked when she tried to turn her tears to relieved laughter. With a sniffle, she said, "It's okay. I'm fine now."

But she *had* been frightened, so frightened —and the residue of that fear accompanied her into sleep and infused her dream . . .

Alone, she waited to be punished. It was unfair. She had done nothing wrong.

She sat in the first seat of the center row, her hands folded on the desk. On the ceiling, the fluorescent lights poured down a cold light as they faintly buzzed, a sound that vibrated down her spine.

She knew very well where she was—and there had to be a mistake. This was the fourth grade classroom in Belford Community Grade School, the realm of the feared and hated tyrant Miss Kostner. Other teachers in the school administered discipline reluctantly, Miss Kostner, enthusiastically. Other teachers sent kids to the cloakroom or kept them in after school. Miss Kostner had a ruler. "Hold out your hand, please."

No! I do not belong here. Beth wanted to tell someone that, to rectify this error in time. She was an adult now and Miss Kostner was a terror consigned to memory. Except *somehow* she did not feel at all grown up. Despite this adult body cramped at the small desk, she was a child. Her world was divided into zones of safety and security, areas of known fears, and yet darker territories of fears unknown.

Young, she was young, and leaden with fright.

Then she understood. *This is a dream, only a dream. A dream cannot hurt you.*

By why did the realization bring no lessening of her fear-misery?

Now she was no longer alone. Her children —*But I am a child myself!*—was here, Kim in the desk to the left, Marcy at the right. *I can see them without moving my head.* Feet flat on the floor, hands folded, they sat stiffly as though mocking her.

And she knew the teacher planned to punish them all.

Then the teacher appeared at the desk, appeared from nowhere as people can only within a dream. The teacher was not Miss Kostner.

Michael was the teacher. He was smiling.

He would be the one to inflict punishment and she knew there was nothing she could do to prevent him.

Michael summoned her with a nod. In the eternity it took to walk from her desk to him, she watched the transformation. It was a surprise, but it had the feeling of something that made perfect, irrefutable sense.

Michael's face lost its familiarity. He might have been a wax statue whose features had been instantly reworked by a sculptor's invisible hand. His mouth became a cruel slash. His nostrils flared. His eyes held the too-bright gleam of taxidermist's glass.

I do not know him, she thought. *I have never known him.*

Michael opened the top drawer of the desk. He took out the ruler.

Trembling, she held out her hand, palm up. Michael slowly raised the ruler, keeping it an unending, frozen moment at the peak of its climb.

She waited for the fiery slash.

The ruler sliced the air, a blur, first the brownish-yellow of wood, then shining steel as it becomes a long, sharp knife that servered her hand at the wrist.

There was no blood. There was no pain. Her hand lay on the green desk blotter, fingers curled up, an insect dying on its back.

Michael-Who-Was-Not-Michael said, "Now the pain. Now the blood."

And he—Michael-Who-Was-A-Stranger—stabbed her, the knife a cold intrusion in her belly, stabbed her, a twisting sharpness in her chest, stabbed her, a rending, ferocious agony in her throat.

This is a dream! Dreams cannot hurt you! Dreamscannothurt! Beth screamed in her mind.

Her subconscious commanded all its resolve, willed her *Out*—out of the dream-horror. Thoughts rushed in to soothe her, comfort her: *All is well and my children are safe I am safe no fear no harm no hurt no danger no killing no blood no death No Death NO DEATH!!!*

The succession of consoling ideas wove together in a heavy tapestry that covered over her dream, hiding it under a thick layered cloth of assurance, concealing it from memory.

When Beth Louden awoke the next morning, she felt tired, a bit achey and cranky, as though she had not had a good night's sleep. She thought she might have had a nightmare.

She tried to recall it.

She could not, not for the life of her.

FOUR

MICHAEL PIERCED the yolk of his second over-easy egg with the corner of a half slice of toast. At the counter, Beth, in her housecoat, poured herself coffee in a yellow "Smiley Face" mug and then came to join him. Through the east window, the sun cast a sharply angled parallelogram between them on the butcher block table.

"Good eggs," Michael said. He performed a Groucho Marx, eyebrow waggling leer. "Eggs help a man restore some of his recently drained vital juices."

Beth laughed. "Michael, you are terrible."

"I yam what I yam and 'at's all what I yam," Michael grinned, left eye set in a Popeye squint.

The portable radio on the counter reported the eight o'clock weather forecast. The start of the work week would be—"What else, Chicagoland?" demanded a manic deejay—another scorcher, temperature near 90, humidity near "hideous!"

Michael said, "We could use a good rain, break this heat wave."

"It would help," Beth agreed.

Same old scene in the same old script, Michael thought. Breakfast: The Husband and The Wife discuss The Weather, and then, naturally, The Kids.

"What time do Marcy and Kim roll in?" he

asked.

"The bus is supposed to be at their school by 10:30. I'll leave here early, though, so I can stop out at Lincoln Junior College for a catalog and registration information before I pick up the girls."

"Uh-huh," Michael nodded, finishing the egg, then saying what he knew she'd be pleased to hear. "I'm glad to see you're excited about going back to school, Beth."

"And *I'm* glad *you're* glad. I think it will mean something important to us both. I mean, our future doesn't have to be more of the present routine, does it?"

"Right," Michael said—and his future definitely would *not* be. As for Beth—*Hey, kiddo, you probably don't want to plan too far ahead, okay?*

Toying with the handle of her mug, Beth pursed her lips thoughtfully. She said, "It's been strange not having the girls home these two weeks. I've missed them and worried about them, but, you know, I think it did work out well for the two of us, Michael."

"I think so, too."

"And I'm sure the girls had a good time at camp."

"Sure," Michael agreed, "ghost stories around the campfire, canoe races and nature hikes. They probably got to weave a lanyard or a potholder in the crafts shop. Say, we're talking about real adventures!"

Beth laughed, then became serious. "You know, living in the suburbs, Marcy and Kim get a fairly narrow view of life . . ."

"Uh-huh, know what you mean . . ."

"So," Beth continued, "I hope they met all kinds of different people at camp . . ."

He was unprepared, for once completely off-guard. He took a drink of coffee and Beth said, "Maybe they learned that not everyone is the same after all."

The laugh corkscrewed up from the center of his chest. He tried to swallow, to smother the laughter, and could not. He coughed and gagged. Coffee sprayed from his mouth and his nose. Tears stung his eyes.

Beth was on her feet, slapping his back. "Oh, I'll get you some water."

Sputtering and choking, he gulped the water. *Not everyone is the same after all*—another volcanic laugh threatened to erupt and he struggled for control. Oh, Beth, not everyone is the same—*I am not*—and summer camp is the ideal place to learn that—*I know. I did!*

Feeling as though there was a fuzzy tennis ball wedged between his tonsils, Michael croaked, "Wrong pipe."

"Okay now?"

"Sure, I'm fine."

But the laugh kept trying to seep out of him, emerging as a clearing of the throat or a mock cough, and he was glad to get out of the house a few minutes later.

When he was in the car, driving to Superior Chemical Company's office in Oakwood—*when he was alone*—he at last had his laugh, fullblown and wild and true.

Michael remembered summer camp, Camp Bethel, and Jan Pretre, and Alvin Burdell, Alvin, the very first.

Michael Louden remembered when he was

57

The screen door rasped like a parrot—
Ahrkee—and the young man stepped into
Cabin Three, the door clack-rattling shut
behind him. He was tall. His black hair was
trimmed in a neat flat-top. A hooked wrinkle
connected his heavy eyebrows above his
straight nose.

The young man's deepset, dark blue eyes
went down the row of beds and the boys
assigned to them on the left, then up the rows
on the right. He had responsibility for eight
boys in all. He was a volunteer counselor at
Camp Bethel, a Baptist church sponsored
program that gave kids low cost fun and
regular religious training.

Michael thought the young man's eyes
spent a second or two longer on him than on
the others, but he could not be sure. He
would be careful. He was always careful.

"My name's Jan Pretre, guys." The counselor had a deep and friendly voice. "We'll be
spending a lot of time together the next
couple of weeks."

"Hi, Jan!" squalled the fat boy who had the
bed opposite Michael's. Michael had sat next
to him on the bus ride. The fat boy was
named Alvin Burdell. There was a huge, red-
brown birthmark over his left ear that
showed through the fuzz of his crew cut, and
he smelled like cheese.

"Howya doin'?" Jan Pretre nodded at
Alvin. He told the boys that once they were
unpacked, he'd take them down to the lake
for a dip.

After their swim, they had free time, and, after that, lunch. The camp director, Pastor Bill, spent so much time saying grace that the unappetizing food turned into barely edible cold lumps.

That afternoon, a kid from Number Six punched Michael on the arm, a good one, knuckle out, twisting into the bicep. He was looking for a fight, but Michael did not fight back; he ran away.

He never fought.

Lights out came at nine o'clock.

At midnight, Alvin Burdell's crying woke up Cabin Three. Alvin had wet his bed.

Steve Dawes, at thirteen the biggest and oldest Cabin Three camper, hollered, "You fat-guts! Stinking up the place!"

"I can't help it!" Alvin wailed.

Michael lay on his back, not joining in the chorus that derided Alvin.

Carrying a flashlight, Jan Pretre came in. He told them all to get back to sleep, that he'd take care of everything. He told Alvin that what had happened was "no big deal." Anyone could have an accident, nothing to be ashamed of. Jan comforted the boy and assured him, "We'll take care of everything."

Alvin Burdell had his accident three nights in a row.

Steve Dawes decided they'd all better take care of "Fat-Guts." He had a plan. If anybody snitched, he'd get it, too, but good.

Michael stayed out of it as much as possible, saying and doing only what he had to do to keep Steve Dawes and the others from turning on him.

On a free afternoon, Michael lay on his bunk, flipping through a *Picture Stories From the Bible* comic book, the only kind of comic permitted at Camp Bethel. The only other boy in the cabin was Alvin Burdell. He didn't want to go out, didn't want to be the "we're stuck with him" clown in a softball or volleyball game or to go down to the lake for a "free swim" where "seeing how long you can keep Fat-Guts's head under" was becoming the camp's newest sports craze.

When Jan Pretre stepped in, he said, "Hello," to Michael. It made Michael feel strange. He wanted Jan to say more to him—to really talk to him—and he didn't understand why that was so.

But Jan Pretre went over to Alvin, sat down next to him, and spent twenty minutes talking with him, an arm draped over the fat boy's shoulders. Michael could only hear a phrase now and then: "It's okay. Don't you worry. We're friends." Then Jan left and Alvin was grinning, scratching the lumpy birthmark over his ear.

It was not until Sunday that Michael had *his* talk with Jan Pretre.

It had been easy for Michael to slip away from the church service in Big Hall. There were a lot of kids, so the counselors couldn't watch everyone. Michael knew how not to be noticed.

Now he was lying down, hands folded under his neck. On the ceiling, in the corner, a spider had nearly completed a web and was shuffling from strand to strand. If Michael watched patiently, he might see a fly fall into the trap, see the struggle and the slow, certain conclusion.

Then Michael heard the screen door and the hush and scrape of sneakers. Alongside the bunk, Jan Pretre stood over him.

Michael sat up and scooted back, his spine curved to the wall. "Hi! I was just sitting here and thinking, you know . . ."

"Thinking? Shouldn't you be with the other good boys in Big Hall, singing praise to Him from Whom all blessings flow?"

"Sure," Michael nodded. "I guess so . . ."

"Oh yes," Jan Pretre said. "You're a good boy, aren't you? That's what you want *them* to think."

Michael felt a fluttery palpitation of his heart. He looked at Jan Pretre, wondering just who he was seeing. Then Michael said, "So I guess I better go on over to Big Hall . . ."

Jan's heavy hand on his shoulder froze Michael, stopped his flow of words.

"No, you stay here, Michael," Jan said quietly. "And don't lie to me. Don't. You don't have to, you know."

Then Jan sat down, turned his head, fixing his serious blue eyes on him. The corner of Jan's mouth rose but he was not smiling. "You said you were thinking, Michael. What is it you think about?"

Warily, Michael replied, "Oh, you know . . . Just stuff, I guess."

"Like who's going to win the world series? Maybe a cute girl you'd like to take to the junior high sock hop? Whether a Chevy is better than a Ford?"

"Sure," Michael said. "Things like that."

Jan chuckled. "That's a fucking lie and I told you not to lie to me."

Michael did not even see it coming. Jan's slap was an explosion of heat on his cheek and a roar in his ear. He nearly tumbled off the bed, but Jan gripped his upper arm savagely and hauled him back up. He saw Jan through a kaleidoscope of tears.

"What you really think about is how hard it is to fool them day after day, to pretend you're like they are."

"Huh?" Michael put on the stupid, big-eyed, mouth hanging face he frequently used at school. "I don't get you."

Jan sighed. "You can bullshit them, Michael, but not me. Should I hit you again?"

Michael cowered and waited, but Jan did not slap him. The counselor shifted his gaze to look through the screened window toward Big Hall. "Amazing Grace" poured from the building, spreading over the camp like sluggish syrup, youthful voices ponderous and discordant.

"They're making noise so God will watch over them, protect them from the terrors of this universe He created. They live their foolish, frightened lives, praying that God, or the President, or the FBI won't let anything hurt them. They're nothing but shit, Michael, animated shit on legs, and they don't mean any more than shit."

Jan turned his head. His eyes caught Michael and held him. "You hate them, you hate their fucking guts and you want them dead, all those whimpering, pathetic, nothing people."

Jan dropped his voice to a whisper. "Michael, you and I, we are the same. Do you understand now?"

Daring to hope, Michael wanted to laugh— or even to cry. So long alone, surrounded always by people whom he resembled but with whom he had no more in common than he did an alien from outer space . . . And now Jan Pretre was telling him . . .

Wasn't he?"

He had to be sure, and he had to be cautious. Michael said, "Are you saying we're friends?"

Jan said, "You don't want friends, Michael. You don't need friends. *Allies,* Michael, different than they are, standing outside and above their moronic notions of right and wrong. We are Strangers . . ."

"Strangers," Michael said. Saying the word brought him a feeling of both excitement and contentment. *A Stranger*—that was what he had always felt himself to be!

"And we are not alone, Michael," Jan said.

Michael's heart pounded, speaking in code within his blood.

"There are others, more now than there ever have been. Oh, we'll hide while we must. We'll pretend. But the wheel is turning. And then, our time, the Time of The Strangers. Our Time!"

"Yes," Michael said, and he realized he was not using the voice of the one he pretended to be; this was his true voice.

He had a question. "How did you know, Jan?"

Jan barked a quick laugh. "I have eyes," he

said. "I can see."

Then Jan stood up. "We'll talk again, Michael. I'll tell you more, teach you." He grinned and tousled Michael's hair. "For now, just you be a good boy, right?"

When Jan left, Michael stretched out on his back. He studied the intricate spider web overhead. He did not see any flies but the flies would come. Flies were created to be killed by spiders. The weak and the stupid were always the prey of the strong and the smart . . . *Our prey. We are Strangers . . .*

And now, twenty-three years later, and The Time of The Strangers was nearer, foreshadowed in newspaper headlines and despairing sociological studies.

Michael Loúden anticipated the promised Time with the voracious joy of a shark about to feed, felt it great within him as he parked the LTD in his numbered slot in Superior Chemical Company's lot.

He took the elevator to Vern Engelking's office, the office of his ally, his boss, a Stranger.

The green glowing readout of the digital clock radio clicked from 9:30 to 9:31. Lying on his bed in his clothes—he hadn't bothered to undress last night before passing out— Brad Zeller was wide awake. He had been since seven, not moving, eyes open, wondering occasionally where the room's darkness left off and the ceiling began. He knew the ache in his head would continue until he drank it away.

Dusty's habit was to wake Brad with a

whine and a paw at seven o'clock. That had not happened today.

There was a click-jump at 9:32. Brad Zeller said aloud, "I can't just lie here all day, can I?" No one answered him. It took another five minutes, but he groaned himself into motion and went to the bathroom.

Then, in the kitchen, he drew the tan drapes of the sliding glass patio doors. The glaring sunlight in the back yard increased the intensity of his headache. He squinted, trying to believe the feeling that, any second, Dusty would come around the side of the house, press his nose to the window, wanting to come in.

No, that was goddamned stupid. Dusty was gone; he felt that. The cop he'd spoken to when he'd telephoned last night was an okay guy, telling him that most dogs that were lost in Park Estates usually got found, but Brad considered that only official optimism.

Brad decided he ought to eat something. Sure, a hearty breakfast to get the day going —going nowhere, as usual. He thought about a morning eye-opener, but rejected it. Okay, he drank, did some heavy juicing in fact, but that didn't mean he was a booze-hound. Hell, he never touched anything until noon, and then, only beer until evening. Liquor helped him get by—and who didn't need something in this screwed up day and age?

Brad started a pot of coffee and put corn-flakes in a bowl. He poured milk on the cereal, but, sitting at the table, he got a warning from his nose when he raised the spoon; the milk had soured. He dumped the mess down the garbage disposal, spilled the remainder of the milk carton after it, and washed it down with cold water.

He opened the cabinet beneath the sink to throw away the carton. The plastic bag in the trash bucket was nearly full. He stuffed the carton in, squeezed it down, and yanked the white plastic liner from the container.

Carrying the tied trash bag, he stepped onto the patio in his bare feet. The humid heat triggered a wave of nausea. He walked toward the back of his lot where he kept the garbage.

From twenty feet away, he heard the high-pitched drone of the flies. There was a light wind at his back, so the odor did not come to him until he'd gone a bit farther.

He'd never smelled anything quite like it, yet he knew what it was, somehow, knew what it had to be. The smell was of death, death and the aftermath of death as heat speeded the process of putrefaction.

Brad shuffled into the stink. He was close enough now to see—*and he had seen.* The black and white fur, the precise shape of paw pads. The cover of the garbage can was slightly raised. Between the lid and the can, the dog's rear leg projected stiffly.

The flies were brazen, clinging to the top of the can when he lifted it; their green-blue bodies were as bright as Depression glass.

If it weren't for the smell, Brad would have thought the moment unreal.

Dusty lay on mounds of garbage inside the container. The dog's head was craned impossibly far back as though he'd been frozen while trying to howl the moon out of the sky. Dusty's tongue protruded, black and swollen.

Brad dropped the bag of kitchen trash. It split open. What a mess, Brad thought; now I'll have to pick that all up.

Then he thought: Dusty is dead and for more than a minute, that was all he could think.

Then he turned and staggered to the house. He had a quick shot of Imperial, felt its promise and needed more and had another.

He telephoned the Park Estates Police. "I found my dog, Dusty," he said. "He's dead." He felt the sweat like ice on his forehead, the flash of tears that were also so cold. "He's dead and someone . . . someone killed him."

FIVE

SOMETHING WAS going to happen . . . something wrong. Claire Wynkoop knew that, felt it now as she had all day. Unable to relax, she sat stiffly on the bentwood rocker on the screened-in back porch and tried to ignore the promise of the premonition that teased her mind.

On her lap lay an open book, *I See Tomorrow's Forevers*, a choice of reading matter that she considered ironically appropriate: an "as told to" autobiography of an alleged psychic. This particular self-proclaimed prophet received her impressions of the future by gazing into a glass doorknob.

Thirty atrociously written pages had convinced Claire Wynkoop, the town of Belford's librarian, that *Tomorrow's Forevers* was "Today's Tripe," definitely not a book for library purchase; the review copy would be returned. Claire considered most of the "studies" of the paranormal to be sheer nonsense, or worse, malicious frauds to generate new fears for the already fearful.

Claire closed the book. Just above the nape of her neck was a pulsing ball of tension and, in the center of her skull, a feeling she could describe only as "an itch impossible to scratch." There was, too, the vibrato of a single, high-pitched note ringing in her ears, the constant sound that had been amplified in the day-long stillness of the library.

Symptoms of her hypertension or perhaps an adverse reaction to the new perscriptions meant to lower her blood pressure? She could not deceive herself. All the premonitions she'd experienced in her sixty years— *Not that many but every one was one* too *many!*—had been heralded by her feeling this way, the way she did now.

She tipped back her head. Though Claire Wnykoop's hair had made the transition to snowy white a decade earlier, she was a woman who wore her age well. Her neck was neither wattled nor excessively wrinkled, and the lines bracketing her mouth were friendly, indicating she'd spent more time smiling than scowling. She prided herself that weight was not a factor contributing to her high blood pressure; she was no heavier at sixty than she'd been at twenty, and while she granted that some of her pounds had "relocated themselves," she carried herself with the erect dignity of one who'd gone to school at a time when posture was a vital part of the elementary curriculum.

Claire's eyes, however, were not what they had once been, so she peered at the western sky through the upper lenses of bifocals. The isolated puffs of white cloud, the fine, golden ball of sun against the tranquil blue, made for a peaceful scene, so lovely that it was hard to accept that something *bad* was on Fate's calendar.

It was. She knew that. *What? When?* She didn't know yet. Nor did she have any guarantee of clear, comprehensible answers; often her visions were vague, as though she were seeing abstract-impressionist paintings in motion. It was only rarely that a premonition jumped into three-dimensional focus.

But inevitably her future glimpses were *not* assurances of glad tidings. Others with psychic gifts might predict winning race horses or know that a tumor would prove benign. Claire's intuitive impressions varied only in the degrees of misfortune they foretold.

She felt this precognition—*You nasty thing!*—lurking just past the border of consciousness. Glumly, the told herself, *I will see what I see when I see it.* That was how the tricky *whatsis* operated. She could neither avoid a look at the future nor hasten its arrival.

When Claire rose, book in hand, she was dizzy and a shower of sparkling angel's hair floated before her eyes. Definitely hypertension, she thought. Her dizziness passed and she went into the house, leaving *Tomorrow's Forevers* on the kitchen table. In the living room, she clicked on the old, nineteen-inch black and white television. She seated herself on the couch for the Channel Nine News. The six o'clock anchorman was smiling as he reported the firing squad deaths of forty-six "enemies of Islam" in Iran. The "close-up" reporter smiled through his feature on teenage suicide. On a commercial, a woman grinned at learning her husband preferred stuffing to potatoes.

Claire had enough of capped-teeth artificiality and she got up and turned off the set. The picture vanished, leaving behind a white dot in the center of the screen, a white dot that glowed and spun as something cold and spider-legged scurried down Claire's spine.

Claire staggered back a step. She straightened, eyes fixed on the pinwheeling, expanding dot. The television screen was smeared with globs of whiteness, then shadow, and Claire thought, *Now* . . .

And *now* became the future as she saw . . . *A mouth and eyes. The mouth is wrapped around a terrible scream and the eyes are screaming, too. A child screams, flies and floats and twists so slowly through depths of air, flying and floating and screaming.*

The child is . . . *All mouth and eyes* . . . *I cannot see. Who* . . . *She* . . . *This little girl so terrified* . . . *I feel her fear* . . .

I cannot see!

I cannot see but somehow I know and this is my grandchild, the child of my child . . .

But Kim? Or Marcy? I hear the scream and I feel the fright but so dark this vision, I cannot see her face . . .

Cannot see!

The scream ends with the thudding brutality of the pain-enveloped fall, the impact on the ground, the darkness . . .

Claire Wynkoop blinked. It was finished.

Shivering, she exhaled and then nodded, her decision definite. She had to call. Beth would laugh and try to pretend there was no reason to be upset. *But you've learned, haven't you, my dear?* One of the children, Marcy or Kim, was in danger, or would be.

71

And this time, oh please this time, let the awareness of danger-to-be prevent it coming to pass!

Claire dialed her daughter's number. Circuits hissed and crackled and then there was a ringing.

Sixty miles north, in Park Estates, Beth Louden answered the telephone. "Michael?"

"It's . . ."

"Oh. Mom."

Claire squeezed shut her eyes. She heard it in Beth's voice. Something *was* wrong—now.

"The children . . . Are they all right?"

"Of course, Mom," Beth said. "Home from camp today. They're fine."

"I saw something, Beth."

Beth's sigh was a breathy dismissal. "Not now, Mom. I'm just not in the mood, okay?"

"Beth . . ."

"Mom," Beth curtly interrupted, "the girls are all right, I'm all right. Michael's all right and that's it."

"Then what's bothering you?" Claire demanded, because Beth's words thrummed with tension.

"Nothing I feel like talking about, okay? I'll give you a call tomorrow."

"All right, then," Claire said quietly. There was nothing else she could do now except worry.

Before she hung up, Beth assured her mother yet again that everything was all right.

No, Claire Wynkoop silently responded, it was not.

Nor would it be.

"Dad's here!" In a Camp PineTop T shirt and raggedy-kneed jeans, Kim shot down the stairs. Smiling, Marcy trailed her younger sister.

Eight-year-old Kim was solid and chunky, able to belt a softball farther than most boys her age. With the short, brutally blunt haircut she'd insisted on before camp—she was then in one of her "I hate Marcy" periods and didn't want anyone saying they looked like sisters—her round face sunburned and peeling, and two missing lower teeth, Kim was straddling the borderline between cute and homely.

Not so Marcy, so lovely that people frequently commented that she ought to model or do TV commercials. Summer sun had lightened the blond hair that tumbled onto the ten-year-old's shoulders. Her oval face was delicately featured and her lip line was finely sculptured so that her mouth didn't have the poutiness common to many children. In green, white-trimmed jogging shorts and a sleeveless yellow top, Marcy radiated the graceful, yet unmannered poise of a ballerina born to the dance.

In the foyer, Michael braced himself fo the children's rush. Squatting, his arms encircling the girls, he kissed them and then, with a grin said, "Don't get the idea we missed you brats. It was so nice and quiet around here, Mom and I were thinking of leaving you at camp for the next ten years."

"Oh, Daddy," Marcy whimpered, clinging to his neck.

Oh, Daddy! Michael thought. Marcy was a beautiful mouse who usually responded to his teasing with a helpless "Oh, Daddy"—unless she failed to realize he was joking, in which case her wounded feelings were likely to prompt tears.

Quavery-voiced, Marcy said, "Daddy, you did *so* miss us, didn't you?"

"Hey, I was only fooling, baby." As Michael assured Marcy, "just how much you kids mean to me," Kim broke in with a *nyah-nyah* inflected, "So what, Dad? There's this camp where you send grownups, you know. I'll put *you* there!"

"Oh, that so?" Michael said. He let Kim wriggle free of his arms. When Kim chose, Michael thought, she could be something else. He'd tease and she'd tease in return. If he yelled, she yelled. And there were times when her high spiritedness led her across the border from the realm of mischievousness to the domain of pure brattiness, times when Michael could almost feel his hand gripping her throat and . . .

"I'll send you to . . . Camp Crummy it's called!" Kim said.

"Never heard of it," Michael said placidly. "Is it a nice place?"

"It stinks. They feed you stale bread with lots of yucky bugs on it. How do you like that?"

Michael pretended to ponder, then said, "Toasted."

Kim doubled over in laughter. Giggling, Marcy said, "You are so funny, Daddy."

"Yup, shore am," Michael drawled. "Yuh

bet yore life I am, l'il Missy." He tickled Marcy, a finger scooting down the ribs, and, still giggling, she jerked away from him.

Michael straightened up. "Where's Mom?" Ordinarily when he came home at the normal 6:30 or so, Beth greeted him at the door.

"In there," Kim pointed, and then led the way into the living room. Holding Marcy's hand, Michael frowned.

Not quite whispering, Marcy said, "Something bad happened today, Daddy. Mom's real upset."

She was; he knew that when he saw Beth seated on the sofa, jerking her head with a sharp start-stop movement like a bird when he and the kids entered. "I . . . I'm so glad you're home, Michael," Beth said, her face sickly pale.

Michael let go of Marcy's fingers. "What's wrong, honey?"

Beth blinked as though the question hadn't registered. It was Kim who shouted the answer as if she had a wondrous secret she'd been saving: "Someone went and killed Dusty, Mr. Zeller's dog. Isn't that gross?"

Oh, that so, Michael thought. How about that?

"God," was all he said. He sat down, turning to face Beth and taking her hand. He sent Kim and Marcy up to their room and then asked Beth, "What exactly happened, honey?"

"It's just awful, Michael," Beth said, shaking her head. "So wicked and senseless."

Michael quietly urged, "Tell me, Beth."

She did not, not right away. Michael understood. Wifey dear had to approach this horrible *thing* at her own slow pace, lessen its impact by creeping up on it with a recitation of the typical, common *normal* things that had preceded it.

"I started out feeling so fine today," Beth said wearily. "Before I got the kids, I did go out to Lincoln Junior College. It was something. As soon as I stepped in the building, I felt ten years younger."

"Sure," Michael said.

"I spoke with the advisor. He was nice. I'm going to take the abnormal psych class."

"That's just great," Michael said. "I'll bet it will be interesting." *Get on with it, you silly bitch,* he mentally commanded.

After the college visit, Beth had picked up the children, and then they'd gone shopping, stopping at McDonald's for lunch on the way home. "Then we got in, oh, it must have been 1:30, I guess."

They hadn't been back five minutes when there was a pounding at the front door—a visitor. "Brad was drunk. I've never seen him like that. I never saw *anyone* that drunk."

"Jeez," Michael said.

"I thought he was going to pass out. Every time I got him to sit down, he'd bounce right back up. He wasn't making much sense at first. He kept asking, 'Who'd want to hurt good old Dusty?' Finally he managed to tell me . . . the story."

Beth squeezed Michael's hand so hard his fingers went numb. "Someone broke Dusty's neck," Beth said. "Killed him and left the body in the garbage."

"Good lord," Michael said. "And the kids heard all of this?"

"Pretty much," Beth said miserably. "I tried to shoo them away, but Brad was so loud . . ."

"Sure," Michael said. "I understand. It's awful. It's just awful for Brad and for the kids and you." Michael fell silent a moment, then asked, "Did Brad call the police?"

"Yes," Beth said. "They came out and took . . . the dog. They're investigating, of course."

Right, Michael thought. No doubt the local version of Quincy was seeking fingerprints on a deader-than-shit dog this instant.

Michael dipped his head. "I'd better take a walk," he said. "See how Zeller's holding up."

"I knew you'd do that, Michael," Beth said. "Are you okay now, honey?"

"Not okay," Beth answered, "but better. I'll try to put together some kind of dinner."

"Not for me," Michael said. "My appetite is pretty well gone."

Before Michael left the house, he told Beth to put the chain on the door. He'd knock when he returned.

Beth's eyes acknowledged the warning and he knew she understood what he wanted her to. Somewhere—outside—*perhaps living in this very neighborhood!* was a person who killed, a person who killed dogs, who could possibly kill . . . Why, it might even be someone they knew very well.

Goddamn, it was funny! Michael Louden, the Stranger, laughed to himself as he went next door to be a "good neighbor."

* * *

I am all alone. Brad Zeller sat in the kitchen thinking that one thought. His hand was wrapped around a nearly empty glass and only three inches remained in the Imperial bottle on the table. But—not to worry—another fifth waited in the cabinet. Sure, it would be a bitch to walk all the way over there the way the floor was pitching and rolling, but then, journey's end! and he'd reward himself with a drink. And a drink. And a drink. He hoped he might eventually pass out.

And then, well, tomorrow would be another day . . .

Another day of all alone. There was a thought for you. The *thought.*

Dusty . . .

Dusty. Was. Dead.

The hurt tore through Brad Zeller all over again. His glass was empty. His hand floated to the bottle's neck. With slow, drunken precision, he poured without spilling a single drop.

When the front doorbell rang, Brad struggled to his feet and managed a wide-legged, swaying stance. He staggered from the kitchen. The walls and furniture became handholds and resting points to keep him erect.

He opened the door. He was not all alone. His friend was here.

"Muh . . . Michael," Brad said, working to control lips and tongue.

The floor thrust up under his heels. He rocked forward.

Michael quickly stepped in and caught

Brad under the arms. "Steady, big fellow," he said, easing Zeller around. Michael draped Brad's flopping arms over his shoulder.

"Sudbody killed Dusty," Brad mumbled, heavily leaning on Michael. "You hear 'bout it?"

"Yes, Brad," Michael said. "Believe me, I know all about it. Let's sit your sagging ass down now, all right?"

"Kitchen," Zeller insisted. "Got somethin' to drink in the kitchen."

"Right you are," Michael agreed. "You're a guy who needs a drink, yessir."

In the kitchen, Michael deposited Zeller in a chair at the table. Brad used both hands to pick up the glass. Some whiskey flowed down his chin but most of it went down his throat.

"Join you for a drinkee, pally," Michael said. He took a can of Old Milwaukee from the refrigerator and popped the top. He sat down across from Zeller. "Drink up, Brad. That's the way."

Brad's head lolled from side to side as though he were undergoing a slow motion *petit mal* seizure. "Dunno who killed my nice dog, Michael. Figure maybe a kid? Figure some teenage punk sonofabitch of a kid?"

Michael shrugged. "I doubt it. After all, there's no such thing as a bad boy."

"A sonofabitch," Brad said, "that's who it was."

"Just remember, Brad, there's some good in the worst of us and some bad in the best of us. That's what I think, anyway."

"Yeah," Brad said, head bobbing. He wasn't really sure what it was that Michael had just told him. It was difficult to make sense of the words, connect them up with one another. It didn't matter, though. Things were better now because Michael was here and someone *did* give a goddamn about Brad Zeller and he was not all alone.

Brad's eyes became wet. "You are my friend, Michael. You are my very good friend."

"Gee," Michael said, "Golly. Holy smoke. It's an honor, Brad. No shit and honest Injun, I really mean that."

"See, a person's gotta have somebody."

"That's true. Everybody needs somebody sometime. Wouldn't that make a great song title?"

"Used to be times . . . I get lonely, y'know? But there was always old Dusty. He was my friend, too. My very good friend."

"Yes, a dog is man's best friend, Brad. A fucking shame somebody killed your dog."

"Yeah."

"Say, you're crying, Brad."

"Yeah." Brad ran his hand over his face, smearing the wetness around. "Got a daughter. Nice kid, Joanie, doesn't give a damn about me. Lives in California. Never calls. Shit, she didn't even show for her own mother's funeral."

Michael said, "Try to be optimistic, pal. Maybe Joanie will drag her ass here for your funeral."

Brad squinted. Michael was smiling. Had Michael made a joke, trying to make him feel better? He thought so, but he wasn't certain.

Brad pushed back from the table, the chair legs squeaking on the floor tiles. "Gotta take a leak."

"Be my guest, Brad. Man's got to do what a man's got to do."

"I . . ." Zeller grinned loosely. "I can't stand up too good."

Michael rose. "Hey, I can't let my chum, my buddy, my *compadre* sit there and piss his pants, can I? That wouldn't be neighborly."

Michael hoisted Zeller to his feet. "Here we go," he said.

As Michael helped him down the hall, Brad Zeller felt the warm, welcome emotion of gratitude filling him. "Thank you, Michael. You are a good man."

Michael laughed, a crisp bark. "Hell, I'm a fucking angel, Brad. Haven't you ever noticed my halo?"

Flicking on the bathroom light, Michael propped Brad against the wall. Michael raised the toilet seat. "Okay, buddy. Piss your brains out."

Brad lurched toward the stool. On his third attempt, he caught the catch of his fly and unzipped his trousers.

"Ah, what the hell," Michael said to himself. Brad was two feet from the toilet when Michael kicked the back of his left knee.

I'm falling, Brad Zeller thought. He tried to ready himself for the impact. It wasn't that bad, he thought, not all that much pain as he went down on his knees.

The pain exploded a moment later. Zeller's head between his hands, Michael grunted with total, all-out exertion, and pushed Brad's skull forward and down.

Zeller's forehead smashed into the rim of

the toilet bowl. Brad felt a steel net of agony squeeze his brain. A black balloon expanded inside his skull and he thought his eyes were going to pop from their sockets.

Then Brad slowly tumbled from his kneeling position, as though he were a penitent yielding to the exhaustion of days of prayer. He rolled onto his side, then to his back.

There was only a smear of scarlet on the toilet rim, but blood welled thickly from the trench in Brad's crushed forehead.

Michael smiled, gazing down at Zeller. "Most fatal accidents occur right in the home, Brad. Think I saw that pleasant little item in the *Reader's Digest.*"

Brad blinked. The pupil of his left eye was so dilated that the cornea had virtually disappeared. Blood seeped from his ears and trickled from the corner of his mouth.

"Yessir," Michael said, "damned near every day you hear about some stupid old drunk taking a flop in the bathroom and fracturing his skill. Sure looks like that's what happened to you, pal."

Brad's left leg jerked.

"Next time, you watch your step, hear?" Michael said.

Zeller's arms flapped. He kicked out, the final actions ordered by his ruined brain. Then the electro-chemical processes of his mind ceased. His chest rose and fell, and deep in his throat, there was the sound of water slipping through a sluggish drain.

"No need to get up, pal. I'll show myself out," Michael Louden said to the dead man—and he left.

SIX

MARCY AND KIM had their eggs, scrambled, and, as usual, Kim considered mealtime "time to talk." If she was at all upset about the killing of the neighbor's dog, she showed no sign of it. Instead, she had so much to tell her mother and father about camp. Camp PineTop was "Neat!" a "real blast;" it was "such a fun place!"

The children were not yet dressed for the day. Kim, to Michael's right at the kitchen table, was wearing her *Star Wars* pajamas; Marcy, across from her, had on Swiss dot shorties. While Kim rattled on and on—" . . . so then the canoe tipped over and everyone was screaming but I wasn't afraid"—Marcy fastidiously sliced her sausage links, her elbows off the table, her manners as refined as those of a child of the British Royal Family.

At the stove, Beth, in her housecoat, slipped the edge of the spatula under Michael's over-easy eggs and put them on a plate. Last night had brought a touch of terror to her life that she did not fully comprehend. Only Michael's assurances and his arms about her in bed, as well as the brandy Michael insisted she drink, had enabled her to get to sleep.

But now, this morning, Beth thought the kitchen had the golden-good feel of bright sunshine and she was working hard to convince herself that what had happened yesterday was . . .

No, not *impossible*, but certainly *the* too horrid, too awful occurrence that brushes by you only *once* in a lifetime. Someone—some inhuman monster—had killed Brad Zeller's dog. That was true, a reality. She would come to accept it, eventually, even if she never understood it. But it had to be the one inexplicable horror that filled the quota for the Louden family—*That's it, The End, thankyouverymuch!*—and now it was time to get on with living their normal life.

"Here you are," Beth said brightly, placing Michael's eggs and sausages in front of him. Returning from Zeller's last evening, Michael had said that Brad was in a bad way, as could be expected. They'd have to keep an eye on him; that was all they could do.

"Thanks," Michael said. "Looks great. This is the kind of breakfast that makes you think morning is a fine time to start the day!"

Primly raising a bite of egg to her mouth, Marcy giggled at his comment. Kim said, "Oh, Dad! That's stale! Morning's when you *got* to start the day!"

"Oh," Michael said, "live and learn. I never realized that."

A moment later, Beth had her own breakfast and was seated opposite Michael at the other end of the table. *Now*, she thought, *here we all are and everything is as right as it can be and there's nothing to worry about, nothing to . . .*

. . . nothing to dread . . .

She was ashamed of herself, an adult, preyed on by those vague and unformed terrors of children, waking them, shrieking, in the thick of night, with a cold, spider-crawl fearfulness that cannot be appeased even by the warm safety of MomandDad's bed.

Beth sipped her steaming coffee. The dog's death—Funny, she did not want to think of the dog as Dusty—that would make it worse . . .

The—dog—was dead for no reason, no reason . . .

No! Not now. She would not allow herself to descend into a nail-biting, mind-whirling worry about this-and-that . . . and-everything. Oh, there was reason to be careful—real reason—*and wasn't there always*—but she wasn't going to go overboard, become a statistic on the "Percentage of Paranoids in Today's Suburbs!"

" . . . So I got in trouble," Kim said. "All it was was funny, and they made such a big deal out of it."

"What did you do?" Michael asked. "Maybe it wasn't so funny and maybe it *was* a big deal. That's a possibility, too, don't you think?"

"Nah," Kim said. She drank milk, nearly upsetting the glass. "There was this wimpy girl in our class, y'know. Her name was Alana. She was real scared of snakes, so I put this garden snake in her bed."

Kim laughed at the recollection of the wimpy girl named Alana who found a snake in her bunk.

"Very nice," Michael said dryly. "I'm really

proud of you."

"Uh-huh!" Kim said. "Did she ever scream!"

Yes, Beth thought, *everything is just fine. There are some men who can't even talk to their kids, but Michael? He's just hanging on every word that Kim says . . .*

"And they found out what you did," Michael said.

"Nah," Kim said, "Alana was such a wimp-o, I wanted her to know who did it so I *told* her and she went and told the counselor."

"Well," Michael said, "honesty is the best policy. Confession is good for the soul. Tell the truth and have no regrets."

Beth watched as Michael moved his hand to his mouth just a half-second too late to hide his smile. Kim didn't seem to notice.

"So anyway," Kim said, "I got punished. They made me clean up the *whole* camp. I had to use this stick with a nail on the end of it and pick up all the papers and everything."

"Sounds like you got what you deserved," Michael said reflectively. "But do *you* think that was a fair punishment?"

"I didn't care, so you know what I did?" Kim said.

"No. What?" Michael responded.

"The next night I put *three* snakes in old Alana's bed! And a toad, too!"

Michael said nothing. Once more, his hand was over his mouth.

Beth thought he was smiling, trying not to laugh at Kim's mischievous adventures at Camp PineTop.

He was not.

Michael was remembering.

There's always a wimp at a summer camp.

The wimp at Camp Bethel, when Michael was 12, was named Alvin Burdell . . . .

It was a Tuesday night, forty-five minutes after lights out, and it was time to get Alvin Burdell, "Fat-Guts" whose inclusion on your team meant you automatically lost the race or the volleyball or softball game, the jerk who couldn't do one thing right but knew how to do a million things wrong, who got you sick just looking at all that wiggling blubber, and who, *just like a big fat baby!* wet his bed and woke up everyone in Cabin Three with that rotten stinking smell and his crying.

In his underwear, Steve Dawes led them, another boy aiming the penlight; they were the "Cabin Three Commandos" and the Target for Tonight was "Fat-Guts." Steve had appointed himself chief of the operation and no one had opposed him. He was thirteen and tough, a schoolyard bully on vacation at summer camp, always ready to do what he could to make life miserable for anyone weaker than himself.

More or less silently, the seven boys surrounded Alvin's bed.

Michael hung back as far as he dared. This wasn't for him, not his way to get involved with these *nothing people*—he had started thinking of them in that way since his talk with Jan—but he couldn't refuse to be part of it, either. He had to keep up the pretense, go on acting like everyone else, *the nothing people!* until . . .

Alvin was asleep. The penlight threw a yellow circle on his open mouth; a thick shadow moved as if something were trying to crawl out of his throat.

"Now!" Steve Dawes gave the order.

It was a smooth surprise as a pillow pressed down on Alvin's face, muffling his shocked cry, and hands held his arms. The blanket and topsheet were yanked down. Hands gripped Alvin's ankles, pinning him totally.

"Fat-Guts" was helpless.

"Yeah!" Steve Dawes said. "Now we fix him!" Steve was holding a can of blue paint and a brush. He kept saying, "Yeah," voice trilling with excitement, as Alvin's pajama tops were unbuttoned, the bottoms pulled down to his knees.

"Lookit that whale blubber!" Alvin's breasts were as bulbous as an over-developed woman's.

Steve laughed. "Itty-bitty prick like that. Way Alvin pisses, he oughta have a damn fire hose!"

Everyone was laughing, caution diminishing at the continuing success of the Cabin Three Commando raid. "Mowf, mowf!" came from beneath the smothering pillow. They laughed at that too. "Sounds like a harelip dog!"

"Move the light," Steve said. He took the lid off the paint can and squatted by the bedside. "We're gonna put a sign on you, Fat-Guts," Steve said. "Right on your titties. It'll say 'Porky Pisspot.' Then we're gonna paint your itty-bitty prick blue and tie you to the flagpole so when they raise the flag tomorrow, there's a big, fat surprise!"

Alvin Burdell heaved; he looked like a giant sea slug. "Mowf, woaa . . ." was his inarticulate plea.

The tip of Steve's brush trailed blue, a shaky line P on Alvin's right breast, then, next to it, an O.

Suddenly, there was a piercing sound—*Ahrkee*—a clack and a rattle.

"Now what the heck is this . . . ?"

Light descended in a sharp yellow instant from the single bare 75 watt bulb overhead and froze The Cabin Three Commandos.

The boys scattered, backing to their own beds, turning and running, as Jan Pretre strode forward. The frightened excuses spilled out. "We weren't . . ." " . . . not doin' nothin' . . ." "It was just a joke, huh?"

Then Jan Pretre had Steve Dawes and Alvin Burdell threw the pillow from his head and sat up, blubbering hysterically.

"Hey!" Jan spun Steve around and Steve dropped the paint can. Holding Steve from behind, Jan cranked the boy's arm up between his shoulder blades.

Steve Dawes yelled, rising up on his toes, eyes bulging, his face as white as breakfast oatmeal. Then he started to peep like a starving baby bird, "Ohohoh . . ."

"Steve," Jan Pretre quietly said, "don't you know it's wrong to be mean to people? You shouldn't try to hurt Alvin." Jan pressed Steve's arm higher still.

"Ohohoh . . ."

Staring, Alvin was pulling up his pajama pants. Tears ran down Steve's cheeks and his face looked as if it were melting. "My arm, my arm, you're breakin' . . ."

"Now Steve," Jan said, "you really ought to apologize to Alvin. Let's hear you say you're sorry and that you promise never to be so mean again, okay?"

Each word of Steve's agonized apology was on a frantically ascending scale. Then he was begging. "Oh, please, my arm, don't hurt me, don't hurt me."

Jan released him. Steve staggered. Then, head down, working his shoulder, he slowly made his way to his bed, not looking at anyone. He crawled under the sheets, lay on his side, and shook with sobs.

"Alvin," Jan said, "there's an extra cot in the counselors' cabin. Come on, we'll get you cleaned up and you sleep there tonight."

When Alvin Burdell smiled, he looked like a jack o'lantern lit by a dozen candles.

On Saturday, after breakfast, Jan told Michael that he was taking him along with their "good pal," Alvin, on a special overnighter. Another counselor would take responsibility for Cabin Three that night. Jan told Michael that the overnighter would be a lot of fun.

Then he told Michael *how* they would have fun.

It was nearly sunset when they camped in the woods, far from Camp Bethel. Their site was near to a steep ravine, rough ground where the grass had lost the battle to stones and weeds.

Jan built a fire. He cooked beans, the open cans heated in the flames, and they roasted hot dogs on sharpened sticks.

"Having a good time, Alvin, old pal, old buddy, old chum?" Jan asked.

"Yeah!" There was a mustard smear alongside Alvin's mouth, more mustard as well as ketchup on his T-shirt.

Alvin's hand splatted on the side of his neck. "Got that little stinker!" he crowed, reducing the mosquito's remains to gooey pulp and flicking it in the fire. "Lot of bugs tonight."

"Hey, no problem," Jan Pretre said, "You kill them. It's easy to kill them, isn't it?"

Sitting with his legs outstretched, Michael saw a rock within arm's length. He picked it up. It was egg shaped, the size of a baseball; he felt its weight.

Nodding toward the ravine, Jan said, "Really a beautiful sunset. Let's go take a look."

Alvin waddled beside Jan. They stood at the edge of the ravine. Jan pointed to where the pink ball of the sun seemed to rest in the V of a tree where two limbs joined.

"That's just like a picture postcard," Jan said. "All that pretty color. It's so fucking beautiful I could just shit."

"Huh?" Alvin said. He began to laugh. "Hey, Jan! I didn't think you talked that way. Hey! Shit!"

Michael got to his feet.

"Sure," Jan said. "I'm just the right kind of guy, you know, with the right language for the right situation. That's the way it is, old pal, old buddy, old chum!" He patted Alvin's shoulder. "You know what I mean, don't you, you fucking 'Fat-Guts'?"

"Hey, Jan, I know you're kidding around, but . . ."

Michael was running. He held the rock tightly, fingers shaped to it, and his arm was back as though he were about to throw.

Michael did not pitch the stone. Just as Alvin was turning his head, Michael planted his feet, locking himself to the earth. He swung his arm, snapped it forward.

He smashed the rock against the birthmark over Alvin's ear and there was a sound like a cantaloupe falling from a supermarket cart and smacking the floor. At the same time, there was another sound, similar to the crunching of the shell of a hard boiled egg.

And there was yet another sound that might have been Michael Louden's heart.

Alvin dropped to his knees, swaying. He said, "Dowah . . ."

Jan stepped in front of Michael, directly behind Alvin, and slammed his knee into Alvin's back. Alvin rolled down the ravine.

"Really a pretty sunset," Jan Pretre said. He told Michael to follow him, warning him to be careful; if they didn't watch their step, it would be easy to fall all the way down to the bottom of the ravine where Alvin lay.

Alvin was on his back, left leg twisted sharply beneath his rump, a pointed splinter of bone shredding the pinkish, oozing flesh of his right forearm. His eyes were wide open. The left side of his head seemed to be covered with thick pudding.

"You . . . hurt . . . me . . ." Each word brought a bubble of red spit to Alvin's lips.

"You are smart, old pal, old buddy, old chum," Jan Pretre nodded. "You are fucking perceptive." He laughed. "Alvin had a fall. Go boom. Looks like you broke your arm and your leg and cracked your little head so all your smarty-smart brains are leaking out."

Alvin's mouth opened and closed. A bright red bubble popped.

"What a bad, bad accident," Jan said. "I'm afraid old 'Fat-Guts' broke his neck, too!"

Jan bent, sank his fingers into the porridgy flesh under Alvin's jaws, and, gritting his teeth, twisted and jerked. There was a series of loud cracks, like a string of ladyfingers, only louder, much louder.

Alvin's chest heaved once and his tongue shot out of his mouth. Then he let out a long, sputtering fart.

"And I thought he liked the beans," Jan Pretre said.

For two hours afterward, Jan talked and Michael listened. Jan told him about aura. Jan could see auras; he understood them.

Michael's aura, that of Michael-The-Stranger, the real Michael! *was very bright, very red. When Michael struck Alvin with the rock, Jan could not even see Michael's face for the brightness of it. Michael had been transfigured by the reality of himself.*

And Jan told him what would happen next —and what would happen in the years to come—in the Time of the Strangers.

Yes, Jan was correct about what happened next. The police were understanding. It was evident that poor Alvin had suffered a fatal accident.

Because Alvin died twenty-three years ago, before it became fashionable and profitable for everyone to sue everyone else, the child's parents did not charge negligence against either the "good Christian camp" or Alvin's counselors. Oh, they knew how their boy had felt about Jan Pretre; all Alvin's letters home had lauded the counselor who had been so good to him, so kind and protective.

You could tell Jan Pretre was crushed; he could hardly stop crying. This was a terrible thing and he would feel guilty forever.

And that young man who'd been with him . . . that Michael Louden . . . The way he carried on, he must have been very close to Alvin. The poor boy would probably have nightmares over this as long as he lived.

That afternoon, when Kim asked if she and Marcy could ride their bicycles to the 7-11 Store in the "mini-mall" two and a half blocks away to get "Slurpies," a concoction of sticky-sweet syrup and ice, Beth's first thought was to say, "No." Then she thought better of it. Rationally, she knew the world was full of dangers, but unless you sealed your children behind walls and denied them their childhood, there was only one talisman a parent could gave a child against peril, the caution, "Be careful."

That's what she told the children.

At the end of Walnut Street, Kim, in the lead, turned right.

"Hey," Marcy called, "7-11 is the other

way . . ."

Kim braked her bike, scooted off the seat, and, holding the handlebars, waited for Marcy to catch up to her. "I don't want any Slurpy. They taste like yuck. That's just what I told Mom so we could get out and do something!"

"What do you mean?" Marcy asked. She looked worried. The "something" that Kim often wanted to do meant trouble. "Let's just go to the 7-11 and get a Slurpy and then go home."

Kim looked at her sister unbelievingly. "That's what's wrong with you, Marcy. You never want to do anything fun."

"I *do* . . ."

"That's why you don't have friends!"

"I do so have friends!"

"Oh, sure," Kim taunted, "you have lots of friends, but you don't have any *best* friends. You're not any fun."

Marcy lowered her head, and then, when she looked up again at Kim, she said, "So what do you want us to do?"

Kim smiled at her "trouble-in-mind" smile. "Let's go see them building the new houses."

Despite the nationwide slump in the construction of new homes, Park Estates West, a new development owned by the firm responsible for Park Estates, was moving ahead, homes going up in the optimistic belief that there would be buyers, eventually, for them. The suburb in the making was on the other side of Highway 394.

"We can't!" Marcy said. The girls were forbidden to cross 394, a four lane divided highway. "Daddy would . . ."

"*I'm* not going to tell Dad," Kim sneered. "And you'd better not, either!" Kim slipped up onto her bicycle seat and began pedaling slowly. She looked back over her shoulder, calling, "Come on and quit being such a wimp!"

When Kim was halfway down the block, Marcy came after her, standing up on the pedals and riding fast.

Wilbert C. Clarkson wasn't joking when he told people that his middle initial stood for "Careful." That was the way he lived his life and he credited that philosophy for getting him through sixty-three years—so far. No, Wilbert and his wife didn't get swine flu shots a few years ago because of the possibility of side effects, and no, Wilbert refused to wear contact lenses because "who really knows what putting them on your eyes could do" and so Wilbert wore thick, unfashionable, old style hornrims.

Nor was it time well spent talking to Wilbert Careful Clarkson about the safety of air travel, either; the engines on a 727 went, say, you didn't pull over to the side of the road and wait for the tow truck! You went down and that was it.

You were far safer in a car, if it was the *right* car. You wouldn't find Wilbert behind the wheel of one of those Honda Civics or Dodge Omnis or whatever; an accident in one of those baby buggies, say "Goodbye."

Wilbert Clarkson drove a Cadillac, trading

it every three years. (Rich? No, sir, his four franchise quick-print shops hadn't made him wealthy, but he did all right—all right enough to afford a sensible car.)

Wilbert drove his Caddy . . . carefully. The speed limit was 55—the gasoline crunch had had one good effect on American society, Wilbert figured—so Wilbert set the cruise control at 55 on the nose.

This afternoon, he was heading south from his home to Oakdale to visit the manager of his print shop in Carmody. Nice guy, that manager. He and his wife, both of them youngsters, were running the place, but they were having trouble. Of course it was trouble they didn't have to have. If they had only been —careful. They just didn't take the extra time, the extra care, to make sure the ink and water were mixed exactly right. You could quick print anything if you just made certain that your equipment was right—so much ink and so much water and the customer had as pretty a copy as anyone could ask for.

Okay, Wilbert would explain it all to them. If you had the right machinery and treated it properly, no sir, you never had problems.

The yellow, diamond-shaped sign on the side of Route 394 warned him: "Crossroad." Wilbert Clarkson slowed down. You couldn't be too careful, you know.

Then his foot, heel on floor, toe up, was ready to hit the brake, because . . . That kid had no brains! Look at her, just shooting out across the highway like that!

Okay . . . He had nothing to worry about. And neither did the kid. She had made it halfway across the road and—a quick glance showed Wilbert—it was all clear in the northbound lanes.

But then the kid lifted a hand from the handlebar and waved and *another* kid came scooting out . . .

And Wilbert had his foot on the brake and he hit the horn and he was saying, "Oh no, oh no," and he had the wrenching, awful realization that, no matter how careful you were, *accidents happened!*

Accidents happened!

He swerved, zigging toward the shoulder, and it made no difference. His foot on the brake pedal made no difference, slowing the Cadillac, but not enough, *not enough* . . . Wilbert C. Clarkson wanted to believe in magic, that somehow the day-shattering blare of the horn would transport the little girl on a bicycle into another dimension where she would be safe.

In a splinter of a second, Wilbert C. Clarkson had a revelation: as careful as he was, as careful as he had always been, he was going to have an accident, an accident—and there was not a single thing he could do to prevent it.

Then the Cadillac hit a bicycle.

There was a sound of shredding and twisting that Wilbert would never forget.

A child flew through the air.

An instant's image burned into his mind: the girl, her face slightly distorted by his thick glasses, the tinted windshield, the haze of hot summer, as she flew from the bicycle seat, riding only air for a suspended moment, her mouth and eyes so surprised . . .

Wilbert C. Clarkson pulled onto the shoulder of the road.

I've killed her. I've killed her. I've killed her, he thought, and then he got out of his Cadillac to do what he could for the child who had not been spared by his lifetime of "taking care."

SEVEN

LIKE so many libraries in the Midwest, Belford's was not air-conditioned, and so the windows were open, a light breeze fluttering the American flag in its socket in the corner of the high-ceilinged room. It was warm, but not uncomfortably so, and there was the pleasant odor of old books and dark woods. Claire Wynkoop's feeling of serenity made her think her personal vision of heaven needed neither angels nor sweet-singing choirs; she'd gladly spend the afterlife in nothing more elaborate than an other-dimensional version of the Belford Public Library.

"Mrs. Wynkoop, is this a good one? Should I take it out?"

Through her bifocals, Claire Wynkoop looked at the book the girl, Nelda Jarvis, placed on the checkout counter. It was by Judy Blume, and, like all the popular Blume titles, a frequent check-out of the junior high age group. Some of the more conservative parents in town didn't like Blume's honest treatment of frank themes, but Claire Wynkoop decided what belonged on the shelves, and besides, you didn't have to worry about what kids read. It was the kids who *didn't* read—or couldn't—who found trouble for themselves and made it for others.

"Yes, Nelda," Claire told the child. "I think you'll enjoy it." Stamping the return card,

Claire was pleased that so many children consulted her about what to read, pleased that she—yes, *she;* nothing wrong with taking credit when credit was due!—had made the library a place that children frequented.

When it happened, it was sudden, so sudden that while she had reason to anticipate it—she'd awakened that morning with "the old brain itch," the cold, menacing, ringing in her ears, her classic harbingers of premonition—it still caught her by surprise. She was looking at Nelda, knowing it was Nelda but not seeing her, seeing instead the face of the little girl who . . .

. . . screamed and floated, spinning in the air, wrapped in the shock of impact and enveloped by the sound of metal twisting and tearing, the little girl who sees now, sees with the ultra-clarity of fear, the ground racing up toward her . . .

Claire Wynkoop braced the heels of her fisted hands on the countertop. The moment of clairvoyance was over but during it and now, in its aftermath, her blood pressure had shot up to 200 over 110. The book stacks were whirling in a soundless hurricane. The ceiling was dropping to crush her. The earth itself was trying to dislodge her from its face.

"Mrs. Wynkoop, are you all right?"

She heard Nelda, Nelda in the here and now.

She couldn't answer, not yet, but a portion of her mind, coolly disinterested, spoke up: *Now? Is this it? Stroke? Heart attack? Is this death?*

And, with ironic detachment, she thought:

Is it going to be the Big Library in the Sky?

No. She could feel her body decide the issue, and she knew . . .

Not this time.

"Mrs. Wynkoop!"

She forced herself to focus, to see Nelda's plain, concerned childish face. The girl was frightened, tugging at a strand of mouse brown hair.

"Yes, Nelda," Claire said, "I just had a spell." Spell, she thought, now that was a word that showed her age; she doubted if people nowadays had "spells." Then she mentally added, *And I also had, no, not a premonition this time, but the*clarification *of one!* Before she had not known exactly what *would* happen, but now she knew what *had* happened, and to which child.

In the office, she telephoned Beth, but there was no answer.

Beth was already at the hospital.

With his silver hair, Vern Engelking looked strikingly like a Santa Claus who'd gone modern and shorn his beard. He projected good humor and fine high spirits as he talked about "Superior Chemical's, ah, difficulty with Mr. Herbert Cantlon."

Michael and Eddie Markell were seated with Vern at the round conference table in Engelking's tenth floor office. "Now," Vern asked Eddie, "just how long has our less than conscientious representative been defrauding us and our esteemed clients?"

"Three years at least," Eddie Markell said. "Maybe longer, but I know for sure three.

Way I see it, he's one of those guys that figures if he's an asshole, everyone else is an asshole, too."

Vern Engelking laughed. "Eddie, you have a unique way of expressing yourself."

Eddie Markell didn't answer. Eddie Markell was forty years old, and when he was younger, he had a passing resemblance to Sam Spade in the definitive incarnation by Humphrey Bogart in *The Maltese Falcon*. Perhaps that was what had led Eddie to become a private detective. What had led him to become a heavy drinker, though, was the pressure of having to hide what he really was —a Stranger. Eddie Markell did industrial investigations for suburban firms, Vern Engelking's among them, and he drank. When he had the opportunity, he killed people. His aura was the telltale red of a Stranger, but he had another aura as well, the internal smell of decay that came from years of mummifying himself with liquor.

"Tell us more unsavory facts about our hitherto trusted salesman, Herb," Vern Engelking said.

"What's there to say?" Eddie shrugged. He had lost weight in the past two or three years and his lightweight sportcoat did not fit well. When his shoulders moved, the cloth bunched up at the collarbone and stayed wrinkled. "Fucker uses his own set of price books for all his territory; he's skimming good coin from southern Illinois, northern Kentucky and Missouri. So I kill his fucking ass and that's that."

Michael had his misgivings about Eddie.

Yes, Eddie was a Stranger, but he might soon prove a liability. Eddie seemed less and less capable of maintaining his disguise, of thinking of every possibility and planning for it. When The Time of The Strangers at last arrived it would only be those who had never, *never once* given themselves away, those who had been as shrewd as Michael Louden, who would partake of the countryside feast of blood and screaming and death.

Vern Engelking raised an index finger. "If you please, *we* kill his fornicating ass. These group endeavors are so rewarding for us all."

"Yeah," Eddie said. "See, Herb's got this nineteen year old sweetie-pie he shacks up with in Mt. Claron. Wednesday night's his usual for getting his cookies. I'll fix it so we can have a surprise party. We can do them both, put some heavy shit on 'em."

"Michael?" Vern asked, raising his eyebrows, "We'll have to go away on business next week. Does that suit you?"

Business, Michael thought, *the business that was the sole reason for a Stranger's existence! Herb Cantlon, pot-bellied yokel with white socks and jokes about traveling saleman and farmboys who loved sheep, a good ole boy hick in hicksville territory—lumpy-dumpy Herby—and a woman!*

A tingling shudder ran through Michael at the thought of what Vern and Eddie and he would do. How could the thrill be described? he wondered. Sex? It was so far beyond any pleasure that the brain or body could know from any of the varieties of *that* act that the comparison was ludicrous. Had he been capable of pity, Michael would have felt sorry for the poor sadist who found only sexual pleasure in inflicting pain; A Stranger knew transendent, illuminating, overwhelming *pure* pleasure—became himself *all* pleasure when the blood poured hot and red and copper-stinking . . .

"Sure, Vern," Michael smiled. "I knew when you appointed me national sales manager that there'd be some travel involved."

"Indeed," Vern Engelking said.

"Yeah, whatever," Eddie Markell said. "See you guys," he said, and left.

With Eddie gone, Michael voiced his concern. If there was anyone he trusted in the world, it was Vern Engelking. "Vern, do you think Eddie could be a problem for us? The way he's drinking, well, his lungs ought to be marked 'flammable.' I'm not so sure he's in control."

Vern nodded, leaning back in his ergonomically designed executive chair. He folded his hands, twiddling his thumbs; he was one of the very few who could do that without looking like an untalented actor in an amateur melodrama. Vern sighed. "The fact is, I don't know. Eddie has his virtues, but your fears are not ungrounded. The man imbibes immoderately and that might create unfortunate situations in the future."

Then Vern smiled at Michael. "But for every problem, there is indeed a solution. If Eddie becomes a problem, we'll—solve him. Let's hope it won't come to that."

"All right," Michael said.

The beige telephone beeped and blinked. Vern rose and went to his desk.

The call was for Michael.

When he hung up, he answered Vern's unspoken question. "Beth," he said. "She's at the hospital. Kid had an accident, got hit by a car. She's in X-ray right now."

"Ah," Vern said, "children can cause their parents ever so much worry. Is she seriously injured?"

"Don't think so. Of course, with my kids, there's no need to worry about brain damage. You can't hurt what you don't have."

"Michael, it's remarkable how you can joke despite your shock and upset."

"Believe me, Boss, I'm only putting up a brave front. You know how I love those kids; no one's ever seen a more devoted dear old dad than me."

"Don't let me keep you. Please hurry to the bedside of your unfortunate infant. But try to look more the grievously concerned parent!"

"Yes," Michael said. He willed his face to change. He could feel it happen, a perfect imitation of fearful anxiety creating worry-dark hollows beneath jumpy eyes, even a tic-twitch along the jawline. Michael Louden had a thousand faces and all—*all but one of them*—the face of a normal man.

Now, he was the father suffering the terrible fears and concerns about his beloved child.

"By the way," Vern Engelking asked as Michael was on his way out, "which precious lamb was injured?"

"Kim," Michael said. "It figures."

It took Michael forty-five minutes to reach South Suburban Medical Center. The moment he stepped into the waiting room, directly across the hall from Emergency, Beth ran to him. "Oh, Michael . . ." He held her tightly, realizing that "Oh, Michael" was a statement of relief and not anguish.

"Kim's—Kim's okay?" he tentatively asked.

"They think she'll be . . . she *is* fine!"

Michael let out a deep breath. "Thank God," he whispered. He looked over Beth's shoulder and saw Marcy, seated in one of the plastic chairs that lined the walls of the waiting room. For a second, her eyes met his, and then she quickly glanced down, moving the toe of her sneaker from side to side on the tile floor.

"Mr. Louden?"

Michael turned, and Beth, standing at his side, said, "This is Dr. Hasselbrink. He took care of . . ." Beth had to struggle to say her child's name as she realized for the thousandth time how near her child, *their little girl*, had come to death.

Dr. Hasselbrink shook Michael's hand. "That is a kid and a half you've got there, Mr. Louden."

"She's . . ."

"She's what I'd have to call a miracle," Dr. Hasselbrink said. "We've got negative skull and chest X-rays, no signs of internal bleeding, and, except for some bruises, Kim seems to be a hundred percent." The young intern had a reddish-blond mustache that was heavier on the left than the right, giving his otherwise pleasant face a disconcertingly unbalanced appearance. In his white tunic, Dr. Hasselbrink reminded Michael of the college kids who used to earn summer money by selling ice cream from three-wheel bikes in the parks.

"We'll want to keep her for twenty-four hour observation," Dr. Hasselbrink continued, "just to play it safe, but I think we're A-OK."

A-OK, Michael thought, *Dr. Kildare goes hip.*

"I . . . I can't tell you how . . ." Michael paused, made himself choke slightly with the emotion he was supposed to be feeling, and then—he congratulated himself for the extra touch—willed his eyes to mist as he put his hand on Dr. Hasselbrink's shoulder and squeezed. "How grateful we are!"

"It's okay." Dr. Hasselbrink blushed, apparently not at all comfortable receiving gratitude. *Just like the Lone Ranger*, Michael thought. *The insecure sonofabitch can't handle anyone saying 'Thank you.'*

"Thank you," Michael said, "I mean that from the bottom of my heart." Dr. Hasselbrink tried to slip free—politely—of Michael's hand; Michael squeezed the intern's shoulder emphatically. "I wish I knew how to tell you how much we appreciate everything you've done."

Hasselbrink turned as red as a high school sophomore who'd just learned he'd given his oral report in American History with his zipper at half mast. "Really," Dr. Hasselbrink said, "I'm only glad I was able to give you good news."

"I want you to know . . ." *Enough!* ordered Michael's mental warning system. "Well, thank you." He released the doctor.

"They're getting Kim settled into Pediatrics now," Dr. Hasselbrink said, backing away. "You should be able to see her in ten minutes or so, okay?"

"Thanks again, Doctor," Michael said, and Dr. Hasselbrink was out of the room, moving like he'd been summoned to perform emergency surgery on the Pope.

Michael glanced over at Marcy. She was slumped forward, elbows on her knees, hands folded, head bowed. "Daddy's girl" was staying away from Daddy, and Michael softly asked Beth to step out into the hall. Keeping his voice down, he asked, "Why is Marcy so down? She knows Kim's going to be all right, doesn't she?"

"She feels terribly guilty, Michael," Beth said. "You know what she told me? When she saw Kim get hit by the car, she wished it was her."

But what had happened? Michael wondered. He asked and Beth proceeded to tell him, leaving out no boring detail: the police came for her, told her about the accident, they were so nice, such polite young men, they even brought Marcy's bike home in the trunk, and, well Kim's bike was ruined of course, and then they took them all back to the hospital . . . *Damn*, Michael thought, *put one quarter in the slot and the goddamned jukebox plays all night!* He tuned out babbling Beth.

Later, when he was alone with Kim (Marcy was too young to be allowed upstairs, so Michael and Beth took turns staying with her in half hour shifts in the main lobby) Michael did learn what had actually occurred. Kim, who had scraped arms and legs and no other marks to show for the accident, and who wanted to know if they could rent her a hospital television for the one night she'd be there, excitedly, but clearly, told her father about it.

The car struck the back wheel of her bicycle. Kim flew over the handlebars, landed on the highway, and "It was like I was doing all those somersaults." She wound up rolling all the way to the grassy median and by the time "this old guy who zapped me" got to her, she was on her feet.

Incredible, Michael thought, the miracle that the intern had called it. But perhaps nothing was incredible, when it came to kids. One little creep drowns in a tablespoon of water, and the next day, you see in the paper that a kid decided it would be fun to jump off the Sears Tower and did so without harming a hair on his empty head.

Kim did want to know if she were going to be punished for riding across—well, *almost* riding across—394. Michael pretended to ponder the question a moment, then said, "Yes. As soon as you get home tomorrow, you're on restriction. That means no bicycle riding."

"Dad!" Kim protested, "Very funny. You know my bike got all squashed!"

"So I guess you can't ride it, right?"

Kim glowered, sitting up in bed. "That's not fair!"

Michael said, "Well, we'll talk this over when we get you home." He put up a hand, signaling the end of the discussion.

Before he left so Beth could begin her visit, Michael said, "You know, I bet you weren't even scared when you were whizzing through the air like Superman."

Kim's face became serious and reflective. Quietly, she said, "No Dad, this one time I *was* scared."

There would be a next time too, the time when she would know fear and finality.

That was The Stranger's silent promise to himself and his child.

They left the hospital at 8:00, the end of visiting hours, and, with a stop at Burger King—they were all hungry—they didn't pull into the drive until a quarter after nine. When they stepped inside, the telephone was ringing.

While Beth spoke to her mother—"Yes, Mom, yes, she's okay now," Beth sighed. "That's right, Mom. You were right. No, I'm not saying you're being an 'I-told-you-so.' I know you're concerned, Mom . . ."—Michael told Marcy to get washed up and ready for bed.

Fifteen minutes later, Michael knocked on the door of his daughter's bedroom. "Marcy?" He turned the knob and went in.

The bedroom, dimly lit by the lamp on the nightstand between the twin beds, was not so

111

much a place the girls shared as it was two "half-a-rooms" divided by an invisible wall. Over the headboard of Kim's, the bed nearer the door, was a poster, a close-up of soulfully ugly E.T.; above Marcy's, a framed picture of three horses grazing peacefully. As always, there was the smell of pinewood chips and guinea pigs—Michael hated the insult to his nose—and in the aquarium-cage on the stand by the window, Kim's brown and white cavy, Chopper, was whistling its unhappiness at being separated from his companion, Snowball, that Marcy was holding.

"We have to talk, Marcy," Michael said.

Marcy slowly nodded. Wearing a pastel blue nightgown with a "rainy day umbrella," design, she was sitting on her bed, her white guinea pig on her lap as she petted its head.

A girl and her guinea, Michael thought. *How goddamned touching*.

"Put Snowball back in the cage," Michael said, thinking *before I smash him against the wall and watch him splatter!*

"Yes, Daddy."

Both of them sitting side by side on the bed, Michael said, "Riding out on 394 today wasn't your idea, was it, honey?"

Marcy shook her head.

"I didn't think so," Michael said, "but you knew what you and Kim were doing was wrong."

"Yes, Daddy," Marcy said, her voice only slightly louder than a whisper. "We shouldn't have done it, and I shouldn't have let Kim go there. I could've come right home and . . ." Marcy choked, "and told Mom and maybe

Kim wouldn't be in the hospital."

Michael slipped an arm around Marcy's shoulder. "That's right, you love your sister and so you feel bad she was hurt. And your Mom and I love you kids, and we don't want you to get hurt. That's why we make rules to keep you safe. Do you understand that, honey?"

"Yes, Daddy."

Now how was that for a "Father of the Year" speech? Michael congratulated himself.

"You broke the rules, Marcy," Michael said, "so you're going to be punished. I'm going to spank you."

In the Louden household, spanking was punishment for only the most serious misbehavior; that meant that every once in a while, *Kim* got paddled. Marcy, of course, never gave her parents cause to punish her that severely, and with Marcy a mere reproving word could bring tears to her eyes.

But this time . . .

"Oh, Daddy," Marcy's lower lip trembled and her eyes watered. "I really am sorry, so sorry . . . Please don't spank me!"

Oh, Daddy! Christ! He hadn't heard her pathetic, puling "Oh, Daddy" in what had to be at least a couple of hours!

He answered by laying her face down across his lap. Marcy whimpered tearfully.

Before he spanked her, he couldn't resist. "This will hurt me more than it does you," he said, and, at the last of a half-dozen stinging slaps to her bottom, he had to add, "You'll thank me for this someday."

EIGHT

It was 5:30 in the morning when Beth awoke. The night had not been restful; she was too tense. She had slept, but it was an uneasy slumber that made her think she was seeing the oppressive, weighty blackness of the bedroom through her eyelids.

What is it? she asked herself in the two detached and disoriented way of those who have just emerged from unremembered dreams. *What is wrong, so terribly wrong?*

Lying on her back, Beth had the sudden, scraped-nerve feeling that she was being watched. She turned her head and in the dark, saw Michael on his side, facing her, his eyes awake and aware.

"Michael?"

How long had he been looking at her without her knowing it? she wondered—and why should that upset her?

"Can't sleep?" Michael asked softly.

"I guess not," Beth said. "There's so much going through my mind, and every time I try to figure out exactly what it is, it all slips away from me."

"Want to talk, Beth?"

"I think so," Beth said, "but I don't know what it is I want to talk about."

"That doesn't matter. I'm a good listener. You know that. Say anything and we'll go from there."

Beth thought. "Everything, well, everything seems to be going wrong somehow."

She paused. No, *wrong* was not exactly the word she meant, she explained. It seemed that suddenly everything was *changing*, changing in ways she did not understand. That frightened her. She had always felt secure, sometimes content, sometimes bored, but believing one day would be much like the next with its minor worries but no great fears, the ordinary small victories and defeats that made up life as usual. Now it seemed that the web of security that enfolded them all, the family—MichaelandBethandMarcyandKim—was being torn away. Zeller's dog, then, the very next day, Kim's accident . . .

But, Michael interjected, they had reason to be thankful, not fearful. After all, they'd come darned close to losing Kim, and, as it worked out, she'd be home from the hospital today, her own sassy, ready-to-raise-hell self.

"I guess," Beth said, but she didn't feel relief. It was as though the killing of Zeller's dog and Kim's accident—*the accident that Mom's second sight, intuition, psychic gift, whatever! had forecast!*—(And would Mom be providing new, dire predictions today, tomorrow, the day after?) —were inexplicably linked events in a chain of catastrophes destined to befall them.

That's how she felt, anway, and she had to admit it was not rational. But feelings didn't have to be reasonable to be real, to be true, did they?

And, another change (*for the worse, of*

course, of course!)—Marcy, their obedient, polite, model child—Beth was just sick, more over Marcy's *punishment* than her crime. Beth believed in the disciplinary worth of a needed paddling, and a couple of times had warmed Kim's bottom herself, not wanting to cast Michael in the "wait till your father gets home," "Dad's the one who hits" role, but physically punishing . . . now it was both girls —always upset her.

"Come on, Beth," Michael said. "Don't make more out of it than it is. Even the best kid goofs sometimes." Beneath the covers, Michael put his hand on Beth's hip. "Marcy did and she took her licks and that's that. Besides, as guilty as she felt about the accident, a couple swats and a few tears put things back in balance for her. She got punished, so she knows we forgive her and now she can forgive herself."

"I know you're right. Everything you're saying to me, I've already said to myself. But believing it is something else." Beth sighed. "I guess things are okay and I'm letting my imagination run wild."

"Honey," Michael said, "it *has* been a rough couple of days. That's not your imagination, and with all the stress of what's happened, you have every reason to feel kind of shaky. I understand that."

Knowing Michael understood and cared *did* help, Beth thought; it helped some, anyway.

"I don't know," Michael went on, "maybe this *is* a period of change in our lives, for whatever the reasons, but there's nothing written in the stars that says the changes are going to be all bad, is there?"

Beth felt otherwise but she answered, "No."

"I mean, next week you're going back to school. That's a change for you, and it's going to mean a change for all of us, but there's nothing wrong with it."

"You're right," Beth said. *He is right and I know he's right and that is that*, she told herself, working at believing it.

Michael patted her hip. "I may not always be right, but I'm always the guy who loves you. Whatever changes come our way, we'll handle them together, you and I."

"Yes," Beth said. Saying the simple word was an affirmation that made her feel better.

"Thanks," she said.

"For what?"

"Being my early morning psychiatrist."

Michael laughed. "The psychiatrist isn't supposed to be in bed with his client, but as long as I am, are you in the mood for some additional therapy"—Michael moved his hand to her belly, then down—"shall we say, a consciousness-raising experience in sensory awareness?"

"You're the doctor," Beth said.

Through her gown, he petted the mound of her womanhood. He said, "I prescribe a deep, intramuscular love injection."

"A wonder drug, Doctor?"

"Wonder-ful, my dear," Michael drawled, his hammy, overdone W.C. Fields impression. "It's is called . . . penis-cillin."

Their initial caresses were slow and, Beth thought, particularly gentle, moving to a lazy, relaxed union well suited to the early morning, Beth on her side, gown pulled up, Michael spooned to her, his front to her back, arm around her, cupping her breast, softly scissoring her nipple between the first and second finger of his right hand.

"There! That's good!" Michael's words were carried on the warm breath that brushed her neck and cheek. Beth drew her knees higher, pushed her buttocks back to feel the regular rhythm of Michael's hips and the smooth rippling of his belly at the small of her back.

It was good to be held and loved, she thought, drifting in warmth and comforting pleasure. A part of her mind continued to think, however, refusing to let her descend into the realm of pure feeling. After all, they had to be relatively quiet—it was really rather funny—so she couldn't let her keen enjoyment be expressed by the gratified moan that threatened to rise in her throat that might be a prelude to a squeal or even a sharp scream, because Marcy was right down the hall! Wake the child and uh-oh, that awkward instant feared by every parent: "What are you guys doing . . . *oh!*"

It was Beth's thinking mind that was invaded by the terrifying idea:

If she twisted her head . . .

Now, damn it! This is absurd and I know it and why do I keep coming up with this non-sense?

. . . and looked at the man whose hairy chest was a silly tickle between her shoulder-blades . . .

I've got to cut it out, stop dreaming up all this frightening, senseless garbage!

. . . at her husband, lover, Michael . . .

No, damn it anyway! Just stop it, Stopit-Stopit!!!

. . . She would not see him, but a stranger!

The irrational thought froze her. She did not yield to it and turn her head, but she was no longer one with Michael, making love. She was cold and alone, and when Michael squeezed her hard, muffling his climactic grunt against her neck, she was glad he was finished.

After breakfast, Beth telephoned South Suburban Medical Center to learn that "Kim had a good night," and, "as soon as we have a final looksee," she could be released, say around one o'clock or thereabouts. Standing at the kitchen counter, Beth realized she had been braced for bad news, and, as she put the receiver back on the cradle, she chided herself. There was no black cloud overhead, no seven years bad luck down the line, and no reason for this utterly unreasonable, melodramatic sense of impending doom that was plaguing her. She had signed up to be a student in the abnormal psychology class, not a case study for it!

It was high time for a "return to normalcy" (she couldn't recall if that phrase was remembered from high school history class or from her single year at college), and that's exactly what it would be.

Michael wanted to stay home, Vern Engelking would certainly understand, and they would all bring Kim home.

No, Beth insisted he go to the office. Though she didn't explain it to Michael, today, Beth wanted the satisfaction of "things as usual," their more or less regular schedule.

Besides—it was hard to admit to herself, but there it was—she needed to be away from Michael for a while, time to make sure she had that ridiculous "I don't know him; he's a stranger" *delusion*—I've got to call it that because that's precisely what it is!—banished from her mind.

So, at 9:30, later than usual, Michael left. Beth telephoned Belford, caught her mother before she left to open the library at 10:00, shared the good news about Kim, and deliberately kept the call brief so she had no disquietude talking with "sees all, knows all, *scares* me" Mom."

Then Beth busied herself doing "normal" things, taking note of how normal and immanently satisfying they were. She read the newspaper, dusted and polished the living room furniture, watered the indoor plants. After straightening up the downstairs rec room, she took a coffee break, listening to the portable radio in the kitchen. WBBM All-News reported that a man in San Francisco, annoyed by a the crying of his two month old son, had beaten the child's head in with a ballpeen hammer. It was horrible, she thought, the act of a madman, shocking and sad, so very sad—and it and all the other senseless terrors that made the news from day to day had absolutely nothing to do with

120

the Louden family of Park Estates.

The weather was pleasant for a change, temperature in the mid-70s, humidity not out of line, and late in the morning, Beth worked outdoors, Marcy accepting the invitation to help. At breakfast, Marcy had said little more than "Good morning" and then gone to her room. With both of them wearing "outdoor grubbys," on their hands and knees in the garden, plucking tiny weeds that were at most an insignificant threat to the thriving flowers, Beth surreptitiously watched Marcy.

"The flowers were really something this year, weren't they?" Beth said. The geraniums, campion, zinnias, morning glories, impatiens, were all still in lively, colorful bloom, and Beth had a flash of a lovely fantasy: Winter would come to the Midwest, the ice, the snow, but alongside the garage, her garden would receive a special grace and be untouched by death-cold, the flowers always living, always beautiful . . .

"Uh-huh," Marcy said, and then, as Beth hoped she might, Marcy accepted the unspoken invitation to talk. "Mom, are you mad at me?"

Delibately keeping her tone matter-of-fact, Beth said, "About yesterday?"

"Yes, Mom."

"No," Beth said. "I think I *was* mad, but I'm not any more. You and Kim both made a mistake, something bad happened that could have been much worse"—*and remember, you're talking to* yourself *as well as your daughter, Mrs. Louden!*—"and that's all there is to it."

"Mom," Marcy said, "you always tell me you trust me. Do you still trust me?"

Beth took a moment to think it over and then her honest answer was: "I sure do, Marcy, 100 percent."

"You know something, Mom?" Marcy said, her voice strikingly somber and adult. "You're the best Mom in the world and Daddy's the best father."

Just as seriously, Beth said, "And your dad and I have the best kids in the world."

The other "best kid" was released from South Suburban Medical Center at 1:30, but, with the paperwork—the insurance forms, the check for the deductible, the waiver of responsibility, etc.—it was 2:20 before they started home, Kim in the front passenger seat on the Chevette Scooter, laughing about having a ride down to the lobby in a wheelchair when "I didn't even break my little toe," Marcy in the back.

Beth decided she'd prepare an especialy nice ending for this thankfully normal day. While the Louden family didn't become enthusiastic over elaborate gourmet meals, they all, Kim included, liked unusual treatments of American standards. The window open over the sink, the kitchen fresh-smelling with a gentle breeze, Beth sat at the table, planning her menu: a tossed salad, zucchini, stuffed meatloaf with twice-baked potatoes and an almond-green been caserole, and for dessert—yes, let's get a *bit* fancy and creative!—a chocolate-mocha roll cake!

The cake would take some time, so she set

to work at it. Next week she would become a college student, a woman in "today's *real* world," but for right now, checking refrigerator and cabinets for ingredients, she was happy to be "a domestic-minded housewife," Mrs. Michael Louden, cooking a good meal for her family.

Upstairs, Marcy and Kim were in their room. Doctor's orders were that Kim take it easy for another day or so, and "Mrs. Louden, if she has a headache, dizziness, nausea, anything at all, call right away," so Beth told Kim to stay indoors.

"You know," Kim said, on her bed, leaning back on her elbows, knees bent and bare feet flat on the spread, "that was real dumb."

"What do you mean?" Marcy said. Like her mother, she'd changed clothes before leaving for the hospital and now, dressed in yellow sun suit, Marcy stood by the open window, back to Kim, the breeze ruffling her blond hair.

"You know," Kim said, "how you waved to me so I thought it was okay and then that guy zapped me."

"I didn't see the car," Marcy said quietly. "I thought it was okay."

"Then you're blind," Kim said.

"I'm not blind," Marcy said. She turned her head and squinted at Kim as a slanted ray of hazy sunlight struck her eyes. "I just didn't see it, that's all."

"For sure," Kim said with a contemptuous sniff.

Marcy moved to sit on the side of Kim's bed. "Kim" she said, "Maybe it *was* my fault you got hurt, but I didn't mean it. And I really am sorry. Don't be mad at me, okay?"

Kim didn't reply.

Marcy leaned forward and, as though sharing a grave secret, whispered, "You know, Daddy spanked me." As soon as she said it, Marcy blushed.

Kim's eyes were big with surprise. "Wow! He spanked *you?* You never get it, you're such a goody-goody."

Kim sat up and tapped her sister's arm. "Hey," Kim said, "I'm not mad at you now, okay?"

"Are you sure?"

"Yeah, I'm sure."

"I want to give you something," Marcy said.

"What?"

Marcy rose and went to the aquarium that housed the guinea pigs. She took out the white one, held it with her left hand under its belly, the other hand beneath its excited, kicking rear legs.

"I want you to have Snowball," Marcy said, handing the guinea pig to her sister. "He's yours now."

Shaking her head, the tip of her tongue filling the gap of missing teeth in the bottom row, Kim said, "I can't! Snowball's yours!"

"I'm giving him to you. I want you to have him."

Kim held out her hands. The guinea pig squealed in fright as he and his ownership were transferred from one girl to the other. "Thanks, Marcy," Kim said. "Sometimes you're a pretty good sister."

"An ex-cellent re-past, my dear," Michael drawled, folding his napkin and putting it to the side of the plate.

They'd had supper in the dining room, white tablecloth and good china, and even candles. Beth, bright and fresh in a green skirt and ruffled, yellow blouse, smiled at Michael and said, "Will you please stop being W. C. Fields!"

Would would you like me to be, wifey dear? Michael asked himself.

"No, thanks," Michael said to the offer of more cake or another cup of coffee. He pushed back his chair, and with the dramatic wave of a carnival barker, announced, "And now, fair ladies, for your delight and pleasure, we have a surprise, for you"—he pointed at Kim as though aiming a pistol— "and you"—Marcy was temporarily in his sights—"and, last but not least, *you!*" He took aim at Beth, letting his thumb-hammer fall.

Beth gave him a puzzled look while Marcy said, "Oh, Daddy," and Kim demanded, "What is it?"

He rolled his eyes at Kim. "I said it's a surprise. If I tell you what it is, then it won't be a surprise anymore. Now that makes sense, right?"

Kim nodded.

Michael rose, gesturing like a choir director to bring the group to their feet. "Come, my three wonderful woman, and follow me." In the kitchen, he opened the door to the basement rec room. "Please go downstairs and await my summons. And if anyone peeks before I've got it all ready, her head will turn into a giant turnip."

Marcy and Kim were both giggling and Beth, Michael noted, seemed as happily confused as the girls. *Yes*, he thought, *wasn't he one hell of a guy to bring such excitement into their miserable, moronic lives? Bet your ass, he had a goddamned warehouse full of all kinds of surprises for his dear family!*

Ten minutes later, Michael led them out the back way. Even as he was saying, "*Ta-dah!*" and waving toward the open garage door, Kim was running, shouting, "A bike! A new bike!"

"Three speeds, hand brakes, everything a girl could want," Michael said.

So thrilled she was actually hopping, Kim asked, "Can I ride it now, Dad? Please?"

Sure, pedal out to 394 and try for a truck this time, Michael thought. "Well," Michael said, "you're supposed to take it easy, so twice around the block will do it for tonight. Is that a deal?"

"You got it!" Kim was off like a shot, zipping down the drive.

"Now Marcy's surprise," Michael said. Inside, he told Beth to wait in the kitchen; she was forbidden to go to the living room under pain of becoming turnip-headed.

Marcy's gift was on the dresser in the girl's room. "A television!"

"Every American kid needs a television," Michael said, tapping the plastic cabinet of the twelve-inch black and white set.

Michael readied himself and, yes, there it was, Marcy's exclamation for all situations:

"Oh, Daddy!" She threw her arms around his neck and kissed him, thanking him again and again.

It hadn't been easy deciding what to buy for Marcy, with her dishwater personality, but hell, he needed to have something for her. He thought she seemed delighted but then again, a mouse like Marcy might have been equally satisfied with a pound of putty!

Beth's surprise—her surprises, that is—were perfect, Michael had no doubt. Downstairs, asking Beth to keep her eyes shut until he told her to look, Michael guided her from the kitchen to the living room, Beth softly laughing about how silly Michael was acting.

"Now, when I count to three," Michael said, "open your eyes! One . . . two . . ."

Beth giggled.

" . . . three . . ."

Beth opened her eyes. Her hands formed a tent in front of her mouth, muffling her exclamation: "Oh, Michael!"

On the end tables flanking the sofa stood the antique crystal lamps Beth had wanted so long. Their brass bases gleamed and the delicate, hanging prisms both captured and reflected a spectrum of diamond-bright, fairy-like colors.

"They're . . . they're beautiful!"

She thanked him with an exuberant hug and a kiss, made the obligatory comment, "You spent so much money!" obviously not displeased that he had, and then Michael said, "Well, glad I made all my ladies happy."

Michael explained he had about a half-hour's work that had to be done, but, as he started upstairs to his office, he turned back. "Beth," he said, "have you seen anything of Zeller today?"

"Hmm, no," Beth said. "You know, I'm really ashamed to say it, but with everything going on, I didn't think . . ."

"Sure," Michael said, starting for the front door. Before he reached it, he called back to Beth. "Say, how about going over to Brad's with me? It might do him good to see the two of us, let him know we give a rap about how he's doing."

"Of course," Beth agreed. At Zeller's, Michael rang the bell twice, knocked, and got no response.

"Maybe he's out," Beth said.

"I don't think so," Michael said. "Car's here and there aren't many places that Brad does go."

Michael knocked once more and then, pausing, he tried the doorknob. It turned.

"Michael," Beth said, her hand on his arm.

Michael opened the door, stuck his head inside, and called, "Brad? You here Brad?"

"Michael," Beth said, "maybe something is wrong."

Something wrong? Michael thought. *Whatever could have gone wrong for good old Brad Zeller?*

"I'll take a look out here in the kitchen," Michael said. "Why don't you step down the hall and see what's what?"

"All right," Beth said hesitantly.

In the kitchen, Michael drummed his fingers on the table and waited. The bathroom was down the hall. Had he not been so intently listening, he would not have heard it. Beth's outcry was pinched and weak, only his name, sliced in two distinct syllables.

Then she screamed, his signal to race to her, a scream that grew louder as the pitch rose like a European police klaxon, that did not end until he got to her.

She was gasping for air to scream once more. Her face was so white that the vein at her temple looked like a tattoo. Beth stood catatonically rigid in the washroom doorway, hands like claws on her cheeks as though she were about to rip at her flesh, eyes glitter-glazed circles of horror and shock.

Michael did all the right things, pushing past her to check Brad—*A corpse is a corpse is a corpse*—taking Beth's shoulders, ordering her to calm down, telling her they would call the police—*"Let me speak to whoever's in charge of the dead drunk squad"*—saying, "Come on, Beth," and "It's all right, Beth," and "That's it, hold on, don't faint," walking her back to their house. "Just a few steps more, that's the way."

And it was all he could do to prevent himself from putting his face close to hers, so close, and saying, "Surprise!"

NINE

Two UNIFORMED officers from the Park Estates Police Department and the paramedics arrived without sirens, their whirling lights fragmenting the neighborhood into coldly iridescent, expressionist angles and objects: a birdbath, jumping shadows cast by the limb of a tree, an advertising circular blowing across a lawn, the eyes of a prowling cat, Beth Louden's face as she stood, with Michael, on the walk by their front door.

"You're the folks who called? The Loudens, isn't it?" asked a slender man in a light tan suit. He'd pulled up in an unmarked Ford shortly after the others. He'd gone into Zeller's home, stayed only a minute or so, and now, offering his hand to Michael, he explained he was Detective Charles Hogan from the country sheriff's office. It was standard operating procedure for the county to check into all "deaths by misadventure."

Michael asked the detective to come in; it would be better to talk inside. And it wouldn't be necessary for his wife to go— *over there*—would it? She was still pretty shaken.

"I don't think so," Hogan said.

Beth thought that, despite a more than slight resemblance to Don Knotts, Detective Hogan projected quiet competence. The three sat around the kitchen table, and Beth, with a perfunctory calm that surprised her, answered his questions. Hogan scratched notes in a pocket-sized leatherette book. Yes, she was the one who found Brad. An alcoholic? She couldn't say that, not exactly, but yes, Brad often drank heavily.

Beth sipped hot coffee. Michael had put up a pot. Hogan's low-key, blandly efficient manner reassured her. He might have been an insurance representative writing up a policy. *This was nothing out of the ordinary to him*, Beth thought, and that somehow made it less awful for her. There'd been a tragic accident, but now there were proper steps to be taken. The world was still in balance.

And then she wondered if, right now, next door, at this exact moment, Brad Zeller was being put on a stretcher and covered over and hauled away so that the right things could be done for him—*to* him. There was a quick and horrible image on her mental movie screen: that dent, blood crusted, in his forehead, and Brad's face, the grinning sneer of his upper lip sucked in and drawn over his teeth, as though death were mocking life.

Beth blinked rapidly, eyes wet.

"I'm sorry, Mrs. Louden," Detective Hogan said. "I'm just asking what has to be asked."

"I know that," Beth said.

"It's all right, Beth," Michael said, his hand on her arm. "The detective has his job to do. We've got to do all we can to help the police."

She glanced at Michael from the corner of her eye, saw him through the diamond lens of a tear. My God, she thought, this is unreal.

Michael sounds as though he's reciting lines from a TV script! Didn't he understand that Brad Zeller was really dead—deadandgone—forever . . .

No. she was *upset.* That's the way she would think of this chaotic desperation-fear-dread she felt, this too real sense not that *she* was going mad but that the world around her had done so. She had to control herself. There was—Oh, God, it was grimly funny how the corniest lines came to mind!—"Nothing to fear but fear itself"—a cliche well suited to this moment, as apt as Michael's "We've got to do all we can to help the police."

"I see," Detective Hogan said, and Beth realized that he must have asked another question and that she had answered it.

Now Hogan spoke to Michael. "You said you were over at Zeller's the other night."

"Yes," Michael said. "Brad was, well, I don't want you to get the wrong impression of him, but he was drunk and depressed on account of what happened to Dusty."

"Dusty?" Hogan said.

"His dog," Michael said. "Brad notified the police. I thought you knew about it."

Hogan shrugged his shoulders noncommittally. "Local report and I haven't really touched base with the locals. What's there to know, Mr. Louden? Why don't you tell me?"

"Sure," Michael said. "Okay, I mean, anything I can do to help."

What is it? Beth demanded of herself. Why did she feel as though she were watching a stage play, a drama in which there was an actor portraying a policeman, and another, Michael, cast in the role of . . . of The Good Neighbor? The Hero?

. . . *or The Suspect! The Man Who Knows Too Much! The . . .*

Beth drank more coffee and scolded herself. Reality was quite bad enough without her imagination—her *paranoia*—adding to it!

"You know," Michael was saying, "it does seem suspicious that one day Brad's dog is killed and then the next day Brad is dead himself."

"Suspicious?" Hogan said.

"I mean, I'm not a policeman, so maybe I shouldn't use a word like that, but it is strange. Don't you think it's strange, Detective?"

"Sure it's strange," Hogan said. "A lot of things are strange but that doesn't mean they're suspicious."

"Maybe I used the wrong word."

"Maybe," Hogan said.

Word games! They were playing word games, Beth thought, with the frustrating feeling of exclusion of a child hearing other youngsters speak pig-Latin, sounding *almost* as though they were talking English, but not quite. No, it wasn't that. She was . . . upset. She was misinterpreting, finding uncalled-for connotations for every word, every phrase, then compounding the error by seeing nuances and new shades of meaning for a raised eyebrow or the tap of a finger on the table.

"What time did you leave Zeller's the other

night, Mr. Louden?"

Michael waved a hand. "I'm not sure. Maybe 7:30, maybe 8. It could have been later."

"Hmm," Hogan said, nodding at his notebook without looking up at Michael. "Just as a guess, Zeller probably died within a couple hours of that. We'll know more after the autopsy. Always do an autopsy for something like this. Would you say that Zeller was into a bad drunk when you came home?"

"Because of what happened," Michael said, "I would have to say that now, but I didn't realize it then. You see, when I first went over there, Zeller *was* pretty out of it. I even had to help him get to the john. But later he seemed to come around. I thought it was okay to go."

Michael's voice trailed off and then, suddenly, he slammed a fist on the table. Coffee sloshed over the rim of the cup he'd poured himself but from which he had not drunk. "I should have done something! It's just that I've seen Brad drunk before and I figured he'd be okay, sleep it off like always, but this time, he'll be sleeping if off forever. If I'd hauled him over here, put him to bed on the sofa in the rec room . . ."

Michael pushed back his chair. He rose, walked away, and then, back to the table, stood with his hands on the counter, head bowed and shoulder hunched. "Goddamnit, Brad Zeller was my friend and I . . ."

Michael turned, pinched the bridge of his nose. His eyes glistened.

Beth saw pain on Michael's face, in his

weary, defeated stance. He was blaming himself, she thought, playing that anguishing mind game "If only I had . . ." She had never seen her husband more vulnerable, more in need of her comfort, and she knew just how very much—trulyandalways—she loved Michael Louden.

She got up and walked to him. Michael put an arm around her.

"I am sorry, folks," Hogan said. He flapped shut the notebook and rose. "I've bothered you enough. Thanks for the coffee."

"It's all right," Michael said. "And I'm sorry I got carried away. It's just that Brad was a good man and . . ."

He didn't continue. Shrugging, Hogan said, "And something bad happened to him. I know. It works that way sometimes and we can beat our heads against the wall trying to come up with answers. The only good thing about pounding your head on the wall is that it feels so good when you stop. So do me a favor, Mr. Louden."

"What's that?"

"Don't put any more lumps on your head. Zeller had an accident. That's what it looks like, that's what the autopsy will show. That's what happened, period. Believe me, I've seen enough of these things to know. You seem to have good memories of your friend and that's something, anyway. Keep those memories and don't blame yourself. It's not your fault."

"I . . . I guess you're right," Michael said, and Beth prayed that Michael—*her good, loving,* gentle *Michael*—did not blame himself for poor Brad Zeller's death.

He did not.

He wished he were free to take credit for it.

"Sorry we came?" Michael asked. It was the mid-afternoon, Saturday of Labor Day weekend, and they were at the Engelkings. There were four lawn chairs arranged in a circle in a corner of the redwood deck over the patio, but two of those chairs were unoccupied now; Laura Engelking, always the hostess, had gone off—"I *must* do something about those empty glasses, Beth and Michael!"—and a moment later, Vern excused himself to greet some new arrivals.

It was a simple question, but Beth did not immediately answer; she thought it over. Michael had had to convince her they should go to the Engelkings' party. She hadn't felt like it. In fact, when she awoke this morning, she felt like doing just what she'd felt like doing yesterday and the day before: nothing. But a grown-up person couldn't lie in bed all day. An adult had responsibilities; there were things that had to be done and not to do them, simply to lie around feeling neither content nor sad, simply feeling *nothing*—that could not be.

So, all Thursday and Friday, feeling no more alive then a zombie in a grade Z horror movie, Beth had forced herself to meet her obligations, shopping and cleaning and cooking—her responsibilities to the household; talking to Marcy and Kim (their younger daughter seemed to be worried about the start of school because it meant "fractions" and she wasn't sure she knew her times

136

tables yet) and to Michael, her responsibilities to her loved ones; even reading a newspaper and glancing through the textbook for her abnormal psychology course that began next week, her responsibilities to herself.

She had done all this while diligently avoiding thinking about Brad Zeller. Joanie, Brad's middle-aged daughter, had flown in from California and had stopped by for twenty minutes. She looked like a character from a West Coast version of *The Wizard of Oz* after it had been re-written by a New Wave, Granola-eating Seeker of Higher Consciousness. Joanie philosophically accepted her father's death. "His time, maybe *karma*, y'know" and "The flesh is merely flesh, y'know," and so with Brad's body released from the country morgue, the finding, "accidental death," Joanie Zeller made arrangements for her father to be cremated. The house would go on sale next week—there were people "getting paid good money to handle it"—and Joanie was off and away. It was as though Brad Zeller had never existed, as though the reality of him had never been.

And oh, oh God, that was just so wrong, *that a man could be blotted out like that! You couldn't let yourself think about it, you couldn't let yourself feel it, the heavy sadness imbedded in your bones . . .*

"Hey," Michael said, "penny for your thoughts and all that. I asked if you're glad we came."

Beth honestly answered, "Yes." The temperature was in the low 80s, the few clouds in the blue sky puffy and picturesque;

it was as if Nature favored America, giving its blessings to plans for beery picnics and softball games and holding hands—feeling young—for believing that everything will go on forever.

There were about forty guests at the Engel-kings' party, neighbors, employees of Superior Chemical, friends. Beth had met some before, others today for the first time. It seemed to her that everyone was genuinely glad to be gathering together here—now. And, of course, Laura and Vern . . . While the Engelkings lived only a half hour due west of Park Estates, High Wood was an exclusive suburb: Old Money and New Money with Taste. Still, Beth had always been more than comfortable with the Engelkings, Vern, so comic with his flamboyantly formal speech, the model of the goofily eccentric favorite uncle in your "pretend" family tree, and Laura, with her constant cheerfulness that never seemed artificial.

Being here—*hereandnow*—with every-body, with them *all*, was like a confirmation of what Michael had said that morning, the final argument that persuaded her they should attend the party: "Life has to go on, Beth."

And Beth felt ready to go on with life.

"Honey," Michael said, "are you getting a little drunk?"

"Yes," Beth answered. She laughed quietly. The wine punch was potent. She felt as though her level of perception had been raised so that sounds—the group in conver-sation at the other end of the deck, the people below on the patio, in the back yard, and at the poolside, the radio somewhere playing easy listening music—were particularly clear. No one sound meant anything of itself but all blended together to form an aural blanket as soothing as the night noises of an idyllic woodland. "A little drunk, Michael, and you know what?"

"What's that, honey?"

"It feels fine."

"Guess I'm a little drunk, too," Michael said. "It's been some kind of week, so you're right. It feels good."

He didn't look drunk, Beth thought. And hey! Had he *ever* been drunk? Had she ever seen Michael juiced to the gills, *el blotto*, wiped out, bonkers? Wasn't one monumental "drunken husband" scene obligatory in every middle-class marriage?

Giggling, she decided she would definitely have to ask Michael to get drunk for her some time. When somebody was totally smashed, you had a chance to see the *real* person— that was simple folk wisdom.

When Laura Engelking returned, handing Beth another cup of wine punch, she told Michael that Vern wanted him to join him in the house for a minute.

"Probably business," Michael said with a theatrical sigh. "Work, work, work, that's all Vern ever thinks about."

"Business?" Laura laughed. "Michael, please! Vern wants to show you his new videogame! Everytime he manages to kill another 'alien invader,' he lets out a whoop like we've won the lottery."

Michael smiled. "You know, Laura, Vern might seem like an easy-going guy, but you have to be careful."

"Oh, What is that, Michael?"

Michael laughed. "The boss has the old killer instinct."

On the diving board, a fourteen-year-old stood poised, arms raised, concentrating, while determinedly paying no attention to the cute thirteen-year-old girl in shorts and a halter who sat in a chaise lounge, working just as hard at not noticing him. The boy took a deep breath, jumped, and smacked the water in a noisy, explosively spraying belly-flop. He didn't look at the laughing thirteen-year-old girl as he swam to the side and hoisted himself from the pool, thighs, chest and belly turning crimson.

In the shallow end, a mother encouraged her pre-schooler to try to float and a heavyset woman sat on the edge, dangling her feet in the water.

The man watched the two children who were in the third lap of a race across the pool's width on the "safe" side of the rope marking the deep end. The smaller child looked like a seal pup in her brown swimsuit, but she fought the water, kicking and splashing, wasting energy, while the older girl, in a flowered swim-cap and two piece red suit, glided smoothly, easily and almost effortlessly staying in the lead.

The man took a sip from a can of Michelob. Without being handsome, he was distinguished looking, tall and tanned, in his mid-forties, his black hair peppered with gray, his full beard neatly trimmed. His eyes were an intense dark blue. There were lines across his forehead that made him look more weathered than worried and a curlicued wrinkle seemed to splice together his heavy eyebrows.

Marcy reached the side of the pool and hooked her elbows on it. "I won," she said.

Kim, sputtering and splashing, gasped, "Oh yeah?" Then, springing on Marcy from behind, she dunked her and kept her under.

The man stepped to the edge of the pool. Looking down, he said, "Okay, that's enough of that. Let her up."

Kim angrily squinted at the interference, but released Marcy, who bobbed up, blinking and coughing.

The man squatted, looked into Kim's eyes. "I understand," he said softly. "She won your race and you're angry. It's all right to feel that, but it's not all right to try to hurt someone else."

A short time later, Beth, who'd decided to see what the girls were up to, found them standing by the pool, wrapped in their towels, animatedly talking to the bearded man who continued to squat, keeping himself at their level.

"Hi, Mom!" Kim called. "This is . . ."

Rising, the bearded man shook her hand and introduced himself.

"I'm Beth Louden," she replied. There were few men she'd met who were comfortable shaking hands with a woman; either they were into light finger-touching, or trying to revise their standard "businessman's hearty grip" to show their belief in feminine equality, but most men didn't find shaking a woman's hand at all a natural experience, and so it made for awkward first meetings.

There was nothing unnatural about this man's hand, holding hers for just the right amount of time and then releasing it. "Mom," Kim said, "is the food ready?"

Beth didn't know, but she said the girls might want to go find out. They scurried off.

"You have lovely children. You must be proud of them."

"Thank you," Beth said. "And yes, I *am* proud of them."

A few minutes later, Beth thought her "handshake impression" had been absolutely right. This "handshaker" was one of those rare individuals with whom one almost immediately felt at ease. Conversation flowed spontaneously, moving quickly from superficial to serious, and Beth found herself talking about some of the pressures of the past week. She wondered if liquor was making her too talkative, deciding that even if it was she didn't mind—and how she hoped that the bad period was over and done. She learned that he had known Vern Engelking for many years, that he had only recently moved to the south suburbs after living out east, and that he was a psychiatrist.

She had to laugh, and then she felt she had to explain her reaction. "You *look* like a psychiatrist."

"I know what you mean," he said, obviously not offended. "People were always telling me that, so I felt I had to get into the field. I'm just glad I don't look like a cowboy."

She told him she was quite interested in psychology herself. In fact . . .

Vern Engelking and Michael walked over. For an instant, Beth thought she saw a startled look cross Michael's face, but then it wasn't there, and he was pleasantly smiling, extending his hand, as she said, "Michael, I want you to meet Dr. Jan Pretre."

"I tell you, I didn't know . . ."

"If you were seeing a ghost? Or whether to shit or go blind? Or if you really *do* prefer butter to the higher priced spread? You were surprised. I saw it."

"Yes," Michael Louden glumly admitted. Surprise was something he hadn't felt in years. A Stranger couldn't afford to.

"It's all right, Michael," Jan Pretre assured him. "No harm done—this time. Just be careful."

Late in the afternoon, there had been a sudden change in the weather, a common occurrence in the Midwest, and the temperature began nose-diving. Now, an hour after sundown, many guests had departed and the majority of those who remained were inside, in the warmth, enjoying the offerings of the Engelkings' well-stocked bar. Michael had slipped away with Jan and they stood talking at the front of the house by the three-and-a-half-car garage.

But how long, Michael asked, would he— *all* The Strangers—have to continue being careful? There'd been so many years of maintaining the sickening guise of one of the *normals*, a meaningless, anonymous blob of humanity. When was the Time, *their* time that so long ago Jan Pretre had promised was forthcoming?

"There are so many of us, Michael," Jan said tonelessly. "More than you can imagine. More than even I ever thought. Every day I seem to find yet another who bears the mark, whose aura burns the color of fire and blood. We're everywhere, Michael. Just be patient. It won't be long, not now. Our Time is coming. You can feel it, can't you, Michael?"

"Yes," Michael said.

The wind blew cold from the north, and on it, he could smell the promise of winter kill, hear the icy shrieks of nightscreams and frigid terror. It was a wind that promised deathblow and bloodspill and the Time of The Strangers.

TEN

NEITHER OF the girls seemed to notice Michael, standing at the open door of their bedroom. Knees up, shoulders against the bed's headboard, Marcy was reading a *Nancy Drew* book. Kim, on her bed, was on her stomach, propped up on her elbows, chin in her cupped hands, staring at Chopper and Snowball. Side by side on her pillow, the guinea pigs were as inanimate as furry stuffed animals and only their brightly glittering eyes were a sign that they were indeed living creatures.

Goddamned double-ugly little bastards, Michael thought, *and that stink from their cage, pinewood chips and guinea pig shit!*

"Hey," Michael said, "you kids finish all your homework?"

Two startled faces peered at him. "No homework, Daddy," Marcy explained. "Not the first day."

It was the Tuesday after Labor Day, the traditional "back to school" date for much of the United States. It was also Beth's "back to school" day; she'd left for her class at Lincoln Junior College fifteen minutes ago, leaving Michael to take care of the girls.

Michael glanced at his watch. "Well, then, I guess it's about bedtime for you two, right?"

"Daddy," Marcy unhappily protested, "it's way too early . . ."

Jesus Q. Christ, Michael thought, she didn't realize he was joking. There were times he was convinced that Marcy had no more sense than those miserable, brainless guinea pigs!

"And I'll tell you what!" Michael said, bobbing his head like a spring-necked dashboard ornament, "I'll even rock you girls to sleep. See, I'll go out and find a great big rock . . ." He finished the sentence silently . . . *and bash your itty-bitty heads in!*

"You know, Dad," Kim said, "your jokes are getting pretty stale."

Michael put his hands on his hips and with the moronic enthusiasm of Steve Martin, uttered the comedian's classic, "Well, Ex-*Cuse* me!"

Marcy giggled. Kim made a derisive sound with her nose.

"Okay, if you don't have any homework and you're not ready for bed, how about we get in the car, zip over to the Dari-Quik, and get some cones. How's that sound?"

"Uh-huh!" Kim said.

"Oh," Michael said, "I am so very pleased that my suggestion meets with your approval, Kimmy dear. You know my one true goal is to make you happy! Put Meatball and Flopper away and let's go."

"It's *Snow*ball and *Chop*per," Kim said, "and that wasn't funny, either."

On the way out the front door, Marcy took hold of Michael's hand and said, "I like your jokes, Daddy."

"Good," Michael said, "So do I."

He wondered how "Daddy's little girl" and "little sister" and "sweet loving mommy" would like the big joke he had planned for them. Now *that* joke—oh shit, they'd think it was a goddamned scream!

She parked the Chevette in the "D" section of the lot. She checked to make sure she had the spiral ring notebook, the textbook *Abnormal Psychology*, and then, opening the notebook to the first, unblemished page, she wrote, "Mrs. Beth Louden" with one new Bic pen, then on the line below added the date with the other pen, making sure both ballpoints worked.

It was foolish how excited and yet somewhat fearful she felt, Beth thought, as she stepped out of the car. The feelings she had, the thoughts racing through her mind, were no more sophisticated and mature than those that used to besiege her as a child starting back to school. *Will the teacher be nice?* All she knew about the course's instructor was that his name—or was it a she—was listed in the catalog as K. Bollender. *Her classmates, would they be pleasant, or even fun to be with? Would there be a class brain and a class wit and a class dunce—and oh, please God, don't let Beth Louden wear the pointed cap!* She so wanted to do well on quizzes and tests and have the right answers when the teacher called on her, and have the right questions that she wouldn't embarrass herself by asking!

Beth had a moment's strong temptation to turn around, jump back in the Chevette, and go home. Who ever said there was anything wrong with simply being a wife and a mother

—and a damned good interior decorator and a fine gardener, too, so there!

She had, she reminded herself. This was *her* choice, a decision to become—to *try* to become—more than she was.

And she was pretty darned lucky to have someone like Michael, as supportive as could be. He'd told her she looked just great for her first class. Well, to tell the truth, she *had* very thoughtfully chosen the crocheted, creme-colored top and the black designer jeans (her only pair but definitely pants that made her feel like a casual jet-setter), completing the image of "college student" with new gold earrings and an extra touch of make-up to banish the dark circles that were her inheritance from the stress of last week.

Of course, Michael, being Michael, had had to do some teasing-joking, too. "But you know, I thought all the kids were wearing poodle skirts and penny loafers and Peter Pan collars these days." But there he was, smiling broadly, waving as she backed out of the drive, calling out, "Excelsior! Win this one for the Gipper!" Beth was sure she knew exactly what he was saying in his own sweet, silly way.

Excelsior, Beth said to herself as she walked into the octagonal shaped building, Lincoln Junior College.

K. Bollender was Kevin Bollender—"and please, make it Kevin and not Mister"—he told the sixteen people who occupied the desks in room 211. He quickly called the roll. Then he said he realized that they probably were wondering about "this guy" teaching a course called "Abnormal Psychology," maybe even worrying if he was the instructor for a class like this because "it takes one to know one."

He had a master's degree in clinical psychology. He'd been on staff for two years at the Manteno State mental health facility. He was working on his PhD, had finished the required course work and had written the first half of his doctoral thesis.

Other things about their teacher the students could observe for themselves. In his late twenties, six feet tall, Kevin Bollender looked like an athlete who had been short-changed by his genetic background—not quite enough height for basketball in an era of giants and too slim for football when even high school second-stringers tipped the scales at better than 220. As he went from desk to blackboard to lectern, he had an easy way of moving typical of runners. His hair was brown and curly and all that prevented his being as handsome as any model in *Gentleman's Quarterly* was a slightly over-sized nose; as though proclaiming a lack of vanity, he didn't mind calling attention to that feature with a thick mustache.

He was, Beth thought, *sexy*— a *hunk* in his blue jeans and checkered shirt and sportcoat.

A hunk? Now hold on! she sternly told herself. She was a . . . WifeandMother! She'd taken one step into middle age—*All right*, two *steps!*—and she had no business getting struck by crazily romantic ideas like this. That was for high schoolers (giggle-giggle, "fer sure!"), hung up on Tom Selleck or

Pierce Brosnan, or for undergrads developing the classic and comical crush on *my* professor . . .

She wondered what his elbows looked like?

Oh, this was utterly absurd! Her thoughts were absolutely shameful!

Now cut it out! she told herself. She was getting all worked up over what was merely a minute's fantasy, nothing more. Everyone had fantasies. That was the reason for the success of everything from paperback romance novels to—what else?—*Fantasy Island!*

And as for her ever acting on this fantasy, doing one single thing to bring it into reality, now *that* would be the real absurdity, just incredible. It could never, would never, not in a million years happen!

Beth made herself concentrate on what the teacher was saying, opening her notebook, raising her pen, looking down at the page.

"Now," Kevin Bollender said, "there was a prerequisite for this class, so everyone in here has had at least one course in general psychology." That had been her *favorite* class in her first (and only) year in college, Beth thought, the one that inspired her dream of a career in the field or in social work "—so you know that the word psychology literally means the 'Science of the mind.' But that's pretty ambiguous. After all, when we use the word *mind*, we've got a vague and abstract term. Uh-uh—if we're going to call psychology a science, we have to be more precise. We need some objective terms. How about this for a definition of psychology: The science of the behavior of organisms. Can everyone accept that?"

In her notebook, Beth wrote the definition.

A man in late middle-age raised his hand. "Wouldn't that definition have to include something about studying thought and emotions?"

"Good point," Kevin Bollender said, "and that's certainly what we tend to think of when we're talking about psychology. But remember, if we're to have a true science, it must be objective. We can directly and objectively observe specific behaviors. We cannot observe a thought or an emotion, can we? Ideas and feelings are abstractions. We can only see a particular behavior and then draw some conclusions about the 'internal' mental and emotional—and let's include chemical—processes underlying it."

Kevin Bollender stepped away from the lectern and seated himself on the front of the desk. "Anybody else have a question?" He looked around the room, and then he smiled.

He had a bright smile, Beth thought, friendly and challenging. He seemed to be totally at ease in the role of a teacher.

"Okay," Kevin said, "if you folks don't ask me questions, then I ask you questions. Otherwise, we'd just sit here for two hours listening to one another breathe!"

Everyone laughed and Kevin continued. "This class is called 'abnormal psychology,' and that obviously means we're going to consider abnormal behavior. But before we can do that, we really ought to try to figure out what *normal* behavior is. That way we won't make a mistake and waste our time thinking about normal stuff when we want to get into the whacked-out, crazy stuff, right?"

Again there was general laughter, more so now that the class was relaxing, realizing that Kevin Bollender was not one of those instructors who monotonously read aloud from yellowing lecture notes and then gave tests measuring one's ability to recall those notes verbatim.

"So the question for tonight, 'What is normal?'"

No one offered an answer. Kevin Bollender, with a mock sigh, said, "The response is underwhelming. Because this is our first meeting, I'd say this group's response to my question is . . . normal."

He hopped down from the desk and waved both hands like a camp counselor getting ready to lead a campfire singalong. "Let's approach it another way, okay? Would everyone who is normal in here please raise a hand—and unless every hand goes up, I'm going to run right out the door."

Sixteen laughing people responded as they'd been asked to.

"Fine." Kevin nodded. "We know it's considered normal behavior in this day and age to own a gun. I think the last survey said something like forty-nine percent of the US population is armed. So would all your normal people who own guns please keep your hands raised?"

There were five gun-owners, among them, the middle-aged man who'd asked the question on the definition of psychology. Kevin

Bollender walked down the aisle to him and stood alongside the man's desk. "Your name again, please?" Kevin asked.

"Lee, Lee Thompson."

"Okay, Lee," Kevin said, "you have a gun? A handgun? A rifle?"

Lee Thompson said, "A pistol. For protection."

"What if you bring that gun to class next week and when I'm calling roll, you shoot me dead?"

Lee look puzzled. "That would be murder," he said hesitantly.

"Murder," Kevin reflectively said, eyebrows knit, hands together. "Killing someone else. Would you call that normal behavior, Lee?"

"Of course not!"

"Hmm," Kevin Bollender rubbed his chin thoughtfully and went back to the front of the classroom. "Can anyone think of a situation in which killing another person would be normal?"

Beth put her hand up.

"Your name, please. The sooner we all get to know each other, the better. That way we'll be having friendly, intellectual discussions instead of impersonal screaming arguments like at the United Nations."

Beth told the class her name—she felt as though she were really introducing herself to the teacher and that made her nervous—and she explained, "Killing someone else is what every war throughout history has been all about. It's legal then, And it's the normal thing to do."

"Good!" Kevin Bollender said.

Beth blushed at his approval and immediately looked down at her notebook and scribbled a meaningless doodle.

"It seems that what is abnormal at one time in a specific situation might be normal if time and circumstance were to change. Here's another situation: What if our friend Lee Thompson shot me dead because he was convinced he was Jesus Christ and I was the Anti-Christ?"

Everyone in the class agreed: abnormal—everyone except for Beth, who raised her hand and said, "Wouldn't that depend on whether Lee really *was* Jesus Christ?"

"That's not what it says on my driver's license," Lee joked from three rows over.

" . . . and if you *were* the Anti-Christ?"

"It might," Kevin said. "And how would you determine that?"

"I think . . ." Beth said, hesitating a moment. She had the heady, exciting realization that she was indeed *thinking,* using her mind for something more demanding than balancing the checkbook at the end of the month. "I think there'd have to be evidence, some proof that would let us judge Lee's claims."

"And that," Kevin said dramatically, "is right on-target! A solid answer. You're asking for measurable, objective proof, *behaviors* that we can observe. Which goes right back to our basic definition of psychology, doesn't it?"

A woman with rhinestone decorated glasses, snowy hair, and a sour turn to her mouth, raised a hand and said, "I'm sorry, but it seems to me that we're going round and round in circles. I don't understand. If there's an answer to your question, 'What is normal?' can't you just tell us?"

"I'm afraid not," Kevin said with a shrug. "I'm a champ at dreaming up questions. I'm nowhere near that good when it comes to giving you answers."

The expression of the woman with the rhinestone glasses clearly revealed that this was not her idea of the way to conduct a class.

"Let's take the idea a step further. Is it normal to kill people because you consider yourself superior to them?"

"Of course not!" was the reply from the slender, long-haired young man who had the first desk in the first row. He seemed to be only weeks out of his teens and his voice still threatened to break into an adolescent squeak.

"Oh," Kevin said. "Here's the situation. You were raised in Hitler's Germany. You've been a member of the Hitler Youth. You believe you are a member in good standing of the master race. Now you're a guard at Dachan . . ."

"Uh-uh," said the long-haired man, "you're talking about an abnormal society. It's not normal for people to believe they have the right to kill others because they're superior to them."

"Some years back," Kevin Bollender said, "in our nice, normal society, we had a couple of guys named Leopold and Loeb . . ."

For the remainder of the class, the question "What is normal?" was the sole topic of discussion. Kevin's prodding questions, his vivid examples, led to a stimulating exchange of ideas and opinions, and, at one point, the long-haired young man got worked up enough to pound his desk with a fist, his voice fulfilling its squeaking promise when he said, "Bullshit!"

Kevin Bollender glanced at his watch. "We've only got a few minutes gang, so, let's wrap it up."

Beth couldn't believe that two hours had gone by. She felt mentally tired in the pleasantly worn way that follows intense concentration, really *thinking*, and she was not only pleased with her "in-class performance"—*Uh-uh, she was no feather-brained housewife scarcely up to the challenge of remembering how many cups in a quart! She was a student—a learner!*—She was pleased at being pleased with herself. That was a new feeling.

"For Thursday night," Kevin said, "read chapters one and two—and hey, don't be surprised if there's a quiz, all right? The college wants me to prove I'm a teacher by giving you grades, you see. Now, before we end, any questions about anything at all?"

Not surprisingly, the woman with the disapproving attitude and rhinestone glasses did have something to ask. "What was the point of all this discussion tonight if we don't agree on what is normal?"

"Fair enough question," Kevin said seriously. 'I do have an answer for that one.

The purpose was to get you thinking, to start looking at human behavior in the way a student of psychology must. You've got to realize that while there are plenty of simple questions in psychology, there are *no* simple answers. There can't be, not when you're dealing with something as complex as human beings."

On the way out of the room, Beth Louden stopped at the front desk. She'd just had one of the best evenings she'd experienced in years. She felt alive and invigorated, and so it was only right for her to say, "Thank you."

Kevin Bollender looked confused. "You're welcome," he said, "but I'm not sure I understand why I'm being thanked."

Beth smiled. Suddenly, speaking to him alone, she was overcome with shyness—*and, let's get it said: I am ridiculously attracted to him, so there, damn it, and now we forget it!*—and, feeling the heat of flush spread up her throat, she muttered, "Thanks for a good class," and hurried out.

She'd had plenty of mental stimulation for this evening, she told herself, and she had better get home to her children and her husband, where she belonged!

On any scale of animal intelligence, the cavy, or guinea pig, does not rank high. Its brain is no more well-developed than that of a rat.

Like all living creatures, however, the guinea pig does respond to stimuli. The response of the white guinea pig as it was lifted out of its cage was typical of all warm-

157

blooded, virtually defenseless creatures. It felt excitation. That excitement was not fear; the animal simply was primed to be afraid if its sensory receptors gave it cause.

The hand under its belly was gentle. The finger stroking its back was light. The guinea pig's excitement became pleasure.

A finger and a thumb became an uncomfortable collar around the guinea pig's neck and the animal wriggled. The grip tightened.

Now the animal was afraid. It would have fled had it been able, but it could not.

In the cage, the brown and white guinea pig furiously ran in circles, pinewood chips flying. It made hissing, whistling, clicking noises, an insane string of sound like an audio tape being played in rewind.

The white guinea pig struggled and then froze. Even so unintelligent an animal as a guinea pig can have a sense of its own imminent death. At that point, the creature surrenders to inevitability. The guinea pig moved again only after it was dead, its neck broken, its nervous system sending out final, convulsive signals to its legs.

The brown and white guinea pig stopped its wild running about the cage. It made no sound now. Only its nostrils quivered in the presence of death.

ELEVEN

WEARING HIS new charcoal gray suit, Michael walked into the kitchen. "Well?" Hand in front of him, right arm bent at the elbow, he adopted a model's pose.

It was 5:30 Wednesday morning. The coffee was perked and Michael's eggs were frying over easy. There was no reason for her to get up so early, he had told her, but Beth said she didn't mind. It was a long ride to St. Louis, close to seven hours, and she wanted to get him on the road with a decent breakfast.

Beth nodded her approval. "You're perfect, the very image of the successful young executive."

"Wa-al, ain't I just?" Michael comically drawled. "Shore 'nuf, yuh gotta look the part."

Beth buttered Michael's toast and served him breakfast. "You really do seem eager for this trip, Michael."

Sipping coffee, Michael said, "I guess I am. It's a break in the routine, something new." He laughed. "Or maybe a meeting with our paper products supplier, a chance to talk about all kinds of paper towels, single and double fold, mechanic's rough brown or quality super-soft, is what you find exciting if you're as dull a guy as I am."

Ten minutes later, Vern Engelking arrived to pick up Michael. Vern's flamboyance and his room-illuminating smile were like orange juice for the soul, Beth thought. You felt good just being in the same room with Vern.

Beth realized that what she felt for Vern was far stronger than mere "like" and was in fact the kind of "happy-love" reserved for a special uncle: the uncle who does magic, reaching behind your ear and finding a quarter, and then gives you the quarter. "Could I fix you some breakfast, Vern?" Beth said.

"Ah, far be it from me to impose," Vern said, "howsomever, before departing my domicile, I had but a cup of coffee, and so. . ."

"One egg or two?" Beth asked.

"Two, if you please," Vern said.

Twenty minutes later, she saw the two men off. Michael assured her he'd be back tomorrow afternoon in plenty of time to watch the kids when she went to her class at Lincoln Junior College.

When she went to refill her coffee cup, Beth saw the hesitant rays of the rising sun through the window above the sink. It was a quiet and *good* time, she thought, and she relished having it all to herself. The kids wouldn't have to be up to get ready for school for another forty-five minutes or so. She didn't even disturb her private sunrise silence time by turning on the radio.

She brought her abnormal psychology book to the table and looked over chapters one and two. She'd already thoroughly studied the material, highlighting important sections with yellow marker and making notes, but she found it a distinct pleasure to look at intellectual data and realized she did indeed have the mental equipment to process it. After years of mental stagnation, nothing more challenging than an occasional *Reader's Diguest* quiz, she had truly feared that she'd no more be able to understand a college level text than she could Einstein's Theory of Relativity.

That was a foolish fear, she told herself. Then again, weren't *most* fears foolish, without basis? That's what she thought, anyway, on a morning that felt as uniquely right as did this one.

But that sense of rightness seeped away from Beth Louden's morning.

Because when the girls were dressed and ready for school, at the breakfast table, Marcy was unhappy and Kim was quarrelsome. Snowball, Marcy said despairingly, the white guinea pig, wasn't in the cage, Mom, and he was lost, and she'd looked all over for him, and Kim had been playing with him last night . . .

Well, Kim protested, she could certainly play with Snowball anytime she wanted to! After all, Snowball wasn't Marcy's anymore. Marcy gave Snowball . . .

But that didn't mean Kim didn't have to take good care of Snowball! Just because . . .

Well, Kim did *so* take good care of the guinea pig and she remembered "for sure" she had put him back in the cage and . . .

Beth in her sternest, no-nonsense, I-am-not-kidding voice told both children to "Stop it and I do mean now!"

"I just don't want him to get hurt if he's out

161

of the cage, Mom," Marcy said. Beth softened when she saw Marcy's worried look.

Beth said, "Don't worry. This isn't the first time we've had a guinea pig decide to take a trot around the house. He'll be all right. I'll be house-cleaning today so I'll bet you I find him real quick."

"It's *still* not my fault Snowball's loose!" Kim insisted, sticking out her tongue at her sister.

Beth sighed. "Kim, put your tongue back in your mouth before that gets lost, too."

Kissing the girls goodbye as they headed off for the corner to wait for the school bus, Beth again reassured Marcy that Snowball would be found.

An hour later, she did find the guinea pig.

After she showered and slipped on "cleaning day grubbies," Beth vacuumed the downstairs, taking time out to admire lovingly Michael's beautiful surprise, the—*her*—antique crystal lamps, then polished the furniture and watered all the indoor plants.

She went upstairs and dusted the girl's room, wondering how she might in a nonjudgmental manner *suggest* that Kim try for a bit more organization, order, and (*ugh!*) cleanliness; dirty underpants did not belong under the bed!

Hanging Kim's lightweight vinyl jacket in the closet, thinking that all too soon it would be time to get out winter clothing, Beth happened to look down.

Snowball was smashed between the dresser and the wall's baseboard. Beth knelt. It looked as though the animal had wedged itself into this spot and then had *killed* itself with frantic, futile efforts to escape. Beth touched the guinea pig's fur. It felt as artificial as the plastic bristles of a hairbrush. She had to move the dresser an inch to free the tiny corpse.

Stiff and cold, the guinea pig lay in her hand. *Marcy loved this furry, innocent thing and now it is dead*, she thought.

And then Beth shuddered and squelched an angry black impulse to throw the guinea pig to the floor, to rid herself not of it but of what it represented—Death!

Death was everywhere! Death was next door, *DustyandBrad*, and Death was stalking the Loudens, the skeletal hand of Death brushing Kim, teasing her when the car had almost . . . And now . . . *Death is inside our house. Death surrounds us, hisses at us, wants us!*

Beth took a deep breath. There were more coincidences in life than there were connections, she told herself, and it was sad that Snowball had needlessly died, but that's all it was.

She found a shoebox for Snowball. When the girls came home from school, there would have to be a funeral, a small grave by the garden. As sensitive as Marcy was, that would be of comfort to her. And a lecture about responsibility for Kim as well? Maybe, Beth decided, although perhaps what had happened was lesson enough of itself.

Beth thought she was all right; she really did. But in the kitchen, pouring a cup of coffee, her hand shook. She looked out the window. The sun was shining.

The sun shone but the day was *wrong*.

There really was a business meeting set for 3:30 that afternoon with the St. Louis supplier of paper towels and so, after leaving Park Estates and swinging south onto I-57, they talked about that. Yes, they were getting the best wholesale price possible; even with a standard eighty percent mark-up, Superior Chemical was able to undercut the price of competing janitorial supply firms. But quality control wasn't all that it could be; towels sometimes jammed in dispensers. Worse, too often the supplier felt free to make substitutions and maybe there was no difference in the feel of "Pure White," stock number 34057 and "Creme," number 34059, but customers did complain, and so the president of Superior Chemical and the national sales manager were going to "iron things out."

Of course the ironing out could have been as easily accomplished with a letter or telephone call. This trip's real business was Herb Cantlon.

Herb Cantlon! Michael thought. *That goddamned bloated piece of meat!* Uh-huh, the *important* meeting—*Surprise, Herby, you fat fucker*—wasn't in St. Louis; it was about an hour and a half back on up the road to Mt. Claron, Illinois. Eddie Markell was arranging it. No severance pay for Cantlon. No meaningless, euphemistically worded letters of reference. Herb's association with Superior Chemical was going to be painfully terminated.

Goddamn! Michael felt a surge of power within him, electrical in its intensity. It was as though the human shell he was forced to wear was far too small and confining for the reality of his being, The Stranger who walked through the world, his invisible aura glowing with the red promise of blood.

A promise soon to know fulfillment! Michael thought, as he gazed out the Buick Regal's window at the endlessly flat landscape of central Illinois that whizzed by. He could picture these drab, quiet farmlands flooded with gore, the United States, the entire world awash in a unifying ocean of blood—the Time of the Stranger.

That was what Jan Pretre had vowed.

Seeing Jan last Saturday had given him renewed hope in The Strangers' destiny of death. It had shaken him as well, caught him off-guard, and left him with question.

"Vern?" Michael said.

"Yes, Michael?"

"I want to ask you something."

Vern turned his head to smile benignly at Michael. "One inquires and one learns, Michael. Isn't that American folk wisdom?"

"I'm serious, Vern," Michael said.

"All right."

"Did you know Jan Pretre and I knew each other, that we met a long time back?"

Now Vern was staring straight ahead, his brows set as though he were peering through a misty drizzle and not looking out through the windshield on a remarkably clear day. In a voice devoid of his typical theatrical enunciation, Vern said, "Yes, Michael. I

165

know all about Jan and you. I've known for a long time."

"Then why didn't you tell me he was going to be at your place, Vern? Is there something I'm being left out of?"

Vern didn't answer for over a mile and when he did respond, he did not look at Michael. "There have been things I've been told *not* to tell you, Michael." Vern spoke quietly but without any note of apology.

"Told by whom?" Michael said.

"Jan," Vern said.

Michael frowned. "I don't understand."

Vern chuckled humorously. "And I'm sure there are things happening that I don't understand, either. That's not important. What is important, Michael, is that *Jan* understands. He's been in contact with me for a long time. Oh, years would pass when I wouldn't hear from him, and then there'd be a letter or a phone call and he'd tell me to do something and I would. We have to trust Jan, Michael. Of all of us, he is the one with the clearest vision, the greatest power."

Vern paused and another flat Illinois mile went by. Then Vern said, "There's something I can tell you now, Michael, that I couldn't before. Years ago Jan told me to hire you because you were one of us. Do you remember that?"

Michael's memory was sharp and vivid. There'd been a letter from Superior Chemical Company, informing him that the firm was seeking a new salesman for the south suburban territory and that . . . blah-blah-blah. Mr. Engelking, the president of the corporation, invited Michael to dinner and they'd discussed floor mats and urinal deodorant blocks and waterless head-cleaners and then, over dessert—Vern had had a Napoleon, Michael recalled, and he himself had ordered cheesecake—Vern had said, "I do think you ought to give my offer serious consideration. You see, you are a Stanger and so am I!"

Later, that evening, Michael had proof of what Vern Engelking had said. They went to Chicago's Rush Street, found a prostitute, and cut her throat, cut it raggedly but so completely that her head was attached to her neck by only stringy tendons and a flap of skin. "I knew you were *our* kind of man, Michael," Vern had said. "Welcome to the company."

But *how* had Vern known? Michael had asked.

"I'm not at liberty to reveal that now, Michael. Can you simply trust me?" Vern Engelking had offered his hand.

Michael could trust him, did trust him then as now. It was enough to know that, condemned as he was to walk among the sickening, weak, and whimpering *normals*, he would have another who understood him, who was, indeed, a brother.

It was enough to know that now, all these years later. Yet he had to ask, "Vern, why are you telling me this now when you couldn't before. You've . . ."

"*Now*, you see, is when Jan said I might tell you," Vern interrupted. "Jan is our leader, Michael. He'll lead those who are worthy when it is our time. Trust Jan, Michael."

Michael suddenly felt himself a child again, or at least the "pretend" child he had once had to be. He remembered the Jan who had sought him out, who had given him a baptism in blood, who had told him what he was and what he was meant to be. Yes, he trusted Jan Pretre.

And he trusted Vern Engelking.

Strangers! They were Strangers, and all his questions were answered with that realization and joyous acknowledgement.

Damn, there was someone knocking on the front door of the double-width mobile home and Herb Cantlon didn't want to be disturbed, not now.

He slipped a plaid robe over his shorts and undershirt. "Keep it hot and juicy for me," he said to Gretchen Waller, the nineteen-year-old woman who lay under the sheet. She was a dishwater blond, with a thin face and sad eyes; whenever she wasn't chewing gum, her expression seemed somehow unnatural. "I'll be right back, hon." He waddled to the living room on legs surprisingly thin for such a corpulent man.

He had good reason to be annoyed at the interruption. Wednesday night was (*heh-heh-heh*) Herb's night for nooky, to get the ashes hauled and the sap off his back—and yeah, there was nothing better than tender young poon-tang to keep a guy feeling like the (*heh-heh-heh*) cock of the walk. His mobile home set-up here at Lake Claron, just a few miles from town, was perfect. It was where he brought the wife and the kids for summer vacations and getaway weekends and where he'd been getting it on with Gretchen once a week for the past six months or so. He had privacy, not another house for nearly a mile, and a good supply of booze, a TV, and a stereo and Gretchen who could get (*heh-heh-heh*) pretty (*Whoo-oo!*) wild in the sack.

Oh, sure, the wife knew, but she acted like she wasn't on to doodley-squat and Herb figured she'd keep on the way as long as he kept her happy with a fur coat or a microwave or a string of pearls or whatever the hell she wanted. And so what that the whole town was aware of his getting some tail? You could damned well bet that Herb Cantlon wasn't the *only* married man who messed around; you don't throw stones at the next guy 'cause somebody might bounce one off your bean too.

Herb opened the door. The man who stood on the wooden deck wore a faded, long-sleeved flannel shirt, jeans, and heavy hiking boots. He was holding a .357 Magnum with a ribbed nine-inch barrel and he pushed the gun into Herb's stomach.

"Don't say word one," Eddie Markell ordered quietly. "Back your lard ass in."

Herb felt the precise octagonal shape of the end of the barrel pressing into his spongy flesh. *Oh God*, he thought. *Oh Christ Jesus!* He was going to die. Sure, he'd considered death before now, the sensible, inevitable death that had to occur someday. He had hefty life insurance, a legal will, even "his and hers" funeral plots for himself and the missus. But it had never really struck him, though, that he could die . . . *now*.

And oh, *Oh goddamnit, oh shit, oh goddamnit!* he did not *want* to die now. He tried to step back, to lift his foot, but he couldn't move; then his stomach rumbled. He felt the intestinal fluttering and the gun and he couldn't help it, he giggled, and stepped back.

Eddie Markell closed the door behind him. "All right, fat boy, let's go say hello to your chick. Lead the way."

Sweating and freezing, Herb nodded. He took Eddie into the bedroom.

"What is it? What is it?" Gretchen Waller kept saying, gaping at the gun, at Herb's sweat-gleaming, porcine face, at Eddie Markell's grin and bloodshot eyes—and gun, the gun . . . She lay stiffly in bed, holding the sheet to her throat, like a hospitalized child watching a hypodermic-bearing nurse approach.

"It's your ass and everything connected to it if you give me any trouble. Get out of bed."

"I . . . I don't have any clothes on," Gretchen said. She blushed.

Do it, Herb Cantlon silently begged her. *Don't argue. Don't say anything. Do what he says . . .*

"Don't worry," Eddie sneered, "you won't catch cold. Move."

Gretchen tossed back the sheet. Her eyes were huge. She stood up. Her breasts were small and her ribs and hip bones sharply outlined beneath childishly pink skin.

"Little tits, baby," Eddie said. He rapped Herb on the shoulder with the barrel of the

170

revolver. "Thought you country clodhoppers liked 'em big-boobed, Herb."

Herb said nothing.

"Going to give me the old line, lard ass? Tell me 'More than a mouthful is pure waste?'"

Gretchen bleated, "Please, mister, whoever you are, don't hurt us."

Shut up, Gretchen! Herb wanted to scream. *Don't say a word and we can live . . .*

"Into the living room, folks," Eddie ordered. When Gretchen didn't move quickly enough to suit him, he gave her a sharp slap across the buttocks.

She yiped. Eddie laughed. "Skinny tits, skinny ass. Herb, putting it to her must be like doing it with a barbed wire scarecrow."

In the living room, Eddie told Herb and Gretchen to sit on the sofa. Eddie stepped across the room to the padded rollaway bar. Casually putting the pistol on the bartop as though he were sure they dared not attempt anything, he found a bottle of vodka, turned the cap, cracked the seal, and drank from the bottle.

"Thanks for the drink, Herb. You're a fine fucking host," Eddie said.

Herb Cantlon swallowed hard. "Whatever . . . whatever you want. I . . . I have some money . . ."

"Turn it off, lard ass," Eddie said. "You just sit there with your chick and keep your mouth closed."

Be quiet! Herb told himself. *Not a word, not a sound. Be quiet and live, live, live!*

"We've got to wait awhile, folks," Eddie

said. He had another long pull from the vodka bottle. "Some friends of ours are coming over for a party."

Some friends of . . .ours? Herb didn't understand. He wasn't even attempting to comprehend what the man had said. He knew he wanted to live and that was all that mattered.

" 'Course, there's no reason we can't have some fun and games on our own until they get here." Eddie snapped his fingers and pointed at Gretchen. She started. "Come here, chicky."

Gretchen didn't move *Get up! Go on over there!* Herb mentally pleaded.

"Now, bitch!" Eddie said. He leaned back, his elbows on the bartop's padding. His right hand lay on the butt of the .357.

As though drugged, Gretchen staggered over to him. "On your knees, bitch," Eddie said. She knelt before him. He held the pistol to her temple. "Do it nice, some good head. You make it bad head and you get bad head, too. I'll splatter your fucking brains all over the room." Eddie grinned at Herb. "How about it, lard ass? Okay with you if your lady cleans my pipes?"

There was the hot sting of tears in Herb Cantlon's eyes. He was helpless, shattered, and *Oh shit!* he didn't care, didn't care what happened to Gretchen or to anyone except Herb Cantlon.

Time that was timeless passed, nearly three hours. The level in the vodka bottle was under half. The console stereo was playing, side one of a Kenny Rogers album repeating again and again; now it was "The Gambler," the smoothly rasped advice "You've got to know when to hold 'em, know when to fold 'em," filling the room. Gretchen was on the couch, head down, hair in her face, silently sobbing. And Herb Cantlon was still alive and that was all he knew or cared about.

There was a soft knock at the door. Eddie called. "Come in."

Herb Cantlon didn't believe what he was seeing. Vern Engelking and Michael Louden, the boss and the national sales manager . . . Then again, he wasn't sure he believed *any-thing* that had happened this night, anything except the stranger with the gun and the tangible reality of death.

Herb had a curious, light-headed feeling of relief. He knew Mr. Engelking and Mr. Louden—he worked for them, for Superior Chemical, for God's sake!

Michael Louden was grinning as he set a duffel bag alongside the bar. "Good evening, Herbert," Vern Engelking said. "I do trust you'll pardon the intrusion!"

"Aw shucks, aw shoot, aw shit," Michael drawled. "See, we all jes' figgered long as we were in this here neck of the woods to drop in on you-all. You glad to see us, Herby? You gladder than hammered shit?"

"Herb, what is it? What's going on? I don't understand," Gretchen Waller spoke in a monotone as though all emotion had been leached from her.

"Herb," Vern Engelking said, grinning broadly, "you've always had a delightful sense of humor. Indeed, so many of Superior

Chemical's clients have commented on your vast fund of jokes."

"You're a goddamn million laughs, Herby," Michael said.

"Come here, Herbert." Vern Engelking beckoned him with a crooked finger and a pleasant tone. "I have a joke for you."

There was a crooked, dazed smile on his face as Herb walked toward Vern Engelking.

Vern said, "So a man came up to me and said he hadn't had a bite in three days. You know what I did?"

It was weird, it was crazy, and nothing made sense anymore, but the boss—The Boss —was expecting him to answer, so Herb Cantlon, smiling, said, "So you bit him?"

"No," Vern Engelking said. "I smartly kicked him in the testicles." Engelking's shoe slammed into Herb Cantlon's crotch.

"Whuu . . ." Herb Cantlon grunted, and then the full force of the pain exploded up from his groin, speared his guts and lungs. He dropped to his knees, hugging himself, eyes bulging, tongue protruding moronically.

Michael stepped alongside him. He sharply pinched his earlobe, twisting it. The sharp needle-like hurt of Michael's fingers kept Herb conscious, prevented his being washed under the heavy ocean of pain from Vern's kick. Herb felt himself rising to his feet like a day old helium balloon slowly drifting upward.

He was making wet, peeping sounds of pain. Michael said, "You fat sonofabitch. Skimming some off the top from Superior, huh? Probably bought yourself this hideaway shithouse with what you stole."

"Oh no, oh no . . ." Herb whimpered, throat tight, squeaking like a mouse in a trap. "Oh."

"I am truly sorry, Herbert," Vern Engelking said, "but we must reprimand you."

"Don't kill me!" Herb peeped.

"Don't kill us!" Gretchen Waller echoed.

They went to the bedroom, Eddie holding the gun, Michael with a butcher knife that he had taken from the duffel bag. Herb was ordered to undress. Sobbing, his belly a rippling white mound, he lay on his back on the bed.

"Give him some head, bitch!" Eddie Markell said, pushing Gretchen toward the bed. "Get him hard."

On her knees at Herb's side, Gretchen leaned forward, blindly obedient. This was not happening, Herb told himself. He was dreaming, dreaming it all. That was it! Listen to the way Mr. Engelking was joking—"I do regret any damage my Florsheim might have done your manhood, Herbert"—and look at how Michael Louden was smiling as though he were at a sales convention and, hey! Out there in the living room, that was Kenny Rogers on the stereo! Kenny Rogers for crying out loud . . . So put it all together and it just wasn't real.

"Get with it, Herby," Michael said. "You've been humping the lady for a long time. Now get it up so you can have one more good one!"

I want to live! Herb Cantlon thought. He no longer knew what was dream and what was reality. He was totally attuned to life-need and life-want—*Obey them and live!*—and his body miraculously responded.

"Get on him, bitch!" Eddie Markell said. "Take him for a ride."

This was a crazy nightmare, Herb thought. Gretchen was crying, stradding him, sinking down, accepting his tumescence into her scratchily dry socket, and circling the bed were three smiling men, saying crazy things, things that made no sense, and Gretchen was moving, her bony hips jutting back and forth, her face as expressionless as a fifty cent Halloween mask, and he felt the tightening within him, so strong now because every nerve was fear-alive and tingling . . .

That's when Michael grabbed Gretchen Waller's hair and jerked her back and cut her throat with the butcher knife. The hot curtain of blood shot onto Herb's face and chest. He screamed. Blood in his eyes, blood in his mouth, *her* blood, not spilling but *plopping* onto his throat and chest and belly while her body convulsed in death.

Herb Cantlon was still screaming when he fainted.

When he came to—and he did not know when that was—he was no longer thinking he wanted to live. He was not thinking at all. He was listening in a disinterested way to men speaking. Vern Engelking, Michael Lauden, and—whatwashisname? No, it couldn't have been Engelking and Louden; they would never have done such . . . He did not know any of these men; they were strangers.

"You'll take care of it, Eddie?"

"No problem. Murder and suicide. It'll look like lard ass killed the chick with the

176

blade and then offed himself."

"Very well, then, Eddie. We'll rely on your expertise."

There was a gun in Herb Cantlon's mouth. He had to shape his lips the way he did at the dentist's because of the size of the barrel, and his finger was on the trigger and there was a hand over his hand.

As though all sounds were amplified, he could hear the breathing of the three men who surrounded him, hear the thick drip of blood onto the carpet from the sliced neck of the woman who now lay sprawled across the foot of the bed, and from faraway, the voice of Kenny Rogers. He did not hear the sound of the explosion that sent the .357 magnum bullet into his mouth, up through his palette, bursting his head like a too ripe, sun-heated melon.

TWELVE

As she drove to Lincoln Junior College through a chill, dreary autumn drizzle, Beth was extra cautious at every intersection. The way she felt this Thursday night, she would not have been surprised if a motorist zoomed through a red light to broadside her. Indeed, she thought she would not overly startled if a Boeing 707 plummeted from the skies and crashed right on top of her!

For a week now, she had felt a vague tension, low-key, but as constant as a chronic toothache. She was not sleeping well, waking a dozen times throughout the night to a "worry thought" that refused to linger long enough in mind to become clear. She was irritable, on edge. Like this morning, at breakfast, as she stirred pancake batter, there was a crystalline explosion behind her, a dropped glass. She nearly went through the ceiling. She whirled, yelling, "Kim! You have *got* to be more careful . . ."

Then there was another explosion, Kim's vocal one, as she hollered, "You're always blaming me! I didn't break it! Marcy broke it!"

Marcy, sheepishly apologetic, said, "I'm sorry, Mom. I did it."

Kim was wound up, getting louder with each outraged word: "If I *do* it, I get blamed! If I *don't* do it, I get blamed! I'm just the one you blame things on around here!"

To Beth, it seemed the girls' voices were blending into a manic, turkey-gobble chorus, Marcy's whimpering apology and Kim's outrage. Beth was on the verge of screaming herself, a wordless scream, a descent into this whirling tumult.

Kim was still shouting, "*Everything* that goes wrong is all my fault, Mom. You've always on my case! It's like with Snowball . . ."

Snowball! Beth thought, as she carefully checked for outgoing and incoming traffic before pulling in to the college's east parking lot. Coming when it did, after a string of disasters and near-disasters, finding poor Snowball was, oh, not the straw that broke the camel's back, but definitely one that bent and twisted a few vertebrae.

When the girls came home from school last Thursday, Beth first took care of the unhappy task of telling Marcy what had happened. Marcy was inconsolable for hours. Then Beth took Kim aside, trying to discuss reasonably and calmly the importance of responsibility and the sad consequences of thoughtlessness. That had sent Kim off on a first class, "You're always blaming me!" tantrum, the equal of the one today at breakfast.

Michael had taken charge of this morning's pandemonium calmly, with almost amused nonchalance, telling Kim, to "quit yelling at her mother," saying to Marcy she'd be better off "cleaning up the mess you made" than apologizing for it, and then offering to take over preparing breakfast, a task that Beth gratefully relinquished.

Later, the kids sent upstairs to get their things together for school, Michael said to Beth, "You really shouldn't get upset over nothing like that, honey. After all, a broken glass is no big deal."

Somehow it didn't seem to Beth that Michael thought anything a "big deal." Last week, when he returned from the trip to St. Louis—"Yes, everything went very well. In fact, I had a fine time!"—she tried to have a serious conversation with him about Kim's outburst and Snowball; it certainly seemed that Kim's carelessness had caused the guinea pig's death.

Was Kim, did he think, going through a phase? Sure he did—ha, ha. (*No big deal!*) Wasn't a kid always going through a phase, from age six months to age twenty one? Perhaps Kim was developing a serious emotional problem, Beth suggested. Michael thought that was ridiculous. Kim was spunky and rebellious the way kids are supposed to be. (*No big deal!*) So, sometimes she was bratty, but Michael was sure, "ha, ha," that any problem Kim had in her head could be solved with a whack or two on the other end.

Yes, Michael had treated the issue much too lightly, Beth thought. At least, that's what she *thought* she thought because, all right, she had to admit it, she was all too ready these days to imagine problems for the Loudens, to believe that there was a mysterious curse of bad luck enveloping them.

And what had she been imagining about Michael all week long? she asked herself as she stepped out of the car, slipping her notebook and text beneath her green slicker to safeguard them from the lightly falling rain and mist. *Oh, the same old thing. The same ridiculous foolish, "He is someone I don't know, someonw who seems to talk to me but isn't really talking to me and seems to listen to me but isn't really listening to me and seems to care for me, care about me, love me, but doesn't give the thinnest sliced damn about me . . . Someone who is a stranger to me —and to everyone!"*

Uh-uh and put an end to that! Beth ordered herself. It was the height of absurdity for her to torture herself with groundless recurring fantasies about Michael. That made no more sense than getting all wrapped up in a fantasy about, oh, shall we say (just for the sake of saying something), her teacher, Kevin Bollender.

Kevin Bollender! Now, he really *was* a stranger, and that was what he was supposed to be. Yet Beth knew she could like him very much. The man was physically appealing, he was intelligent, and he was sensitive; you could tell because . . . Well, you could just tell.

Of course, Kevin Bollender was *only* her teacher, nothing more, and certainly he wouldn't ever be anything else but, yet still . . .

Beth stepped into the school's fluorescent lighted entranceway. She had the disoriented, stomach-fluttering sensation that her eyes weren't exactly seeing what she was looking at. It was, she thought, like being on an abruptly ascending elevator in a sky-scraper.

Then the non-existent elevator arrived at a non-existent floor. This floor, Reality, Beth told herself. She took a deep breath, smelled the cleanliness of the rain that had accompanied her into the building. Her head cleared.

She went to her class.

"Well, we've had a chance to consider some *bona fide* weirdos so far," Kevin Bollender said. "There's your basic, run-of-the-mill schizophrenic who's convinced he's a pitcher of orange juice. You've got your paranoid who knows you're out to get him but figures he might just be okay because his friend, God, is personally looking after him. And let's hear it for the catatonic, the manic-depressive, and, the ever-popular multiple-personality!"

With the class's appreciative chuckle, Kevin Bollender sat on the edge of his desk. He stroked his moustache with his thumb and forefinger. "But seriously, folks," he said, "tonight we're going to consider the *weirdest* of the weird, the strangest of the strange, an anomaly to even the most abnormal. I'm talking about the psychopath."

Beth wondered if Kevin had ever thought of a career as a stand-up comedian or a newscaster. He was a natural communicator, approaching what could well have been a cut and dried subject with bantering humor, never letting the study of psychology become stuffy. As usual casually dressed, tonight in jeans and a tan chamois hunter's shirt, he seemed less an academic than an old-time carnival pitchman pulling a crowd for the sideshow. But there was no question Kevin Bollender was a *real* teacher. His joking manner kept you laughing, but his questions made you *think*.

And he definitely was quite good looking . . .

Beth ordered herself to pay attention to the lecture and not the lecturer.

Rising, Keven went to the board, and with his right hand took chalk from the ledge and lightly tapped the knuckles of his left hand.

"The psychopath," Kevin said, his tone becoming more formal, "has been termed a 'moral imbecile.'

That brought a raised hand, that of the snowy-haired woman in the rhinestone decorated glasses. Everyone else in the class was addressed by his or her first name but she was, as she had requested, always called "Miss Fletcher." Had Kevin Bollender stated, "Icebergs are cold," she'd have challenged it or asked for a clarification of exactly what he meant by "cold."

"Are you saying that a psychopath has a low IQ?" Miss Fletcher asked.

"Uh-uh." Kevin shook his head. "In fact, I'll say the direct opposite. The intelligence quotient of a psychopath is typically far above average, near genius or even genius."

"Then why," Miss Fletcher persisted, "would he be an imbecile?"

"A *moral* imbecile," Kevin replied. "A

psychopath might have the brain-power to solve the country's inflation problems or to discover a cancer cure, but when it comes to morality, to a deliberation of ethics, that's where Mr. Psychopath gets a failing grade."

Lee Thompson, the middle-aged man whose questions always had a purpose, said, "The psychopath doesn't know the difference between right and wrong?"

"Oh," Kevin replied, "he knows what society deems right and wrong, but that has no bearing on what he himself does. Laws and codes of conduct are for others."

Kevin turned to the board and drew a large circle with three smaller circles within it. "From your previous classes in general psych, you're all familiar with Sigmund Freud's theory of personality. Let's say the large circle represents the whole of one's personality structure. Within it, we have the *Id*"—he so labelled one of the smaller circles —"and this is the inborn drive for gratification. It's a raw and aggressive instinct, nothing but an unrestrained pleasure seeking impulse. It lusts for control, for total power. Then there's the *Ego*, right here." Kevin wrote the word in the second small circle. "The ego is the rational segment of the personality. Ego is the *thinking* mind, the mind that figures out how to meet the demands of reality and finds way for the id to achieve its necessary gratification.

"But, aha!" Kevin said, as he wrote the word *Superego* in the third small circle, "The superego, last component of the personality to develop, is basically the conscience. Here we store all the ideas of right and wrong and good and bad we learn from parents, from authority figures, from our own experience in society. The superego limits what the ego is free to do to gratify the raw, aggressive wants of the id."

Kevin drew an "X" over the superego circle. "Zip! The psychopath isn't burdened with one of these. That means he's free to do what he pleases—and that's anything he thinks he can get away with that will make his id purr with happiness."

Rob Gretsh, the long haired young man who often posed the most difficult questions, raised his hand. "What causes someone to become a psychopath?"

"Hmm." Kevin Bollender slowly nodded. "That's a wonderful question, Rob. Too bad I don't have a wonderful answer. Instead, I can give you all kinds of theories. Yessir, psychology is loaded with hypotheses, variables and theories!

"Here's one: If a kid is raised in conditions of near-total rejection and neglect, he could become a psychopath simply in order to survive without becoming psychotic. His 'coping behavior' is lying, cheating, stealing, and so as a child, he learns to get what he wants and needs in the most cunning ways. As an adult, he goes into the world doing the same thing, following the pattern that has been successful for him.

"Then we've got the theory that psychopathy, like any other form of mental illness you can name, is caused by a chemical imbalance. That's a popular notion. You know, 'better living through chemistry.' The chemists are sure that once they determine the formulas, they can turn a schiz, a paranoid, or a psychopath into Norman Normal. That means that many of my colleagues who make fifty bucks an hour and up will have to get themselves honest jobs!

"And here's another theory for you. I guess you could call this the 'Bad Seed' concept if you'd like. Just the way some people are born to be tall, a psychopath is born to be psychopathic. Maybe the mass murderer with a tattoo that reads 'BORN TO RAISE HELL' is showing he has real insight into who he is and how he got that way!"

Rob Gretsch couldn't accept the last concept. "Uh-uh, that's blaming it on Fate. That kind of thinking is right out of the Dark Ages!"

Kevin shrugged. "Actually, the idea belongs to Carl Jung, and he's right up there with Freud and Adler."

People totally without a conscience, Beth thought. *People who lived in Atlanta, Georgia, or Lincoln, Nebraska, or Clearwater, Florida or right next door, doing what they wished without the slightest consideration for others, without fear of law or morality—without guilt.* Considering the number of psychopaths who might be on the loose was not, Beth reflected, the way to develop a sense of trust in your fellow man. And yet the subject was intriguing. She had a question.

"How can we tell if a person is a psychopath?"

Kevin said, "That's extremely difficult to

determine. The psychopath seems to be normal—in fact, *super* normal. He's a terrific actor. His relationships with others appear to be intense and involved but are actually cold, calculating, and without any emotional intimacy.

"So the only time a psychopath reveals himself is when he acts in illegal and immoral ways. He's the charming con man who sells the sweet old lady the Brooklyn Bridge. He's the regular churchgoer who steals every penny from the church's building fund. Or he's a bluebeard who murders twenty wives before he gets caught. And that's a specialty for psychopaths: murder. It's a chance to exercise total dominance over another human being.

"I'm saying, then, that we can recognize a 'moral imbecile' only when we have proof of his actions."

"There's no, oh, predictive test or anything?" Beth said. It seemed there ought to be. A tendency toward schizophrenia, for instance, could frequently be shown by a standard projective test that psychologists had employed for years.

"I'm afraid not," Kevin said. Then, laughing, he added, "Oh, maybe God does put the brand of Cain on 'em, but it doesn't seem He gives others the ability to *see* that mark. So it's only when the psychopath's actions have been found out that we have proof of the psychopathic personality."

"But if psychopaths are so smart," questioned Rob Gretsch, "right at the genius level, *do* they get caught?"

"They do indeed," Kevin said. "You've heard the old expression, 'Pride goeth before a fall.' After he's had a number of successes, the psychopath comes to believe he's invulnerable, much too clever to be caught by the police or found out by anyone. He gets careless, makes mistakes without realizing it or takes chances he previously would have avoided. Then, zap!"

It was all fascinating—and frightening, Beth thought. Anyone, anyone at all, the mailman, the bank teller, the television repairman—*Doctor-Lawyer-Indian Chief!*—could be . . .

No! The thought was there and she did not want to think of it, did not want it to emerge because that would give it a touch of credence, bring it into the realm of possibility, and it was the out-and-out craziest (*and so terrifying!*) thought she had ever had, *would* ever have . . .

And vowing she would not think it, she of course *did* think it, the horrifying totality of it expressed in a single word hiss-whispered in her mind:

Michael!

She recalled when she was a child, maybe five, perhaps not that old. Late one winter night, a terrifying idea had jerked her from sleep, led her to walk down the hall to her parents' room. She silently stood at the door, studying them, wondering *Can I be sure they are* really *Mom and Dad?* Illuminated only by the soft silver of the moon that seeped in through the west window, the two people in bed—*Mom and Dad?*—did not look right, did not seem to be the same people they were during the day. For weeks after that, she stared at them when she thought they weren't noticing, trying to be sure they were not the pretenders that sleep and moonlight had made them seem.

Oh, she had been one silly kid!

And wasn't she still the same silly kid, thinking that Michael . . .

She welcomed the question that came to her mind in response to the classroom discussion she was only half-hearing. If she were seriously thinking about this question, focusing her entire mind on it, then she could not be considering anything else—*Michael! MichaelTheStranger!*—and she was *not* thinking about anything else. She had something to ask Kevin, and only after she had done so did she feel the embarrassment that came from not having first raised her hand and being recognized.

"But all that psychology knows about the psychopathic personality," she said, "comes from studying the psychopaths who *have* been caught. Isn't that right?"

"True enough," Kevin nodded. "And all we know about any of the individual mental illnesses comes from studying those who have been identified as being mentally ill. So . . . I'm not sure I get your point."

Beth's mind was racing. So was her heart. She felt the heady elation of intellectual discovery and challenge, one that she had experienced so many years ago in college and then had not known again during her brain's "dormant years." She stammered, striving to express herself clearly.

"Isn't it possible that there are psychopaths who are not detected and might never be found out? They'd be even smarter and shrewder than the others, real supergeniuses. They . . ."

She paused. She wasn't sure where her ideas were going and she feared following it to a dead end or a corner, a corner where the dunce would have to stand with her back to the class.

Kevin Bollender frowned, his brow wrinkling. He smoothed his moustache, first the left side then the right. Then he said, "That's very good." He smiled, and when he spoke his tone was jocular but genuinely complimentary. "What you've given us, Beth, is what psychologists love: a theory. We can call it Beth Louden's Theory of the Unknown Psychopath."

For the remainder of the class session, "The Unknown Psychopath" was the topic of conversation. Could he exist? Did he? What possible evidence might be found throughout history? In philosophical works? (Rob Gretsch mentioned Nietzsche and his *Ubermensch*, the Superman who was above "the law" that governed the masses. No wonder the Nazis had made Nietzsche their philosophical justification. In today's newspaper headlines and 10 o'clock TV newscasts?

When the class ended, Kevin Bollender asked Beth if she would wait just a moment.

"I want to thank you," Kevin Bollender said. "I mean because of your sharp question, there was a lively discussion tonight instead of a lecture, one of my patented 'Bollender's Boring Bombasts.' "

"I . . . I just had something to ask," Beth said. She realized she was blushing, felt a flare of heat on her cheeks that reminded her of schoolgirl days. It was embarrassing, she thought, to be praised for having an idea, especially when you were not exactly accustomed to having your intellect complimented. Beth felt uneasy—*Actually, excited-happy uneasy*. talking to Kevin Bollender, listening to him commend her for her question and then say, "We could talk about this some more if you'd join me for a drink, say, in the cocktail lounge just down . . ."

Because she was taken aback, without time to think it over, Beth said what she really wanted to say.

"Yes."

THIRTEEN

CLAIRE WYNKOOP was nestled comfortably in her living room's upholstered wing chair. A book lay open on her lap, but she had read no more than a few pages when the words ran together. Claire's head was bowed. She thought she really should remove her bifocals before they fell off but somehow it didn't seem worth the bother. She was pleasantly warm, as though the chair were an enfolding cloud, and she could feel the regular beat of her heart throughout her arms and legs. She was not asleep but she knew she wasn't far from it.

Across the room, atop the antique sideboard, the compact phono-radio that Beth and Michael had given her for Christmas five years ago, was tuned to an easy-listening FM station. Claire thought that every song, whether performed by the twin pianos of Ferrante and Teicher, the 101 Strings, or the Johnny Mann singers, had a lulling sameness. It would be perfect music to doze off by, music that might give her good dreams.

It was 8:30 Friday evening, and for the first time all day, Claire Wynkoop relaxed. She'd awakened that morning with a headache that was not really a headache. At the library, she had listened to *that* sound, the vibrating tuning fork in the center of her brain.

It had been a day that promised premonition, a tense, uneasy, and just out-and-out bad day. Why did the future insist on forcing glimpses of itself on her? she'd asked herself today as she had so many times previously. She was quite content to live in the here and now. There should be impregnable territorial lines separating past, present, and future.

She wondered if she were asleep yet. No, she couldn't be. She could still hear the music . . .

Music that grew louder, then louder still. It filled the room, reverberated in her mind. Gone now was the soothing, floating lyricism, the gently rippling stream rhythm. The music was fiercely, unrelentingly atonal: blaring horns, strings pain-screeching beyond the highest notes of the octave. There was a chorus, voices that yowled fury, unreasoning anger, and hate.

Claire's head flew back. Her glasses had slipped to the very end of her nose and she peered over the top of them. She gripped the arms of the chair.

She saw the future.

Michael! He was standing still. His hazel eyes stared at her, but his face was otherwise utterly expressionless, a blank.

She waited for him to speak. She felt he had something to say, something to tell her.

Her son-in-law, this Michael-in-the-future, said nothing. Then, the crinkles around his eyes deepened and he smiled.

That smile! That is—I do not understand—not the way Michael smiles. I've never seen him look this way!

Michael lifted his hand. He slowly waved.

He is saying goodbye. He . . . No, I don't know what he means, what he is telling me.

Then Michael changed. His face, the face of the son-in-law she loved as dearly as a son, was gone. She was no longer seeing Michael. She was looking at . . .

I am Death!

Death was not a skeleton brandishing a scythe. He rode no ghostly steed. Death occupied Michael Louden's body, but Death's head . . .

Death's head was hellfire, a lunatic pinwheel of pulsing red. It was the writhing, black-scarlet flame of a great infernal candle. It was an evil blazing ruby, the color of the blood of victims, martyrs, innocents.

Though he had no eyes, Death's gaze fell on her. Though he had no mouth, Death spoke to her:

Soon! My time is soon!

Then Death and the future were gone. The FM station was quietly serenading its listeners with the Andre Kostelanetz version of The Beatles' "Yesterday." The slowed chirping of end-of-summer crickets flitered in through the window.

Claire's head ached. Her heart literally felt as though it were within her mouth. She did not fully understand what she had seen but she fully believed it. She knew better than to doubt the miserable gift of second sight that was hers.

She pondered her presentiment of what would be. Michael. Michael and Death. She had seen Micheal become Death. No, that wasn't right. She had watched as Michael had

194

been blotted out, taken over by Death!

That was it! Michael was going to die, and Death had even revealed when: *Soon!*

"Forewarned is forearmed." Like all cliches, that was good commen sense. Claire couldn't allow herself to believe that what she discerned in her intuitive flashes was an inevitability. Couldn't she have seen—and God, she prayed it were so!—merely a possibility, an event that did not have to occur if precautions were taken?

There were people who had testified that they had a "feeling" and so cancelled their passage on *The Titanic, The Lusitania, The Hindenburg*. Who knew how many lives had been saved by a wife's saying to her husband, "I want you to drive to work instead of taking the train," on the very day the 8:05 commuter de-railed; by an intuitive mother's deciding to let her child skip school on the day a school fire claimed hundreds of lives?

She had to warn Michael. Oh, her son-in-law had always pooh-poohed her premonitions. He no more accepted her psychic ability than he did the Flat Earth Theory.

But Beth . . . Beth did not *want* to believe, tried like anything to make light of "Mom's crystal ball bazing," but Beth *did* know. In her heart of hearts, against her will, Beth believed.

She would call right now and talk to Beth.

Claire took the book from her lap and placed in on the drum table alongside the chair. She stood up and the room whirled. Her blood pressure must have shot right up into the stratosphere during her vision, she thought. The dizziness would pass in a moment.

The floor rose up. It was like . . . She remembered being a youthful visitor to the carnival funhouse, the "topsy-turvy" room. She dropped back into the chair.

She felt strange. She looked around the living room. There was a heightened vividness to everything: the chandelier, the couch with the tired middle cushion, the sentimental knick-knacks in the shadow-box . . . She saw it all with an increased acuity. It was as though she could perceive the faint, ghostly traces of another dimension that lay beneath reality. There was an actual thickness to the distance between the sideboard and her wing chair. The room was crowded with depths of air.

Claire tried to rise. God! She was weak! Just sitting upright required so much of her strength. Indeed, her head was tipping to the right and it took her all her effort to keep it level.

Bracing herself with the heels of her hands on the chair's arms, locking her elbows at the right moment, she managed to stand. She took a step.

As a child in grade school, she had learned about gravity. Now, for the first time, she actually understood gravity; it was an overwhelming force working to yank her down.

All around her was a hissing-popping noise, as though she were staggering through a sea of champagne. The giant bubbles of carbonation touched her, burst against her.

The right corner of Claire Wynkoop's

mouth drooped, dribbling saliva. Bent at the elbow, her right arm was pressed to her side, the hand turned up, fingers curled in a rigid talon.

Her numb right leg trailing as though it wanted nothing to do with her, Claire reeled into the kitchen. She had to call Beth, to warn her about Michael . . .

But she couldn't, not yet. Suddenly—*right now*—death was reaching out for *her*. She had to get help.

She used her left hand to take the wall phone from its cradle. She locked the receiver between shoulder and her cheek and awkwardly dialed the "Emergency" number.

When she tried to speak, her tongue filled her entire mouth. That is funny, she thought; I know good and well what I want to say but it's coming out lumpy blocks of noise!

She tried once more. She focused all her concentration. The words were halting and thick but coherent. "My name . . . is Claire Wynkoop." She had to search her mind for her address but at last she had it. Then she explained the problem. "I think I am having a stroke."

She managed to hang up the phone and unlock the back door so that when help arrived there'd be no problem getting in. She tried to get to the kitchen table to sit down but weakness—not at all unpleasant, actually just a warm weariness radiating from her bones—hit her and she sank down onto the linoleum floor, her right leg stuck out before her.

She wondered if she were dying. She did

not think so. Though she had virtually no strength, she did not feel *bad* so much as *different*. She sensed changes within her mind, profound changes. The way she viewed the world was being transformed. She had the impression that for the very first time in her life she was *seeing;* the "scales were removed from her eyes." She understood the meaning of what she saw. On the wall, the ill-sewn sampler that Beth had made when she was in third grade, GOD BLESS OUR HAPPY HOME, was vibrating with a child's love and the joy of creating and the determination to make something "nice."

When the paramedics arrived, Claire Wynkoop was unable to answer any of their questions. She was conscious, but could not speak. Yet her glazed eyes were seeing, seeing not only what existed but the essence of it that transcended mere existence. Her brain, in which millions of cells were dying, was interpreting what she saw.

"Don't worry, ma'am. You're going to be all right."

Claire heard what was said, but more than that, she heard the concern and sincerity in the paramedic's voice.

Her head lolling, she studied the two men.

They shine! I can see the light. I understand their natures. The glow around their heads ... They have auras, bright golden, and that means they are kind and caring ... and good.

Claire Wynkoop's self-diagnosis was correct. She had had a massive stroke.

But now she could *see.*

She could see human auras.

And she could understand them.

It was five-thirty Saturday morning when the telephone rang. Michael sat up in bed, his heart racing. *The call? At last, the call?* Since seeing Jan Pretre at the Engelkings, hearing the renewal of the promise of the Time of The Strangers—*Soon!*—the ringing of the telephone sent an anticipatory tingle down his spine.

But, shit, he should have known. A pre-dawn call was probably a dumbass playing a prank or . . .

Beth had the telephone. She wasn't saying much. "Oh," mostly, but every "Oh" was more worried than the one before and she was crying.

"Beth, what is it?"

Even as Beth said "Mother," he realized what the call had to be. So good old, dear old, sweet old Moms had bought the big farm, over and out and call it a wrap, huh? Hypertension had finally popped the cork in her brain and bye-bye!

He slipped an arm around Beth's shoulder. He said, "She isn't . . ." then paused as though he couldn't bear to face the possibility that Claire was dead.

But goddamnit, and how about that? Claire was not dead after all! The old broad clung to life like gum stuck to your shoe in a fleabag movie house.

After she'd hung up the telephone, Beth, sobbing, gave him the details. Mother had suffered a major stroke, and, by the time she got to the hospital, she had yet another—

not so severe, that one, the doctors thought—on the other side of the brain. She was paralyzed. Right now, they had her in intensive care. She was drifting in and out of consciousness and, while her condition was serious, they called it stable, not critical.

"We have to . . ."

"Of course," Michael said. "We'll get right down there."

"The children, I . . . I don't want them to see Mom when she's like . . . like she is."

Right, Michael thought, *have to spare the impressionable wee ones any nastiness, don't we?* "Okay," he said, "You start getting ready and I'll wake the kids in a few minutes. I'll give the Engelkings a call. Vern's an early riser, even on weekends. I'll ask if they would keep Marcy and Kim until tomorrow evening. I'm sure it will be okay. You know how they feel about the girls."

"Yes," Beth said. "Laura and Vern are like family, Michael"—Beth choked—"Mom . . ."

Of course the Engelkings would look after the children for the weekend. No problem. So sorry to hear what had happened and if there were anything at all they could do . . .

An hour later, the kids dropped off at the Engelkings', Michael and Beth were on the road to Belford. Beth had hurriedly packed, taking a week's clothing for herself. That way she could be with her mother—*"I keep praying she'll be all right, Michael, but that's not what I feel"*—and Michael could probably—*"If only Mom is . . ."*—return home Sunday evening. The girls, of course, had school on Monday and he had to

200

work. It would be better not to upset the children's routine any more than necessary. Once they knew what was what, that Mom would be okay, they'd figure out what had to be done.

And just how the hell "okay" was the old lady likely to be? Michael wondered. *She was probably going to wind up a vegetable, and a goddamned vegetable belonged in the ground.*

"I'm sure things will be all right, Beth," Michael said. "People can make remarkable recoveries from strokes. Your mother is a strong-willed woman; that will help. I'll bet a year from now, you won't even know she had a stroke." To himself, Michael added, *A year from now, you won't know anything!*

Beth did not answer.

Overhead, the sun was a hazy blob in the sky. There were few cars heading south. The highway markers ticked off Monee, Kankakee, Chebanse, the exotic Illinois place names of small towns that had little more to offer a vistor than, as the signs promised, "Food," guaranteed bad, and "Gas," definitely over-priced.

Michael glanced at Beth. She was sitting as far as possible from him, pressed to the car door. He said, "Try to think positively, honey."

"Please be quiet, Michael," Beth said. She turned her head, not looking at him.

Well, please excuse him all to hell! He said, "Beth, I'm sorry if I said something to offend you. That's the last thing in the world I'd want to do, especially now."

In a monotone, Beth said, "You didn't say

anything wrong. In fact, you said just the right thing. You always say the right thing, Michael. But, it's funny, right now I'm having a hard time believing you *mean* any of the right things you say."

Michael's sigh was wounded and apologetic. "I . . . I don't understand." He *didn't* understand, either. Beth couldn't . . . No, he dismissed that idea. Wifey had the keen intuition of a cow at the slaughterhouse. His masquerade was too perfect, had been nothing less than perfect since the day he first met her and decided to make her a part of it.

"Beth," Michael continued, "if you'll tell me what . . "

"Do me a favor, Michael," Beth interrupted flatly. "Just be quiet. I don't want to talk, all right?"

"Whatever you say, dear," Michael said.

"She's awake now and I'm sure she's so glad you're here." The nurse's smile and tone were as artificial as her blond hair.

Propped up in bed at a thirty degree angle, an oxygen tube in her nose, wires running from beneath her hospital gown to the heart monitor on the shelf, IV needle in place in the back of her left hand, Claire Wynkoop looked like a science-fiction mummy, an aged creature kept alive for centuries by medical science rather than magic. But her eyes were open—really open.

I used to get an occasional look into the future. Now I can see the present, see people as they are . . .

Rushing toward the bed, Beth blocked Claire's view of Michael. Beth said, "Oh, Mom," and then she coughed wetly. She leaned down. Claire saw the dusting of freckles across Beth's nose, her quivering lower lip, the glittering tears in her brown eyes, and she saw her aura.

Clear light, but tinged at the edges with jagged lines of yellow. Spikey, angled streaks like crab legs . . . Yellow . . . the color of sickness, of anxiety and fear.

Beth was in an emotional upheaval, Claire realized. *How do I know all this? Oh, that doesn't matter. I know!* While some of Beth's distress was, of course, a daughter's normal concern for a seriously ill parent, there were other reasons as well; Claire sensed that.

Beth kissed Claire's cheek, then took a step back from the bed.

"Claire," the nurse said, "I know you're happy to see your family, but we don't want you to get too excited." The heart monitor showed Claire's pulse rate had nearly doubled and the wavy graph turned into ferociously steep mountains and plummeting valleys.

"Hello, Mom," Michael said. He stood at the foot of the bed.

I understand! Now I understand!

"It will be all right, Mom," Michael said. "You'll see."

You monster! You killer! You murderous bastard! I do see!

. . . the poison red glow about his head! The halo of hate! He was wicked, he was Evil in the form of a man, he was a hideous secret to the world, to everyone, to Beth and the children . . .

She had to give a warning!

"It's not good for her to get worked up like this," the nurse said. She patted Claire on the shoulder. "Please take it easy. You'll have plenty of time to be with your folks."

That brief glimpse of the future that had preceded her stroke—her *change*—she now fully comprehended. Death was coming for Michael . . . God, a grim joke! Michael *was* Death and *his* time was soon!

Claire's lips moved. Her chest heaved. She felt the air rise from her lungs, up her throat, and she tried to order her larynx, her tongue and teeth and lips into a revelation. The only sound that issued from her mouth was a gargled groan.

"Oh, Mom," Beth said.

"Now don't you try to talk, Claire," the nurse said. "Once you're better, I'm sure you'll have all kinds of things to say!"

Claire felt tears of helpless frustration run down her cheeks.

"There, that's all right," the nurse said. She wiped Claire's face with a tissue. Then turning to Michael and Beth, she said, "It would be a good idea for you to step out in the hall for a while until she calms down. This is really emotionally overwhelming for her. She must love you both a great deal."

Michael moved to the side of the bed to stand alongside Beth.

Claire knew. *He is going to kill her. He wants to kill . . . everyone!*

Inside Claire Wynkoop was a shriek. She

could feel it. It was a massive tumor of sound filling her chest, and the only way it could emerge was as a thin moan.

"Please, Mr. and Mrs. Louden," the nurse said.

Michael glanced at his wristwatch. "The doctor said he'd be able to talk to us about now," he said to Beth. "Let's go visit him."

At the doorway, Michael turned back. He gave Claire a brief wave and a smile. "Don't worry, Mom. We'll see you soon."

Fourteen

HER MOTHER was "coming along." That was
what Dr. Rhinehardt, the head of the rehabilitation unit, was continually saying. It was
what Beth wanted to believe. Claire
Wynkoop, however, seemed to prove it was a
lie.

Staring straight ahead, Claire sat in the
plastic cushioned armchair by the window.
With Beth's help, she had teetered the few
steps from the bed to the chair in the private
room.

After she had spent ten days in the Belford
hospital, Claire was out of danger. There was
nothing more the hospital could do for her.
She needed twenty-four-hour-a-day care and
intensive therapy and so she was taken by
ambulance to the Ridgewood Convalescent
Home and Rehabilitation Center. Ridgewood
had a good reputation and was only ten
minutes west of Park Estates so Beth could
visit her often.

Claire had been at Ridgewood for three
weeks. There was no way to predict how
much longer her stay would be. Fortunately,
money was not a problem. Mom had always
"taken care of things," so her comprehensive
health insurance program was adequate even
in an age of skyrocketing medical costs.
There was money in Mom's bank account,
too, and . . .

Damn it, Beth thought, her mother had been so independent all her life. It was heartbreaking to see her like this, so utterly helpless. With the weight Mother had lost, she seemed a dried-out shell in which remained only a germ of life.

As for the "progress" that made Dr. Rhinehardt so optimistic . . . Well, Mom could walk at least as well as a one-legged drunken sailor and could clumsily hold a spoon with her left hand. Her right hand and arm were totally paralyzed. And she couldn't talk, not a word. When she tried, the sounds she made were scarcely human.

And Beth was worried that—*Worst on top of worse!*—Mom's mind was deteriorating. Often when she spoke to her mother, there was a too-bright glassiness in Mom's eyes, as though nothing were registering. And when Mom saw the girls and Michael those first few times, anyway, she had become inexplicably excited, almost hysterical, violently tossing her head from side to side and gibbering frantically. It was almost as though she were terrified of them, horror-stricken at their presence.

Now, Beth forced herself to talk, telling her mother—*Can this woman be my mother?*— what the girls were doing at school, how Michael was—well, he seemed preoccupied, had to be work pressures, she assumed —about her psychology class, the alternator belt on the Chevette that had to be replaced last week, a new recipe she wanted to try. As though speaking normally would somehow bring her mother back, Beth chattered on and on: *Gee, here it was only the start of October and the kids were already starting to get excited about Halloween, but, well, with the world being what it was, maybe it wasn't such a good idea to let them go trick or treating because, oh, you know, there were some cruel and dangerous crazies who . . .*

Claire Wynkoop stared at the wall.

From the hall came the sounds of supper-time carts and trays. "Dinner's on the way," Beth said with forced enthusiasm. "The food here always smells so good."

Beth had been sitting on the edge of the bed and now she rose. "Mom," she said, "would you like me to help you with your dinner?"

Claire did not answer with even the slight-est movement of her head.

Beth had nearly asked, *Would you like me to feed you,* but caught herself in time. She frankly doubted that it would have hurt Mom's feelings, doubted that Mom even understood most of what she said, but some-how acknowledging just how totally helpless Mother was would have meant to Beth her-self that she had simply given up on her.

She couldn't. She had to have faith.

Beth glanced at her watch. It was a few minutes after six. "Well, Mom," she said, "I'd better be on my way to my class and let you have your dinner and get some rest . . ."

Beth was interrupted by her mother's sud-denly lifting her left arm. Claire slowly turned her head over and, fingers curling, beckoned Beth closer.

"Yes, Mom?"

Claire licked her lips. She swallowed, a too

large lump moving down her throat beneath line-worn flesh. Her eyes met Beth's and held them.

Beth squatted. She reached for her mother's hand but Claire pulled it back.

Mom was trying to tell her something, Beth realized. Her mother's eyes were clear and knowing and . . .

Claire moved her hand around her own head as though tracing the outline of an invisible diving helmet. Her lips moved. The sound she made began as a harsh consonant and ended in a whimpered open vowel.

Beth stood up. It was a grim game of charades they were playing. Was she saying she had a headache? Or maybe she wanted a scarf! Beth had to squelch a sudden, angry desire to grab her mother's shoulders, shake her and yell, "Say it, damn it!"

Instead, she merely sighed. So did her mother, a long, weary sigh that soundlessly continued as she seemed to collapse within herself, shoulders and head drooping.

I have to get out of here! I can't stand being with her another moment! Beth was ashamed of the thought, ashamed of how quickly she slipped on her jacket, snatched up her purse, and perfunctorily kissed her mother's forehead. Lingering only long enough to say, "I'll be back tomorrow, Mom," she fled.

She forced herself to walk normally down the hall to the elevator, not to run from the convalescent home to her car. Her heart pounding, she put the key in the ignition but did not start the engine.

She looked at the mask of her eyes in the

rear-view mirror. A motion picture vampire priestess? A prisoner in a South American torture cell? Good God, who was this dead-eyed woman?

She was someone whose world has fallen apart!

She yearned to talk to someone, to spill her guts. "I am miserable and I am afraid. It seems I'm afraid all the time now. I'm afraid of telephone calls and door to door salesman and truck drivers who pull up alongside me at red lights. I'm afraid of strangers taking my kids for rides. I'm afraid of the man behind me in the grocery check-out line. I'm afraid of electrical storms and tornadoes and car accidents and heart attacks and cancer and dreams and death. I'm afraid of things I cannot even imagine."

Her throat tightened as she felt the sting of not unwelcome tears to her eyes. She *did* want to cry but feared that if she began, she might never stop.

She was so terribly *alone*.

There was no one she could . . .

Not Michael. She could not talk to him, not anymore. Michael nodded seriously when she spoke seriously, he murmured consolingly when she needed consolation, and he was just as he had always been—*wasn't he?*—the guy with the pleasantly cornball jokes, who usually remembered to re-cap the *Crest* after brushing his teeth, who read the morning paper, who belched, who yawned, and who was, somehow, an engima, a stranger.

The world was full of strangers.

The thought hit her with the sharp-sweet

intensity of a religious revelation.

There *was* someone!

I think . . .

She had a friend.

Isn't he?

She could talk with him.

She drove to Lincoln Junior College.

The volume of the television was turned up to a window-rattling, kid-pleasing level. They were watching a syndicated rerun of *Mork and Mindy*. Each time Mork uttered his brainless "Na-Nu, na-nu," the studio audience howled appreciation and so did Kim. In her pajamas, she lay on her stomach on the carpet, not more than a yard from the set, chin propped in her hands.

Michael sat on the sofa. It was his night to mind the children. He was tense, keyed up. He wanted to kill.

Killing! That was his reason for being; it was what he was meant to do. Now, knowing that the killing time was not far off—The Time of the Strangers—he felt like a meta-morphosed caterpillar burning to break free of the constricting cocoon of mundanity that had imprisoned him for so long.

Michael crossed his legs. The TV screen presented a closeup of Mork as he declared, "I'm only trying to be a normal guy like everyone else, na-nu, na-nu." The laugh track proclaimed his comment incredibly hil-arious. So did Kim's burst of laughter.

Michael glared at his daughter. Not so long from now—*but when? When?*—he would not need her. He would not need her sister or her

211

mother. They would see him then, see him for the first and last time in their lives, and know him as he was, Michael the Stranger. Good-bye to this goddamned self-denying lie: Dear Old Dad and "Happy Husband . . ."

. . . And say, Beth was kind of blowing it as "Wonderful Wifey" these days. Most of the time she moped around like she'd had a lobotomy on her peanut-sized brain. And every time she hesitatingly tried to get into one of those "meaningful discussions" that she used to half-paralyze his ears with, working for "real communication to keep us in touch with each other," blah-blah-bullshit, well, he'd say something—something quite reasonable, goddamnit! and Gong! She'd come up with a tired, "Oh, never mind," or "Let's forget it," or end the conversation by turning away from him in silence.

Hell, he was saying all the right things and making all the right moves. He'd tried sex and while in the past the old push-rub-tickle had usually done the job, convincing Beth that all was ginger-peachy, super-fine, and hey-hey okay, not so of late. He couldn't call her frigid; she didn't get that worked up.

So she was all bent out of shape about her old lady. That was real sad. Sure too bad. What a goddamned shame . . .

"Hey, Dad?"

"Hmm? What's that?"

There was a commercial and Kim rolled over and sat up. "Don't you like *Mork and Mindy?*"

"I do," he said. "It's a wonderful show. Brilliant comedy. Superb acting. Yessir,

America *needs Mork and Mindy.*"

"Then why don't you laugh?"

"I *do* laugh, Kim," Michael said. "Believe me, your dad is laughing his head off on the inside."

Kim gave him a puzzled look. "You know, Dad, sometimes I just don't get you."

Really? he thought. Sometime I am going to get *you!* Michael rose. In fact, he thought—and pleasure chills bubbled down his spine—*now* would be a wonderful time. You'd hear Daddy laugh, Kim. He'd laugh like you never heard him, but you wouldn't think it was all that goddamned hilarious!

He actually took a step toward her but then stopped. Calm, cool, and collected, that was how he had to be. Patient and enduring—and waiting. The call *would* come, Jan Pretre's call and then, yes then, surely then . . .

Michael went downstairs. In the kitchen, even after shutting the door to the stairway below, he could still hear Kim's gales of laughter and that infuriatingly moronic "Na-nu, na-nu."

He opened the drawer to the left of the sink. There it was, the butcher knife, its long, triangular blade keen and pointed. It was part of a set, steak knives, a potato peeler, a julienne knife, a bread knife, any damned knife you could think of, sold by direct mail and advertised in shrill TV commercials: "You'd think this superb cutlery collection would cost several hundred dollars but it can be yours for the low, low price of only $29.95, that's . . ."

Smiling, Michael picked up the butcher

knife. It was perfect.

He was vibrating like an engine at top racing speed. So *fine* to do it now—the thrill and rush and waves of imcomprehensible joy! Marcy and Kim, and then . . .

Beth's class was over at nine but, she'd told him, there was a group from the class that got together afterward for a drink, so he didn't expect her home until 10:30 or 11. He would say, "How was school?" and she would say, "Okay," and then he'd say, "You know, I don't think the girls are feeling too well. Maybe you ought to look in on them."

He imagined Beth's face as she looked at the dead children.

Her mouth falls open! Her eyes bulge! She tries to scream but she's too shocked, can only make a dry coughing noise! She stands swaying, stares at him as he grins, does not believe, even as he plunges the knife into her chest and belly and throat!

No! Not yet and not now, damn it, no matter how strong the urge, the want and the need. The killing time would come.

Michael put the butcher knife back and closed the drawer. Shit, he understood why Eddie Markell drank like a skid row winehead. When it was in *your* blood to spill the blood of others, the nothing people, and you could not, you had to find solace in other ways.

He walked into the living room. From upstairs, he heard the sound of water splashing in the tub. Marcy was getting ready for bed.

He clicked on the antique crystal lamp on the end table and sat down on the sofa. Then he smiled. So Beth was irritable and out of sorts, huh? He'd give her something to be unhappy about! And might as well spread the misery around a bit—a little something for the girls as well!

A minute later, he was yelling upstairs, "Marcy, get down here!" Then he went to the kitchen, opened the door down to the recreation room, and ordered Kim up.

In the living room, he pointed at the end table. "Kim, Marcy, look what we've got here."

"Oh, wow!" Kim exclaimed. "One of Mom's lamps is all smashed!"

The lamp lay on its side, precariously close to the edge of the end table, its shade crushed, the dangling glass prisms shattered into jagged bits and gleaming dust like diamond twinkles atop a new snowfall.

Marcy, in her nightgown, glanced nervously at the broken lamp, then at her father, then back to the lamp.

"Those lamps were expensive," Michael said, "but the money isn't the important thing. We've got a broken lamp. Your mom is going to be heartsick. I don't think we can have it repaired and I'm sure it can't be replaced. So, who did it?"

Neither child answered him.

"All right," Michael said. He ran a hand over his hair and then said, "Accidents happen. I understand that. So we've got an accident and I'm not happy about it, but I am going to find out who caused it. Once I learn that and when I hear an 'I'm sorry,' that will be the end of it, okay?"

He paused for a few seconds, studying the

children. They were on the spot, he thought, and that was a good place for them to be. Uh-huh, and a bit of hurt and unhappiness at the old homestead.

"Okay," he said, looking at Kim. "What about it?"

"No," Kim said emphatically. "I didn't bust it, Daddy."

"Marcy?"

"No, Daddy."

Michael folded his arms across his chest. "It seems we have a mystery here, young ladies. Something is broken but nobody broke it. Now how can that be?"

Marcy tentatively said, "Maybe it fell over by itself, Daddy."

"Oh," Michael said, with an exaggerated nod. "That's an interesting theory. Or maybe there's a stranger in the house, somebody we don't even know lives here, and *he* knocked it down. That's a possibility too, isn't it, Marcy?"

"I . . . I don't know, Daddy," Marcy said.

"I always get blamed but I *didn't* . . ."

"Quiet," Michael ordered. "The both of you, go to your room." He made a show of looking at his watch. "It's a quarter to nine and nine is bedtime. I'll see you then and one of you had better have something to tell me. Girls, I'm angry now and I'm on the way of being angrier, but if someone owns up to this, it will be okay and nobody gets punished. I don't punish you for telling the truth. But"—he waited a moment to give the threat extra impact—"if I don't hear a confession, then you're both getting spankings—and I mean

216

good ones."

It was five minutes after nine when he went to their room. He gave them extra time to ponder his threat, to sweat over it. *And hey! Wasn't paddling your children one of the requisite parental duties in this 'Forget Dr. Spock' conservative era? Yeah, smash your kid in the face with a fist and you were a bastard of a child abuser; wallop that kid's bottom with an open hand and you were a caring, concerned disciplinarian.*

In response to his "Well?" Marcy only shook her head, but Kim blew up.

"You *are* going to blame me! I know! You're not fair! You're mean!"

"That's enough," Michael warned, but he didn't end Kim's tirade.

"You're plain mean and you want to hurt . . ."

He nearly smiled. Uh-huh, the little toad had *that* right without even realizing that she did!

" . . . I don't care! You can't hurt me. You can spank me as hard as you want and I'm not going to cry!"

Michael slowly rubbed his chin. He somberly said, "I don't have much choice then, do I?"

Kim lay on his lap as rigid as a broomstick. "Are you sure you have nothing to say to me, Kim?"

She arched up, twisting her head to glower defiantly at him. She kept her vow. She didn't even say "Ouch." Afterward she said, "I *told* you you couldn't make me cry and it didn't even hurt and I really hate you!"

He paddled Marcy. She shed all the tears he expected and then some.

With the girls in their beds, he stood at the door. "I'm sorry you made me do that. And whichever one of you *did* break the lamp ought to think seriously about apologizing to her sister for getting her paddled. Good night."

Walking downstairs, he reflected it had not been a bad evening, not bad at all. And there was still the scene to come when Beth saw that "oh so lovely" lamp!

"What are the signs"—she hesitated, sipped her old-fashioned. It was her second. The first was a subtle glow within, just enough relaxation to give her courage—"of a nervous breakdown?"

Across the small table in the corner of the dimly lit lounge, Kevin Bollender stirred his scotch and water. Quietly, he said, "Beth, am I right in thinking that's not a theoretical question?"

She smiled glumly. "Does it show?"

Kevin said, "You've got a lot on your mind. There's something bothering you, probably a number of 'somethings.' That shows. Feel like talking about it?"

"Feel like talking?" she answered with a shrug and a melancholy laugh. "I feel like I *have* to. My whole life is a mess. It's like being on a treadmill in quicksand. I keep on walking and walking and I don't go forward, only down."

"Please go on."

Whatever floated up in her mind came

spewing forth as words, the orders of events no real order at all, her silent lulls made less awkward by swallows of her drink: Brad Zeller and Kim's accident and the death of a dog and a guinea pig and—*It's good saying this. He is really listening to me*—Mom's stroke and always, always now, this heavy sense of dread . . .

She hit an abrupt dead end. She thought there was more she wanted to say but she had no idea how to say it.

She felt a jumble of emotions: embarrassment, foolishness, annoyance at herself for burdening someone else with her troubles—and relief. She stared at her glass. It would be hard to look at Kevin right now; she had revealed more of herself to him than she ever had to anyone else.

Even to Michael, way back when she could believe everything was fine between them? She wasn't sure. She searched her memory for those times of closeness and intimacy between herself and her husband that surely had to be there, but moments like that seemed so long ago, so ethereally distant, that they had no more substance and reality than a dream.

Kevin said, "Things have been going badly for you. You're under a great deal of pressure. You're hurting. I understand. And there's something I want you to know."

"What's that?"

He took her fingers from her glass and held her hand. She had to look at him then. She saw the solicitude in his eyes, heard it in his voice. "I care."

219

She wished she could freeze time, hold onto this moment and the near-magical assurance she felt that "Everything was all right."

Then she pulled away her hand. There was something wrong in her sitting in a cocktail lounge, holding hands with this young man, her teacher, telling him her private woes. She had a husband and children at home. She felt adulterous and immoral and . . .

While she couldn't abandon her guilt, she did manage to set it aside for the time being.

"Why?" she asked.

The corner of Kevin's mouth twisted. "Sorry, afraid I don't get the question."

"You said that you care, Kevin," she said. "I . . . I'd like to believe that. It would help me right now." She went on in a rush, realizing he might construe what she said as insulting but having to say it nonetheless. "*Why* do you care about me?"

Kevin raised his hand. "One," he said, ticking off points on his fingers, "you're intelligent. Maybe I'm funny that way, but I have always liked bright people. Two, you're articulate. Half the people you meet nowadays can't express a simple thought. Three, it so happens that you're easy to talk with. How's that for starters?"

She had to smile. "Please continue."

Her smile was returned. "Okay, let's not forget that you laugh at my jokes, in class and out. We've discovered that we like the same old movies. Besides, when my poor jade plant at home was on its way to the Great Greenhouse in the Sky, you were the one who told me to lighten up on the watering and saved the little critter's life."

Kevin rested his elbows on the table. "I like you, Beth," His voice dropped and grew husky. "I like your brown eyes and those freckles. There's something woman and little girl about you, Beth, and that appeals to a man who . . ."

He suddenly leaned back against the booth's padded backrest. Not looking at her, he too lightly said, "Oh, you know what I mean. It's just that, well, we're friends, okay?"

Friends, Beth thought. That was what they were, and so there was no reason for her to have an ounce of guilt about being with Kevin Bollender. *But I do.* Certainly no one would condemn her for having a drink twice a week with her friend. *Then why did I tell Michael only that some "people from class" stop for drinks, without mentioning that the "some people" are Kevin and myself?*

"Okay," Kevin said, "let's take a look at some of what's bothering you." His tone became more formal, almost as if he were lecturing to a class of one. "People have what we term a nervous breakdown when they're overwhelmed by free-floating anxiety. You're experiencing anxiety, but it's *not* free-floating. There are real causes that triggered your feelings of depression and apprehension. To put it simply, some rotten, painful, out-and-out bad things have happened to you. You've taken an emotional clobbering. You've gone through the grinder, so naturally you feel all ground up. But you're dealing with it. You're handling it. You're meeting your responsibilities and getting along from day to day."

"But why do I keep thinking more out-and-out bad things have to be on the way?"

Kevin pursed his lips to draw in a whistle. "Because that's the way people *do* think, Beth. They look for reasons in the unreasonable and patterns in the random events that make up all the crappy stuff that occurs in life. Years ago, someone wrote *The Book of Job* to try to understand the 'why?' of human suffering. You take a look at today's bestseller charts and the big book is called *When Bad Things Happen to Good People.* Same old 'Why' question, same attempt to find answers."

"I see, *Dr.* Bollender," Beth said with a nod. "So I am not—what's the clinical term—becoming a loony?"

"*Nein,*" Kevin replied with a comic Viennese accent. "It is *nicht* crazy to be depressed when *der* depressing things give you *der* kick in *der keister.*" He grew serious again. "I can't consider you a likely candidate for a nervous breakdown. I sense a real strength in you, Beth, probably more strength than you know is there. You've got internal resources, that ability to cope and to keep on coping."

"Kevin?"

"Yes?"

"Thanks for . . . for the free psychotherapy."

Kevin laughed. He held up his empty glass. "Not free. The workman is worthy of his wages and all that. You can buy me a drink."

It wasn't until the waitress brought Kevin's scotch and water—"No, no thanks, the lady doesn't want another"—that Beth gave him the thanks she'd originally intended to.

She said, "Thank you for being my friend."

FIFTEEN

MICHAEL TURNED west onto Elmscourt Lane. In the back seat, Kim yipped, "Good! We're almost there!"

"You like visiting Laura and Vern, don't you?" Michael asked.

"Yeah," Kim answered. "They've got great video games!"

"Oh," Michael laughed, "*they* do? I wasn't aware that Laura was a video game addict. How about you, Marcy? Glad to have a sleepover at the Engelkings'?"

"Sure, Daddy. It's always fun with Aunt Laura and Uncle Vern."

Beth smiled, wondering when the Engelkings had become "Aunt and Uncle." She had to admit that she herself thought of them in much the same way.

Gazing through the windshield, Beth admired the impressionistic beauty of the setting sun that splashed the hazy blue sky with ripples of orange and pink. Her window was open an inch or so. Today, Friday, had been warm, with a light breeze that seemed left over from summer, and she thought she smelled the lazy-crisp aroma of burning leaves. A moment later, she realized that could not be so. Like most suburbs, High Wood had ordinances against leaf-burning.

Funny how the mind works, Beth thought. For a day as lovely as this, she had naturally conjured up a fitting scent of fall. Well, that was certainly better than dreaming up all that dire, threatening, terrible garbage that had made her feel like a basket case without a basket!

She was realizing just how much_ last week's talk with Kevin—*Bless him*—had helped, giving her insight into what she had been feeling and why. She'd vowed to take one day at a time, accepting whatever "bad" might occur if there were no other choice, dealing with it, but no longer forgetting to see the "good" of each day when it was there. She could handle life; she knew she could. (In fact, several times, when she felt herself slipping back into the blues, she gave herself a "chin up, shoulders back" pep-talk: You're okay, Beth Louden. You're making it and you're going to keep right on making it.")

The power of positive thinking? Or maybe a ridiculous attempt to be Pollyanna? She didn't think so. She was simply seeing things as they were, and that made all the difference For instance, when she got home after her conversation with Kevin last week and learned that one of her antique crystal lamps was smashed, she was angry, upset, and sad. Case closed. It was *not*—multiple choice: A) the worst disaster since the destruction of Pompeii; B) a certain portent of imminent catastrophes; C) part of a Cosmic Plot against the Loudens; D) all of the above.

She wasn't sure if Michael had been correct in punishing *both* children but he had and what was done was done. The girls didn't seem to have any lingering bad feelings, anyway. Everything was settled, everything was normal, everything was "all right" for the Loudens; that was how it felt to Beth.

And she was hopeful that tomorrow, her mother would take a giant step back to "all-rightness," too. They'd pick her up in the morning and keep her until Sunday evening. While Dr. Rhinehardt was pleased with Claire Wynkoop's progress thus far, he believed it important that she start moving back into real life.

"She needs to be with people she cares about," Dr. Rhinehardt had explained, "and who care about her. She ought to see something besides sickness. It could help snap her out of her lethargy, make her work harder in therapy. It will give her a goal, you see, remind her that as soon as she's able, she can resume her place as an active member of your family."

Claire would have the girls' room. So she could rest in a quiet house when she needed to, Marcy and Kim were spending tonight and tomorrow night with Laura and Vern. Vern would bring them home late Sunday morning; that way the kids could visit with their grandmother before she had to be taken back to the convalescent home.

Michael pulled into the long, winding driveway. "Ladies, we have arrived," he announced, putting the LTD in "Park" and switching off the engine.

Her train of pleasant thought broken, Beth turned her head in his direction. Michael was smiling; Beth thought he looked as handsome as he had in those carefree days of

"UsedToBe," when she was a college freshman and he was always the joking senior—
"I'm trying to woo you, Beth, and make you
my *woo*-man, woo, woo, woo!" More than
that, his face was endearingly familiar. Those
crinkles around his eyes, she had been with
him through the years as time had etched
them, and that slightly discolored canine
tooth, a root canal three years ago . . .

Her throat tightened. She and Michael
shared a past, all the moments, important or
insignificant, that comprised a life together:
watching late movies, painting a kitchen,
catching a cold and passing it back and forth
like a game of "hot potato," making love,
raising children . . .

Kim had pushed open the rear door and
was racing toward the house. Marcy followed
at a walk.

"I love you, Michael," Beth said.

Michael waggled his eyebrows dramatically as he slipped the car keys into
the side pocket of his sportcoat. "That's
always fine to hear," he said, "but could I ask
what prompted it?"

She knew she couldn't explain all of it, but
she summed it up with, "You're a good man."

*He was, he was; she knew he was. He was
warm and considerate and loving, and any
other feeling she had about him was sheer
idiocy. Michael, her Michael, a stranger?
Please . . . and, let's face the truth, Beth
Louden. You isolated yourself from him,
sealing yourself inside a shell of unhappiness
and crazy imaginings, and then you blamed
him!*

"Michael, kiss me," she said.

He did, leaning down to her, his hands on her shoulders.

"Uh," he said, "I believe we're expected for dinner."

"Yes," Beth said. She shivered. "Let's try to get home early, Michael. I want to make love."

Michael clicked his tongue against his teeth. "Honey, seven minutes after we finish dessert, we're out the door!"

Beaming, Vern greeted them. "Enter, enter and welcome! If the adults will accompany me to the family room . . ."

"Huh!" Kim interrupted, "you're going to have drinks, I bet!"

"Indeed," Vern laughed. "We'll partake of a potable while Laura finishes preparing the repast, and if you young ladies would like, it so happens there's a new cartridge in the *Atari*, awaiting the touch of a youthful hand on the joy-stick."

"Is it *Ms. Pac-Man?*" Kim asked.

"Far better," Vern said, "an outer-space adventure in which you get to blast meteorites, missiles, and many-headed monsters."

"Sounds like an educational game," Michael said.

Vern guffawed. "It's good for the kids to have a chance to create their own television violence."

In the family room, the electronic sounds of asteroids and spaceships being blasted floating down the hall, Vern mixed Beth an old-fashioned, Michael a Seven and Seven, and himself a whiskey and soda. "Beth,

Michael," Vern said quietly, "I know there've recently been some rough times for you, so"—Vern raised his glass in a toast—"to better days, and to the friendship that gets us all through the bad days."

Clicking her glass against Michael's and Vern's, Beth wished she could somehow take them all in her arms right now, embrace all the people she loved: Michael and Marcy and Kim and Vern and Laura and Mom . . .

She dipped her head so they couldn't see the tears. "Vern," she said, "we can't thank you enough for looking after the girls this weekend."

"Hey," Michael said, "remind me to get their suitcase out of the trunk before we leave, okay?"

"They're beautiful children and we're glad to help," Vern said. He squeezed Beth's upper arm. "You know, well, Laura and I always wanted children and we could never . . ." Vern suddenly turned away, facing the huge stone fireplace, his back to them. "Let's say we feel very close to *all* the Loudens, all right?"

The door chimes rang. From the kitchen, Laura called, "Vern, get that, please! I'm busy."

Vern turned back to Beth and Michael, setting his glass on the copper-topped bar. "That has to be . . ."

The chimes sounded again and Laura called out, "Vern!"

"Excuse me," Vern said, and he left the family room.

"I don't know," Michael said in answer to

Beth's unspoken question. "Vern didn't mention they'd invited anyone else this evening."

"I'm sure you remember . . ." Vern said when he returned with the new arrival.

"Of course, the Loudens," Jan Pretre said. "We met at the party over Labor Day. It's Beth and Michael, right?" He shook their hands.

"That's right, Dr. Pretre," Michael said.

"Please, call me Jan," he said.

Beth recalled how interesting and easy to talk to she had thought the psychiatrist when she'd first met him. Now he seemed a different man, tense and brooding. He was holding himself stiffly, as though he didn't feel right in his blue suit, and his eyes were sunken with weariness. The sharply trimmed salt and pepper beard that she had originally thought gave him a distinguished appearance now made him look weathered and aging.

"A drink, Jan?" Vern offered.

"Scotch rocks," Jan Pretre said. "A hefty one, please. I need it." He leaned an elbow on the bar and when Vern handed him the scotch, he took a good swallow. "I'm sorry," he said. "I didn't want to come in here like Captain Gloom, but I just had some disturbing news. That's why I was late."

"What is it, Jan?" Vern asked.

"I lost one today," Jan Pretre said flatly. "He was seventeen, a nice kid. Super-bright, played guitar and wrote poetry. I really thought we were making headway. He was getting himself together."

Jan Pretre paused to drink. Then he tiredly

said, "He had a one o'clock appointment. We talked about a girl he was dating and his decision to apply for admission to Yale. He told me things were working out. He thanked me for working with him. Then he went home and took a razor blade and slit his wrist. It wasn't your typical teenage play for attention. There was no one else home. He didn't just nick himself for a bit of blood and a lot of melodrama. It was a long cut, lengthwise down the vein. He was serious and now he's dead serious."

Jan finished his drink. "So chalk up one more for Freud, Jung, Adler, and yours truly."

Vern refilled Jan's glass without asking and then insisted on "freshening up" Beth's. He patted Jan on the shoulder. "You can't consider it your fault, Jan."

"Why, of course not," Jan said bitterly. "As a psychiatrist I'm supposed to be objective and uninvolved. That's what it says in the "How to Be a Headshrinker' book. But it doesn't work that way, Vern. A young man came to me, trusted me to set him right, and now he's dead."

"Jan," Beth said, "I *know* you're a very good psychiatrist."

Jan Pretre's brow furrowed. "What makes you say that, Beth?"

She'd surprised herself by speaking. She knew she was at an emotional high, more open than she ordinarily would be, and in addition the old-fashioned was a potent tongue-loosener; one more might be a tongue-twister! Still, she wanted to say something to

Jan.

"You give a damn. I can tell that. People matter to you. That's the kind of person I'd want to be my psychiatrist . . . "

She laughed at herself then and then everyone else was laughing, too. She felt silly and felt it was okay to feel that way with these special people. Michael kissed her on the nose. "You ever think you're Napoleon, honey, we'll ask Jan to fix you right up."

The tension Jan Pretre had brought with him seemed broken but if any of it did remain, it was left behind in the family room as Laura Engelking summoned everyone to the dinner-table.

They were in the family room. The door was closed. It had been, as Vern said, "a veritable banquet:" French onion soup, tossed salad, prime rib and double baked potatoes, and a glazed peach tart. Beth and Laura were doing the dishes while the men, as Vern put it, "withdrew for brandy and talk of Parliament, the troubles in the colonies, and other such matters of interest to high-born gentlemen."

Michael sipped his *Courvoisier* and then, shaking his head, said to Jan Pretre, "That was some sad story about the kid's suicide. I mean, I was almost in tears."

Framed by his beard, Jan Pretre's teeth shone white in a predator's smile. "It was a goddamned tragedy. The poor prick came to me with his penny-ante problems. All he needed to hear from me today was that he shouldn't kill himself. Well, let's say he didn't hear that. I gave him a push, a nudge, led him to gawk at a mirror and see a useless piece of shit staring back and I knew he was gone. I talked him into suicide and he obliged."

They all laughed. "That's it, you know," Jan Pretre said. "That's why I became a nut-doctor. Society hands you a license granting you power over its nothing people. You haul them onto the rack, you twist them and bend them and listen as they scream and cry, and you're a fine guy because you're *helping* them.

"That's why so many Strangers wind up as cops or social workers or preachers or surgeons. Or dentists. Or chiropractors. You see John Doe and Jane Dip when they're hurting like hell and you can make them hurt even more if you handle it right. John and Jane don't suspect a thing. Cop Stranger who blasts the ass off an old bum in an alley gets a commendation for stopping an armed robbery and Doctor Stranger who slices away three-quarters of your guts becomes 'the wonderful man who saved my life.'"

Vern's laughed boomed. "Conventional folk wisdom: the surgeon loves the knife."

"So do we," Michael said. There was silence for a minute. Then Michael said one word—the question: "When?"

Jan Pretre answered the question with a question. "Growing impatient, Michael?" His tone was chiding.

"No," Michael said, and then, more quietly, changed it to, "Yes."

"Don't," Jan Pretre said, and now he was speaking in a warning voice. "Don't get

232

impatient, Michael. Impatient means careless. Careless means you don't think like you should. It means you do things you shouldn't and you don't notice what you had damned well better notice. Do you understand me, Michael?"

"Yes, Jan."

"Michael, Michael," Jan Pretre said, his tone changing again. "It was so many years ago when we met, when I first saw the blood-fire around your head. I told you who you were, Michael, told you that you were not alone and that you'd have to wait, wait for Our Time, wait and never let the nothing people have a hint of who you were. That's just what you've done, Michael. Only a little while longer, a single tick of the Eternity Clock, and the waiting is ended. You will be with us *then*, Michael, if you stay completely in control of yourself, not losing patience or forgetting caution."

"I understand, Jan," Michael said.

"That's good, Michael. That's fine."

A half hour later, Michael and Beth went home.

At eight o'clock Saturday evening, he stepped out of his home office. There was work he'd had to do: write a memo about a new oil absorbent, a note to the Indiana sales rep expressing his disappointment at the drop in last month's sales, a letter to go to the clients of the late Herb Cantlon stating that it had been Superior Chemical's pleasure to serve them and that it was hoped that . . . It was meaningless make-work, he thought, the banal time-wasting he had to do.

He walked down the hall. The washroom door was closed. Beth was bathing. She was happily singing in a childish, off-key soprano, "She's a maniac . . . Mane-EE-Ack!" the main theme from the movie *Flashdance*.

Beth was back to her old self, he thought, loving Wifey Dear. In fact, you could make that ultra-loving WD. In bed last night she had been burning for him. He hadn't heard her squeal and moan that way since . . . hey! Maybe since *ever!*

It was easier for him if Beth weren't acting as though she started the day with a glass of vinegar. Let her keep on smiling a *Good Housekeeping* Seal of Approval smile right up until . . .

The light was on in Marcy and Kim's room. Michael glanced in. In a quilted blue and white housecoat, Claire Wynkoop was seated on Kim's bed. Her right arm seemed confined in an invisible sling, the fingers rigidly curled. With the slow, exaggerated blink of an animated cartoon character, she looked at Michael.

Michael stood in the doorway. "Are you doing all right, Mom? Anything you'd like me to bring you?" He doubted Claire Wynkoop even understood the question. All day she'd been little more than a clumsily animated mummy without its wrappings.

The tendons on Claire's neck twitched spastically. One, two, three, she blinked at him.

Christ, Michael thought, the old crone really acted weird around him. Big change

now that her gray matter had turned to Jello.
He'd always been the number one boy, the
dearly devoted son-in-law, and bet your ass
he'd worked hard for *that* image.

"I know you can't really say anything yet,
Mom," Micheal said. *Sure, Mama-in-law, I
want to do all I can for you now that you're a
fucked up wreck!* "So if there's something
you'd like, how about you nod your head and
we'll figure it out from there, okay?"

Claire Wynkoop didn't nod her head nor
shake it from side to side. Her eyes zoomed in
on Michael's, clicked and locked onto that
invisible "here to there" pathway, and
blinked: one, two, three.

"What is it, Mom?" Michael said. He
stepped into the room.

She seemed to shrink, cowering, as though
she were somehow trying to recede so far
into herself that she disappeared.

Michael said, "Mom . . ."

Claire glared at him. Her back straightened. She didn't blink. There was no mistak-
ing what he saw in her steady gaze. *She hated
him! She feared him!*

Claire raised her left hand. Around her
head she made a motion as thought drawing a
wild profusion of Little Orphan Annie curls.
Then she pointed at him. The index finger of
her left hand was accusing—condemning.

Hate and fear—and she was telling him
why!

His heart raced. He had a strange sensation, completely unlike anything he had ever
known: the skin around his eyes, his nose, the
corners of his mouth, felt as though it were

tightening.

For a fraction of a second, he wondered if he were afraid.

Micheal moved closer. He bent at the knees, squatted, the tips of his shoes almost touching her slipper-shod feet. His voice was gentle, soothing, reassuring. "Mom, I think you see something and it disturbs you. I'm sorry, Mom. I don't want you to be upset. Mom, I love you. You know that."

Her eyes were an icy denunciation.

"Mom," Michael said, "this is Michael, okay? I married your daughter. I'm the father of your grandchildren. Mom, I think you're all confused and upset. You've been sick, Mom. It could make you see things that aren't there, or things that aren't true, that don't make any sense. So, Mom, you trust me, okay?"

Whether she did grant him her trust or if she simply decided that she was weary and worn down and could no longer cope with her knowledge, he would never know, but Claire raised her left hand. Then around his head she traced the outline of his aura. *God-damn her! She* does *see it! Goddamn her, goddamn her. She's touching it—I can* feel *her touching . . .*

Claire's lips moved. Her voice tiredly emerged with the timbre but not the volume of a long un-oiled door-hinge: "Ruh-hed."

Ruh-hed. Christ, there was no doubt in his mind. She was somehow seeing his aura! For a moment, he envied her seeing what he himself had never seen either on himself or on anyone else.

Then he knew he had to kill her.

But careful, he had to be careful. He could not give himself away, not now, when The Time of the Strangers was so close. He had to be sure there would be no suspicion, that Beth would not think . . .

Yes, he had to kill her.

Now.

And he did.

SIXTEEN

"WHY DID you decide to see me?"

"My husband thought it was a good idea. And I talked it over with a friend"—she was spitting out the words, one tumbling into and over the next—"who knows a lot about psychology. I mean, he *is* a psychologist and he teaches psychology. Really I guess that's it."

She crossed her legs, smoothed her skirt, dug at the cuticle of her thumb with the nail of her index finger. Her gaze skittered across the office; she didn't want to look directly at him. There was a Miro lithograph on the wall, a Mr. Coffee on a stand near the picture window, a mahogany desk. When she'd stepped in, she had almost expected a Victorian leather sofa, just like all the psychiatrist cartoons. No couch, though, just the two Danish modern arm-chairs they occupied, set at angles on either side of a low, tiered lamp table.

"When I ask questions, Beth, I'm seeking information so that I can help you," Jan Pretre said. "You didn't answer my question at all, did you?"

"No," she said softly. "I'm sorry, Jan."

"Not Jan, if you please, Beth," he corrected. "Not here. This isn't a social situation. We both want this to be a profes-sional relationship and that means you've come to see Dr. Pretre. Is that all right?"

She nodded.

"Very well. I'll ask you again. Take all the time you'd like thinking about it, but give me a real answer. What are you doing here? Why do you think you need a psychiatrist?"

Forcing herself to speak slowly, to put a pause between each word, she said, "I need help, Dr. Pretre."

She did; she had no doubt of that.

That was why she had agreed to Michael's suggestion: "I don't know exactly what's happening to you and I don't know why it's happening but we've got to do something, Beth!"

That was how he'd begun, three days ago, Monday morning, at the breakfast table, after the children had gone to school. Michael spoke calmly, saying precisely what she herself thought, but the sound of his voice made the skin at the nape of her neck feel as though it were being pricked by dozens of tiny needles.

"Beth," Michael said. "I don't think I can help you. You don't talk to me and you don't listen to me."

Talk to him? God, it required all her will to remain sitting there in the kitchen with him. She wanted to run out the door in her night-gown and slippers, jump into the Chevette and drive away, not giving a thought to a destination, or maybe yanking the wheel hard, the gas pedal to the floor, sending the car zooming from the highway into a telephone pole and ending it, ending this nightmare that possessed her during sleep

239

and enshrouded her by day.

"Remember Jan Pretre, the psychiatrist, Beth?" Michael said.

She did. That afternoon, she'd made the appointment and now she was here, blurting still more of an answer to his question: "I feel, oh hell, I feel like I'm going crazy."

"Go on with that, Beth," Jan Pretre said.

"I have these recurring, obsessive thoughts, these delusions . . ."

"Why don't you tell me about it *without* the jargon."

"Oh, I've been thinking these crazy, crazy things I can't get out of my mind, about Michael."

"I want you to be more specific, Beth. Tell me one particular crazy thing."

Head down, Beth studied her hand. She had ripped her cuticle bloody.

She took a deep breath. "All right, this was about a month ago, right after we saw you at Engelkings. Well, it was the day after that."

It came back to her as it had been coming back, repeating itself again and again, as the totality of the experience, its sights and sounds and smell—and terror. "I was bathing," she said. "It's funny because I remember thinking how happy I was. For the first time in a long time, yes, I was happy."

The smell of rose-scented bubble bath made her think of flowers she would see again next spring. She swirled a fingertip in the water, watching the islands of dissipating white bubbles break apart and then lazily link together in new shapes and sizes.

"You know, it felt so fine that it was me

there inside my skin that I started singing. Oh, I can't carry a tune if it has only one note, but I was singing away, and slipping down in the tub so the water lapped at my chin, and then I heard . . ."

Even with the bathroom door closed, the sounds were perfectly clear: There was a bump and then another so like it it might have been an echo. Something slid down the wall, like the sound of a rat's running feet, and she heard the tinkling crackle of breaking glass, and she knew precisely what had happened: a picture falling from the wall by the staircase, the glass shattering. Then there was a bump—it was no louder than that—and then, just as Michael screamed, "No!" so heavy a thud that the house actually shook. At least, she thought she felt that. Footsteps pounded down the stairs. Michael screamed again, this time, "Beth!"

She leaped out of the tub. She snatched a bath towel from the rack and tied it around her. The bathroom rug slipped underfoot. She fell against the vanity. It didn't hurt then. Two days later, the bruise on her hip was a gloomy rainbow of color; it was still there, faded yellow and green.

"So I ran out into the hall and I saw what had happened."

Mother lay at the foot of the stairs. Michael was beside her on his knees. Mother was dead. She had to be. She looked broken, as though if you tugged at her hand it would come loose at the wrist, as if a touch would send her head rolling across the floor.

"I just stood there. I guess I was in shock.

241

Michael looked up at me. 'She fell. I saw her. She was right at the top of the stairs. Then she went down.' That's what he said."

Beth put the heels of her hands to her temples. Her mind was exploding. She pressed hard, holding her head together. The towel around her became untied, slid down her body. She felt the humiliating vulnerability of nakedness and there was her mother—deadeadead—and there was Michael and she was caught in a debauched surrealistic painting: Death and Michael and Nude on a Staircase and then she screamed.

" 'What did you do to her? What did you do?' I kept yelling that at him and then the next thing I can clearly remember, I was dressed and we were at the hospital and Mother was DOA—I heard someone say that at the emergency room—and then a doctor, maybe a nurse, gave me something, and everything started to blur together . . ."

"I see," Jan Pretre said. "Tell me, Beth, have you had feelings of, let's call it 'mistrust' about your husband in the past?"

"I . . . I'm not sure what you mean."

"Aren't you?"

"Maybe I *do* know," Beth said slowly. "Okay, I've sometimes had this idea that Michael isn't at all what he appears to be, that he's, well, a different man entirely. It's hard to put into words."

"You're doing fine," Jan Pretre assured her.

She went on, telling him what she could in the best way she could. It sounded insane, she realized, but . . . *Hey, he's a headshrinker*

242

and you're supposed to tell a shrink your insane thoughts!

"All right," he said. "Let's talk about your father."

"What? I thought we were talking about my feelings about my husband."

"But now it's time to talk about something else," Jan Pretre said. "We're on an investigation, Beth, looking for clues to help us determine *why* you think what you do about Michael. You've labelled those thoughts 'crazy,' and certainly they seem irrational. We have to hunt for the roots of your fantasy so that we can deal with the cause of the problem and not merely this symptom."

"You're the doctor," Beth said weakly.

"Yes, I am," Jan Pretre said, "and it's important you remember that, Beth. I ask questions, offer suggestions, and sometimes flat-out tell you what to do and how to do it because I have reasons. You've come to me for help and if I'm to provide that, you'll have to have confidence in me."

Beth said nothing.

"Is that hard to do, Beth?" Jan Pretre said, "Is it difficult to trust me because I'm a *man*, a man just like Michael? Maybe you don't trust men at all, Beth."

"That's not true!" She bristled.

"Strong reaction, Beth. Why are you so angry?"

"I feel like you're attacking me!"

"I'm attacking you?" Jan Pretre said, "And Michael attacked your mother? Are you frightened that that is what men do—attack women? Do all men want to hurt you, Beth?"

"You're . . . you're confusing me!" Beth gulped. There was a dry, hard lump in her throat; she kept swallowing but it would not go away.

"If you're going to cry, there are tissues on the desk." From the corner of her eye, she saw that he was pointing.

"No," she said. She hadn't cried since her mother's funeral. Her tears then had been endless, but afterwards, she was empty. She felt as though her very guts had been scooped out, leaving her hollow.

"Then tell me about your father, Beth. That's what I asked you in the first place and that's what you've been avoiding dealing with. Your father—did you love him?"

"Yes!"

"Very much?"

"Yes!"

"Were you Daddy's little girl?"

"I don't understand."

"Did he give you all the attention you wanted?"

Beth turned in her chair. She glared at Jan Pretre. Slowly, she said, "Why are you doing this to me?"

"Beth," he said, "don't you see? I'm trying to help you." His warm, rumbling voice and his compassionate blue-black eyes reassured her. He cared about people; she knew he did. She had to trust him. She needed him.

"Can we continue?" he asked.

She nodded and they went on: *Was her father an affectionate man? To her? To her mother? Was she jealous of her mother? Oh, she didn't think so? Really? What about late at night, that wicked time when wicked children prayed their wicked prayers, did she ever wish that mother were out of the way so she could have Daddy all to herself?*

"All right, that'll do it for this session." Jan Pretre was looking at his watch.

Beth felt physically weary, like she'd spent hours moving the furniture to shampoo the living room carpet. She didn't mind. Weariness was far preferable to the numbness that had invaded her body.

"Do you think we're . . . we're making progress?" she asked as they both rose.

"Yes, Beth," Jan Pretre said. "For the first session, we've accomplished a great deal. And Beth?"

"Yes, Dr. Pretre?"

"Don't expect miracles, all right? Your problem didn't develop overnight. It will take time for us to discover solutions to it, and it's often going to be a painful process, but believe me, you'll be a stronger person for it." He held out his hand. "Trust me?"

She was touched. She shook his hand. "Completely," she said.

"Good," he said. "That's just fine. Let's see you again next week, same time."

In his office, Michael answered the telephone.

"She left here ten minutes ago, Michael," Jan Pretre said. "She's on to you. She knows."

"What?" Michael sat forward in the black leather desk chair. It was impossible, he thought. Tell him you could fly if you flapped

your arms hard enough; he'd believe that before he would Beth's knowing.

"Fortunately," Jan Pretre continued calmly, "she doesn't *know* that she knows. She's one very screwed-up woman, Michael. What she told me today is a classic example of an obsessive paranoid delusion. That's what any shrink would call it and that's exactly what Beth thinks it is."

"Right," Michael said. "Beth isn't going to realize the truth. She doesn't have the sense."

"Don't underestimate her, Michael," Jan Pretre said. "She's no fool. And she has a remarkable adaptive strength. If she didn't, she'd have had a breakdown by now. Take this as a warning, Michael. She could give you problems."

Michael leaned back. A car wreck? The standard suburban housewife suicide—a bottle of pills and alcohol? "Yes, I knew she was depressed—in fact, she's been seeing a psychiatrist—but I never thought for a moment that she . . ." He'd choke then, call up gallons of tears, the bereaved husband surrendering to his grief, while his secret self laughed like a manic hyena. There were ways to guarantee Wonderful Wife didn't give him any trouble.

But Goddamnit! He had waited so long, and he had promised himself that they—Beth and Marcy and Kim—would be the reward for his patience. The Call. The Time of the Strangers. Exult in the shock of their terrified eyes, laugh at their agonized screeching, and kill them, their destruction his farewell to the nothing, normal, mindless life he had been forced to endure, as he strode from that house of death and loosed his bloodlust on the world: Michael, Stranger.

"Are you still there, Michael?"

"I was just thinking."

"All right, then," Jan Pretre said. "I put Beth through a real psychological inquisition today. I'll keep running the same type of play on her. By next week, she'll wonder if *she* really wished her mother dead and then, unable to accept such a terrible thought, projected it onto you. There are 1,001 tricks shrinkers have and I've got a couple of my own. Beth will get so wrapped up in a self-examination that she won't have much time to ponder the man she married."

"Good," Michael said. "Thanks."

"All right," Jan Pretre said. "And Michael?"

"Yes?"

"Take care of yourself."

They were both parked in the same section of the lot. Walking together, they left the building a few minutes after nine. Yes, she was in the mood for a drink. She wanted to tell him about her session with Jan Pretre.

The night was clear, moon and stars radiating a lifeless cold. The parking lot's orange-yellow lights gave a false promise of warmth. As they walked past the "Authorized Parking Only, Section D" sign, she watched their stretched shadows. There were two distinct heads but their shadow bodies were merged.

But was there an invisible shadow that followed their shadow?

Suddenly, she was stricken with fear.

"I'm over this way," Kevin said, pointing.

"No," she said. The sound of her own voice scared her. It was the helpless, desperate bleat of an abandoned child.

She stood stock still. *You're all right, you're in control of yourself, now stay calm,* she told herself, a relentless panic squeezing her chest. Her heart hammered. She couldn't breathe. She sucked in air that stabbed like knives.

This was it. She was coming undone. She quivered, felt herself fragmenting—*All the king's horses*—cobweb cracks running through the fabric of her self—*all the king's men*—jagged edged tear-lines ripping her apart—*cannot put her back together again*—rending her—*back together again*—destroying her . . .

"Hold me!" She tried to scream it but it was a whimpered whisper. *A faraway voice as she dissolved into splinters and shards and . . .*

"It's all right, it's all right." Kevin wrapped his arms around her.

Through her coat and his quilted jacket, she felt his beating heart. She pressed against him, against that warm solidity. "It's all right, Beth."

He was holding her, holding her together, keeping her all in one piece.

He said, "I love you." He kissed her.

He was strong. She was safe with him. She was sobbing, kissing him, his mustache cold-wet with her tears tickling her, his lips demanding and loving.

He pulled away from her. From the corner

of her eye, she saw their shadow on the concrete, an empty distance separating them.

"Beth, I . . . I'm sorry," he said. His face, Beth thought, the way he was scraping the toe of his shoe on the pavement, made him look like a third grader who had to apologize for disrupting class. He was wonderful—beautiful. "I forgot myself for a second. It won't . . ."

"Be quiet," she said, laughing and crying. "I don't want you to say anything that neither one of us wants to hear. Just take me with you, Kevin. Now."

"Are you . . . Do you realize what you're saying, Beth?"

In answer, she held out her hand.

In his Dodge Aspen, they drove to his apartment, five miles away from the college. She sat so close to him on the front seat she felt the heat radiating from his body. He smelled of soap and lime-scented deodorant. She watched his hands on the steering wheel, saw the bony bumps of his knuckles under the delicately taut flesh, the veins invisibly carrying his life's blood, the workings of tendons.

She studied his profile, the profusion of curly hair, his sloping, intellectual brow, the over-sized nose. She had to be sure. She couldn't afford to mistakenly cast him in the role of Knight in Shining Armor, Prince Charming, or Personal Saviour. No, she was convinced. Kevin Bollender was who he was. There was no lie beneath his skin. When he talked to her, *he, Kevin and no one else,* talked to her and when he kissed her, *he—*

KevinKevinKevin! kissed her and when he'd said he loved her, God! She felt loved!

In the bedroom of his small apartment, she insisted on leaving on the lights. She wanted to keep on seeing him.

When they were naked and in bed, she felt as though all of her world were bordered and defined by him. Her arms were full of him, his sides, his ribs, his shoulders, her thighs held his hips, her heels rubbing his calves, the backs of his knees, and her innerness absorbed him, gripped him and played with him and stroked him and loved him.

When it happened, it was so intense that she left her body. It was the delicate, singular instant of death and it was the explosive, peak moment of life. She was consumed by it and she writhed and moaned and cried at its exquisiteness.

He hit his release. She tightly held him, wanting to cling to him in those shattering seconds when his strength vanished and he was a slave to his pleasure, a pleasure that she'd brought him. Then he was smiling down at her, guileless and content.

Afterward, he said, "We ought to talk . . . talk about what happened."

"No," she said. "Not now. Maybe not ever."

"Beth . . ."

"I'm afraid talking would ruin it and I couldn't bear that." She was lying curled in his arms, her hand on his chest. His skin was warm and damp.

"But Beth, I . . . I have to know. Are you all right? Will you be all right?"

She laughed quietly. "Yes, I am all right.

And I don't know if I'll *be* all right, but maybe nobody does."

He took her back to Lincoln Junior College. She got in the Chevette Scooter and drove home.

"Beth, it's past midnight! I was getting worried!" Michael said.

She looked at him and said, "Were you?"

"And what's that supposed to mean?"

She did not answer. She went upstairs, undressed, slipped on a nightgown, and got in bed. She could still smell Kevin, still feel the touch-memory of him.

She had been loved. No matter what happened, that was *real*, and she would sleep easy knowing that.

SEVENTEEN

AT TEN o'clock on Friday morning, Michael stepped into Vern Engelking's office. "You wanted to see . . ."

"I did, Michael," Jan Pretre said. He stood at the floor to ceiling window, hands behind him, his back to Michael.

Seated at his desk, toying with a round glass paperweight, Vern said, "Jan has some news for you."

At last! Michael thought. His public life had been borne and his secret one lived for this, Jan's proclamation!

Jan turned around. Behind him, the early November sun was a blinding wash of light, silhouetting him, blurring the outline of his form. Looking at him, unable to discern his features, Michael remembered their first meeting, long ago, the first stirring of the sense he'd had that Jan Pretre was like him—and was something even more as well.

"You know Beth had her second appointment with me yesterday," Jan said.

Michael nodded.

"Beth thinks, of course, that you can say anything at all to your therapist in strictest confidence. A shrink's office is as sacred as a confessional. She told me something interesting, Michael."

"Okay," Michael said, "what did Beth tell you that you think I ought to know?"

"She's alienated from you," Jan Pretre said. "I think you realize that. She refuses to believe what she thinks are her paranoid fantasies about you, but she's emotionally cut herself off from you. Right now, at best, she views you as a casual acquaintance with whom she lives. Nothing more."

Michael shrugged and then he grinned. "W'al shucks, I guess I jes' ain't been workin' hard enough at keepin' that l'il ole gal o' mine happy and content."

"You haven't," Jan Pretre said. He walked closer to Michael. "Someone else has."

"What's that mean?"

"Beth's having an affair," Jan Pretre said. "She has a lover."

Michael tugged at his earlobe. He said, "Bullshit."

"No, Michael. Fact."

"Beth screwing someone else? For Chrissake, she was a virgin, I mean complete with cherry in place, until two months before I married her. She wouldn't. She's not the type."

Vern chuckled. "It appears the cuckholded husband cannot accept the truth of his mate's philandering."

Michael snapped a quick look at Engelking. Vern's face was a grinning puzzle. Something was wrong here, out of balance. Jan and Vern were his allies, yet they seemed to be united against him in a way he did not at all comprehend.

Jan pointed an accusing finger. "Michael, you transformed her into the type."

"No," Michael protested. "I've always

acted like the super-supportive husband."

"Yes, Michael," Jan said quietly, "but she saw through the act."

A lover! Beth was fucking someone! Only now was the full impact of Jan Pretre's revelation hitting him. He should have known, goddamnit, should have realized she had a private game going. For just about a week now, she'd been out of her hang-dog depression but acting icily civil to him. From time to time he'd seen an expression on her face—a look he should have interpreted as an almost childish gloating, "I know something you don't know, naa-naa-naa . . ."

Goddamn her! There was a surging heat within him. He tried to determine just what he was feeling and then he had it: Outrage! *The bitch had deceived him!* He had spent half a lifetime fooling her and now she'd made a fool of him.

He was suddenly tired. He sat in the chair alongside Vern's desk.

"Last week Beth suffered a major anxiety attack," Jan Pretre said. "With all that she's gone through, she was overdue for something of the sort. She desperately needed somebody, there was somebody there, and they wound up in bed."

Michael quietly said, "And this weekend, last Saturday, she was with him, too, wasn't she?"

"That's right," Jan answered.

The clues were there and he'd missed them. The long time in the bathroom, the perfume and make-up and clothing. Then she was off. She knew he didn't have anything scheduled for the afternoon; he could watch the kids. Well sure, fine, no problem, and he reached for his wallet because she would need money to go shopping. No, she didn't want money, and who said she was going shopping? Well, say, where *was* she going?

She hadn't told him but now he knew. The bitch! She was going to go spread her legs!

"All right," Michael sighed, "and I suppose that in a week or so, after she's had her itch scratched, Beth will come to me with the guilty weeps, confessing her sins and asking to be forgiven."

"I doubt it," Jan Pretre said. "I told you your wife has a strong will. She's severed her emotional ties to you. She's not feeling guilty. She's not even guilty about not feeling guilty. Oh, she's flying right now, that first heady whirlwind feeling of romance, but she's already considering a life without you, thinking about divorce."

She was going to divorce him? Hey, lady, Ms. Shit-for-Brains, you could bet the ass that you were pumping in some guy's bed that *Hubby* would be the one getting the separation. No alimony, no child support, and nothing but a final settlement. Bitch!

A question occurred to him but he did not ask it because the answer simultaneously came to mind: Why had Jan chosen to tell him about Beth this way, in front of Vern? They were both warning him: *You fucked up, Michael.*

"So that's the situation, Michael," Jan Pretre said. "Now you know . . ."

. . . and before I didn't know jack-shit, and it

took you to tell me, right?

" . . . so it's up to you to handle it as you choose."

It would be handled. There was only one more thing he needed from Jan Pretre: a name.

Jan told him.

Kevin Bollender. Michael hoped that Beth truly loved him dearly, completely, totally "need him," "can't live without him" loved the sonofabitch.

Then he went to his office and telephoned Eddie Markell.

In his office in the narrow wing off the library, Kevin Bollender had his feet up on the desk. He burped, tasting the onions from the burgers he'd had for lunch. He had an hour until his two o'clock "Intro to Phych" class and he thought about spending it napping.

There was a knock at the door and before he could get his feet down, a handle turned, the door opened, and Eddie Markell stepped into the office. He was wearing a dirty trench coat and his right hand slipped inside it and came out with a .357 magnum.

"You're the professor, so you've got to be a smart guy. Be smart and be quiet and I don't blow your fucking head off."

"I'm not a professor," Kevin said and then he could no longer say anything. The full effect of cold terror hit him. Jesus Christ, he'd worked at the Manteno mental institution and there'd been some pretty damned inchy doings there, including one raving maniac who'd tried to rip his face off, but he knew that never before this moment in his life had he been utterly, paralytically afraid.

"We're going for a ride, professor," Eddie Markell said. "You do what I say and your curly head stays right on your shoulders where you want it."

Kevin thought that whoever this man was, he sounded as though his entire vocabulary consisted of clichés from old gangster films. Kevin looked at the gun, realized his mouth was as dry as if he'd spent three days lost in the Sahara desert, and thought of a cliché himself: *He'd as soon kill you as look at you.* The man was drunk, you could see it and smell it, and that made him even more dangerous.

"Put your feet on the floor," Eddie Markell said. "You stand up slow, put on your jacket, and take a walk with me."

"This is all a mistake," Kevin said. The instant the words were spoken, he anticipated what the response would be: *Yeah, and you made it.*

He had a dizzying flash of unreality, an impossible answer to all the questions that were leaping like grasshoppers through his mind. This was a 1940s tough guy film and somehow he'd been plugged into it. Boing! *Twilight Zone time* . . . He was going to be all right then. He was the good guy, after all, and . . .

Kevin tried once more. "You'll never get away with this."

Eddie Markell said, "You know, I don't give a shit. And if the marines bust down the door to save your sorry ass, professor, I still don't give a shit. So how about you shut the fuck up and we get out of here."

Kevin walked down the corridor. Eddie Markell was a half-step behind him. He'd put away the gun and a dozen times Kevin thought *Run!* He did not run. The man would shoot, Kevin had no doubt, and there were people in the halls, the custodian with his broom, that guy in a wheelchair, maybe a crippled vet using his GI benefits to further his education, that old woman who was probably on her way to a class in data processing so she could re-join the work force. They were the "innocent bystanders" who always seemed to get hurt, whose injuries and deaths were duly noted in network newscasts and whose names were forgotten during the first Ken-L Ration commercial.

They took the elevator down and stepped out of the school. There had been a change in the weather, the skies clouding over, and now a light cold rain was falling.

Eddie Markell took him to a rusted-out green 1976 Chevrolet Impala. Glancing around the parking lot, Eddie unlocked the trunk. "Get in," he said.

Kevin didn't move. "Look," he said, "someone's going to see . . ."

Eddie slammed a knee into Kevin's crotch. The pain fanned up, twisting his guts and spearing his lungs. He whoofed and Eddie toppled him into the trunk, forcing his legs inside.

The trunk lid slammed.

The darkness was total. Breathing hard,

Kevin lay on his side. The stink of gasoline and grease curled around him. The roar of the engine as the car started was as loud as the rushing cylindrical hurricane in a wind tunnel.

The car was moving, picking up speed. He had to do something.

The wires to the rear lights! He had them, cold and plastic-feeling. He tugged, ripped them loose.

Now he had a chance! A red light, a stop sign, slowing for a crossroad, an intersection, merging traffic, and a cop would be there. "That guy's brake lights are out. Let's write him a ticket!"

Except how many cars without brakelights or headlights, taillights, turn signals traveled a zillion miles every day without being stopped? And who in the hell didn't know that "There's never a cop around when you need one"?

He kicked. He yelled. "Help me! Help!" He pushed against the trunk lid.

The car slowed, pulled to the right, and then stopped. The trunk opened. From the corner of his eye he saw the gray sky and felt the welcome cool rain.

Eddie Markell leaned down. "Shut up!"

Kevin tried to move, to sit up, and Eddie hit him twice, on the temple and then on the cheekbone. The pain was a kaleidoscopic burst behind his eyes.

"I said shut up and I mean shut up," Eddie Markell said.

In the putrid closeness, he lay silent. He drifted from full consciousness to a state of mercifully dulled awareness that let him view what was happening in a detached way. He decided it was very possible that he would be killed. It was numbly bothering that he might not learn why.

It was sometime later—*sometime* because fear has its own clock and a minute might be a day or an hour the sharp finger-snap that connects terror *then* to terror *now*—that Kevin Bollender's claustrophobic journey ended.

The rain had stopped. On shaky legs, he climbed out of the trunk into a wet coldness. They were in the woods, a forest preserve, Kevin thought. The battered Impala stood alongside a Ford LTD on a gravel parking patch. Kevin thought it might be the Glenvale Forest Preserve but he could not be sure.

"That way," Eddie Markell said. He gestured with the pistol at a picnic shelter fifty yards away. The wall-less structure had a concrete floor: a gently pitched roof was supported by redwood columns.

Kevin saw a man there. He was of average height, sandy-haired, wearing mechanic's baggy, dark green coveralls. At his feet was a canvas bag.

"Move it, shit-heel," Eddie Markell said.

An adrenalin-spiked hate coursed through Kevin. He was bigger and stronger than this motherfucking sonofabitch! He could pick him up and snap him, toss half of him north and the other half south.

But there was the gun.

Kevin walked to the picnic shelter.

"Glad to see you, Kevin," said the man in the coveralls.

"I don't know you and I don't know what this is about," Kevin said.

"You don't know me? You know my wife. You've fucked her, you sonofabitch!"

"You're . . ."

"I'm the Lone Ranger," Michael said. He punched Kevin in the jaw.

Kevin staggered back. He had no doubt now. They meant to kill him. He felt like a dead man and because he had nothing to lose, not anymore, when Michael swung again, Kevin grabbed his arm and the wrist and elbow and spun him around into Eddie Markell.

"Sonofabitch!"

Kevin tried to run. Off-balance, Michael whirled, caught him around the waist. Kevin shot his elbow into Michael's mid-section. Michael grunted.

Eddie Markell smashed the long ribbed barrel of the magnum against the side of Kevin's head.

Kevin's knees buckled. Once more, Eddie hit him.

"You can turn the pus-bag loose," Eddie said. "He's not in the mood for the hundred yard dash."

Michael unfastened his grip and Kevin dropped to his hands and knees. Kevin ordered himself not to surrender to the churning undertow that was trying to pull him down into unconsciousness.

"Get up, asshole," Eddie Markell said. "Take your clothes off."

Kevin tried to rise but couldn't. They hauled him up, stripped him. They pushed him against one of the shelter's roof supporting beams, cranked his arms back around it, and tied his wrists with picture-hanging wire.

Michael said, "My wife a good lay, Kevin? You make her suck your cock? You know, I taught her that. That your idea of fun? Having another man's wife give you head?"

Michael drew back his fist. There was nothing Kevin could do to avoid the blow or lesson its force. Michael smashed him squarely in the mouth. "Well, *my* idea of fun is killing shit-heads like you."

Kevin's mouth opened bloodily.

"I think he's interested in some conversation," Eddie Markell said.

"Beth," Kevin croaked. "Don't . . . hurt her . . ."

Michael patted himself on the chest. "My wife has broken my heart, but no, how could I hurt that dear sweet lady? Shit, what kind of guy do you think I am?"

Kevin glared at him with pain-slitted eyes. "Bas . . . tard . . ."

From the canvas bag, Michael took out a jack-knife and opened it. He touched the point to Kevin's chest at the center of the sternum. Then he pressed just hard enough to pierce the skin.

Kevin jerked, slamming the back of his head into the column. Tears rolled down his cheeks as Michael slowly sliced a shallow line down to his navel.

"He's going to scream," Eddie Markell said.

"He's got damned good reason."

"No, let's keep him quiet," Eddie said. "I don't think we're going to be interrupted by any goddamned nature-lovers on a day like this, but just in case, we don't want to have to leave the asshole until we're finished with him."

They gagged Kevin by shoving one of his socks in his mouth. Then Michael began cutting, not hurrying in the least, talking to Kevin with the tone of a shoe store clerk saying, "Have a good day." After a time Kevin couldn't stand it, couldn't bear hearing the cold whisper of the blade opening his flesh so that the pain could hellishly flower along new lines of nerve-endings. He passed out.

He came to to biting cold and a smell so stingingly sharp that it overpowered the scent of his own blood.

Michael's coveralls, saturated with gasoline, were draped over his neck and wrapped around Kevin's lacerated chest and stomach.

Michael struck a match.

"What's up, Doc?" Bugs Bunny asked the hapless Elmer Fudd. With the door to the basement open, the rabbit's question carried up from the rec room, where the girls were watching Saturday morning cartoons, to the kitchen.

Michael sat at he kitchen table with the newspaper. Beth was at the sink, finishing the breakfast dishes.

Michael checked the front page of the *Sun-Times*, then opened the newspaper and skimmed the headlines until he found what he was looking for on page five.

"Beth?"

She turned around.

That smile . . . he thought. All right, in about five seconds, she was going to swallow that grin and get puking-sick on it!

"Don't you know a"—he glanced down at the paper—"Kevin Bollender? I think you told me he taught your psychology class?"

She tipped her head to the side, reminding him of a parakeet contemplating a new cuttlebone. She was still smiling. "That's right," she said.

He stood up, walked over to her, and handed her the paper. "Here's something about him. Bottom of the page."

Nothing happened quite as he'd been expecting.

A half-minute later, Beth threw the paper at him and as he started back, the pages flying around him, she screamed, "You killed him! You son of a bitch!" and punched him in the nose.

"Ow!" Michael cried out. Tears flooded his eyes. He touched his nose; there was a trickle of blood seeping through the left nostril. "You hit me!"

"You . . . You killer!"

Footsteps banged up the stairs. Kim stuck her head in the door. "*Who* killed someone? Hey, Dad, you got a bloody nose!" Marcy peered over her sister's shoulder.

"Nobody killed anybody . . ."

"Your nose—did Mom pop you?"

Michael pointed. "Both of you, scoot back

down there and stay put until I tell you otherwise. *Now!*"

With the children gone, he closed the door and leaned his back against it. He wiped the half-mustache of blood from his lip. "Look," he said, "I don't know what the hell is going on with you, Beth . . ."

"Don't you?" She rigidly stood at the sink. A tic in her cheek twitched and fluttered like a mouse's beating heart.

"No," Michael said, "I do not. You smack me in the nose, call me a killer . . ." Shaking his head—*He was the long-suffering husband doing his damnedest to be patient and understanding*—he walked over to her—*but he was angry now, angry and hurt!*—and, raising his voice said, "If I killed someone, this Kevin Whatshisname, then you'd better call the police, Beth."

She stared at him.

"Go on!" His voice got louder still. "You don't want to be in the same house with a murderer. Call the cops. Now!"

She maintained her stare for only another second and then she lowered her head and her shoulders drooped. "I . . . I'm going to call Dr. Pretre," she said in tight, barely audible whisper. "I feel like I have to talk to him. Today if he can see me."

"All right," Michael said. He sighed deeply.

"If I can get an appointment, Michael . . . would you take me to his office? I don't want to drive myself."

Now what happened to the independent New Era woman Beth thought she was? Michael asked himself. *And all because her*

265

between-the-sheets buddy got barbecued!

"Of course," he said. He was extremely pleased with his next gesture. He put his hands on her shoulders and she flinched but did not pull away. In the most sorrowful, syrupy voice he could produce—*It was a goddamn shame he couldn't cue the violins*—he asked, "Beth, what's happening to us?"

It was an emergency, she explained over the phone, and Dr. Pretre agreed to see her at one o'clock. Marcy and Kim were dropped off at the Engelkings. Michael drove her to the psychiatrist.

During the one hour session, Dr. Pretre said, "I see," and "I'm following you," and "I understand," or echoed her statements rephrased as a question. What she needed more than anything else, he told her, was rest, relief from this crushing anxiety. He handed her a plastic pill bottle. "Here, this is one of the samples I get from the drug company. Take one as soon as you get home. If it makes you groggy, that's fine. Sleep would be good for you."

Later that afternoon, Beth sound asleep, Michael telephoned Jan Pretre. They spoke for five minutes. They agreed that Beth should go on a vacation where there was no chance of her saying something that might cause anyone any trouble.

Dr. Pretre had just the ticket to send her on her trip.

EIGHTEEN

It was a few minutes after eight on Monday night. The Loudens were in the rec room, watching *MASH* like most of the United States. The girls were already in their pajamas. Michael and Beth sat on the couch and she was losing her mind.

On Saturday, when Michael had brought her home from Dr. Pretre's, she took a pill and fell asleep within minutes. After that, Beth knew only that she awakened some time later—*Was it still Saturday?*—and there was Michael with another pill, and she went back to sleep: awake, a pill, asleep, a cycle, repeated and repeated.

Beth thought she had to have eaten during that time—all *that time:* awake asleep a pill—gone to the bathroom. She didn't think she had washed her face. She knew she hadn't changed out of this faded nightgown; she wanted to be flannel-warm in something that held her own scent. It was like wrapping up in an additional layer of self.

When had she last brushed her teeth? she wondered.

"Brush your teeth!" says Mr. Hap E. Tooth. *"Curses!"* says Mr. Tooth Decay, *"Foiled again!"*

She remembered the children had gone off to school this morning—it *had* to be this morning—and she was with them at break-

fast—was that this morning or last week?—
and that Michael had stayed home from the
office today to give her pills.

It was again pill time, not more than a half-
hour ago. She did not feel sleepy, not now.
She was marvelously alert, attuned to everything around her. She heard the sudden flare
of the burner of the hot water tank in the
utility room, the delicate-alive breathing of
the girls—*Marcy exhaled when Kim inhaled
and when Kim exhaled, Marcy inhaled; they
were so opposite in every way*—even the
hydraulic rush of blood through her own
veins and arteries.

There was a wondrous precision to this
moment of intense hearing and her muscles
were taut with the effort of holding onto it.

She realized, then, that she was not breathing. Everyone else in the room was breathing
—she could even hear Hot Lips and Colonel
Potter on television—but she was not. She
had to breathe! If you stopped breathing, you
died.

She tried to pull in air and could not. Her
head was pounding. Her blood rolled in
angry, desperate demand.

I am dying!

No! A moment of calm and pause and
internal hush. She had slipped out of the
natural rhythm of respiration and once she
regained it she would be all right. She
focused on the pulsations of her wrists and
temples, behind her ears, at the back of her
knees, and she tuned in to the messages sent
to these contact points by her racing heart.
She had it then.

In *goes the good air*, out *goes the bad air*, in *goes the good air* out *goes the bad air* . . . She was fine, just fine, breathing so deeply that she could feel the oxygen saturating the cells of her lungs. *In and out and in and out* . . .

"Beth," Michael said, "are you okay?"

Okay can't you see? She said that, or thought it, she wasn't sure which, to the tune of the first line of "The Star Spangled Banner."

She knew that if her hearing was so sharp, her vision was probably no less acute. There was a trick, however, to seeing well, *to seeing the everything that is the all*, and that was instead of squinting the way most people did when they tried to focus on an object, you had to *open* your eyes as wide as possible.

I see Eye See . . .

The picture on a television screen was not a real picture. It was exploding dots of red and green and blue. She studied the dots, first the red, then the green, then the blue, and then let them merge into something more, a picture.

The camera zoomed in for a closeup on Alan Alda. He was drunk, slurring an anti-war monologue: "What it is, is it's all crazy, you see . . ."

Yes, Hawkeye, I do see!

" . . . it's like a joke, but the thing is, the only way you can handle the joke is to come up with a few jokes of your own."

Hawkeye was—*of course, of course*—talking to her. He had probably tried to speak to her before but she had ignored him. She hoped that she had not hurt his feelings. Now he was telling her what to do.

"Beth," Hawkeye said, "believe me, if I could, I'd save you. I'd save everyone, Beth."

I know that, Hawkeye.

"I can't, so it's all up to you, Beth. You've got to be the one to save yourself and those you love. Can you do that?"

Yes, I can.

"Beth . . ."

It was not Hawkeye who spoke; it was Michael. She turned her head, saw his lips shape her name after she'd heard it like a badly dubbed foreign movie. Then she heard the cold echo:

> *Beth*
> > *Beth*
> > > *Beth*
> > > > *Beth . . .*

"Are you all right?"

He was the one who had played the jokes, all the vicious, heartless, monstrous tricks. But she could trick him! Whatever he said was certain to be a lie—*Liar, liar, pants on fire!*—and so she would not let herself hear it.

"Look, Beth . . ."

There! She'd turned him off. It was no more complicated than clicking the knob on a radio. Michael was talking to her, his mouth was moving, but she heard nothing. Beneath the aqueous surface of his eyes lurked the dark specter that was the *real* Michael—*Cruel Michael! Wicked Michael! Stranger Michael!*

She could feel the evil radiating from him. It was draining her of strength. She would get away, but calmly, so he would suspect nothing, and then she would concoct a scheme of her own, a trick of salvation, of rescue.

She stood up and went to the stairs.

"Beth! What in the hell!"

Careful! She was not concentrating as intently as she had to and so his words broke through her barriers. She did not have to walk; effortlessly, she was carried up to the kitchen by the stairs that had become an escalator.

She knew then that Michael did not control the house; it was on her side. In the kitchen, she stood with her head cocked, listening to the house, to the hidden messages it wished to share with her. The chilly night pressed against the windows and she heard the glass panes whisper "Courage" as they refused to allow entry to the dark and the cold. The quiet hum of the refrigerator was the house wiring's electrical energies. She tuned in to that power, and felt it indomitable within her. The plumbing vibrated with liquid secrets and confidences meant for only her.

She went to the sink, turned on the water. Bluish-gray steam rolled out, a heavy fog filling the entire kitchen. She had a place to hide. She was invisible within this dense cloud. She was concealed from Michael.

She saw him—*I see* him *but he can't see me* —as he came upstairs. The girls were right behind him. Beth held out her arms. "Come to me, children."

Within this surrounding mist, they would all be safe. He could not find them, could not harm them.

"Mom," Kim said, "you're being real weird!"

Michael said, "Kids, your mom's sick . . ."

"Liar!" Beth screamed.

" . . . so you get up to your room. Don't worry, I'll take care of her."

No! The children were leaving, gazing back at her. They didn't understand. If they did not come to her, she could not protect them!

"All right, Beth. Everything is all right now. You calm down. Get a hold of yourself."

With his hands on his hips, he stood on the wispy perimeter of the fog. He was grinning —*the flesh of his face peeled away and his skeletal head was of itself a horrifying smile*— as he said. "Shit, Beth, looks like this is it. You've slipped your trolley, kiddo." He laughed. "You're freaked out. Your belfry if chockful of bats. Wifey dear, you are one hundred percent, stem-to stern goofus. You are fucking *nuts!*"

Hands balled into fists, she charged him.

He quickly grabbed her wrists, spun her around, and, keeping her arms pinioned, crushed her to him in bear hug. Her tears exploded and, with them, a string of profanity. Michael laughed. "That's great. Nice and loud so the kids can hear you call their daddy twelve kinds of fucker. They'll have an interesting story to tell at school tomorrow. 'Hey, teacher, my mommy went crazy last night.' "

"I am not crazy!"

"Tell that to the men in white."

The men in white arrived twenty minutes later. They stuck a hypodermic in her arm, strapped her to a stretcher, rolled her out of the house, and took her to Prairie Hills Sanitarium.

He was strikingly handsome, she thought. In his brown, three piece woolen suit, the stylishly thin tie knotted in a precise half-Windsor, his beard sharply sculpted, he had the rugged but intellectual appearance favored by advertising men's apparel in the more conservative men's fashion magazines.

She hated him. He was plotting against her, he and Michael . . .

"Beth," he said, leaning his shoulders against the door frame, "when I ask a question, you are supposed to answer me."

She gared at him. She was sitting up in bed, wearing a scratchy, white cotton hospital "johnny." She was numb—empty—from her hairline to her toes.

Beside her bed, there was a toilet bowl and a sink in the ten by ten isolation room. The floor tile was white and unpatterned. There was an observation window in the door. From time to time, eyes had suddenly appeared at it, always catching her unaware.

She remembered how when she was eight years old, her father took her to Chicago for a visit to the famous Shedd Aquarium. She peered at the sharks, those incredibly flexible torpedoes, behind the glass, and their glacial eyes looked back at her and she'd wondered who found who stranger. It was nearly inconceivable that both sharks and men shared a planet; they were so impossibly different. There in the aquarium, the sharks swam and she felt confusion, and fear, and even the hate prompted by the totally alien.

Dr. Jan Pretre, she thought, was a shark. He belonged on the other side of the glass.

"Beth, I want to help you. I can't do that unless you cooperate."

His help? she thought. *Perhaps he might help her choose her own casket!* She said nothing.

"Do you know where you are?"

She said, "In an insane asylum."

"We don't use that term nowadays," Jan Pretre said. "This is a private institution, Prairie Hill Mental Hospital, and you're my patient. How long have you been here, Beth?"

"Monday," she said. "That's when they brought me here."

"Very good," Jan Pretre nodded. He folded his arms across his chest. "You're far more in touch with reality today than you have been, Beth. Now, can you tell me what day of the week this is?"

She thought about it. She wasn't sure. Without a window in the room, no clock, the light overhead that never went out, the constant dim illumination in the corridor, there were no ways to measure the passage of time. None of the people who unlocked the door to give her pills and shots answered her questions or even spoke to her. (And what were they drugging her with? Something that turned her blood to molasses and made it impossible to hold onto a single thought for more than an instant.)

"Don't you know what today is?" Jan

Pretre said.

"I know that you can't keep me here. You have to let me out. I'm not a prisoner," she said slowly and clumsily.

"No, you're not," agreed Jan Pretre. "You voluntarily committed yourself . . ."

"I did like hell!"

"That's your signature on the admission forms, Beth."

It was a memory or a dream or a fantasy *or an hallucination:* someone was telling her to sign something, that if she signed she would be safe and the girls would be safe and that everyone would be safe and she was signing, looking at her name and thinking *That is all there is left of me, there, on that line* . . .

"I signed myself in so I can sign myself out!"

"You could indeed," Jan Pretre said. He put his hand to his bearded chin. "I'll bet a lawyer would have you released in an hour." Then he glanced around the room. "What a shame, no telephone in here so you can seek legal counsel."

Beth said nothing. She tried to think, but her mind was cluttered with bits of nonsense —a line from a nursery rhyme, the items on a shopping list, the remembrance of the way smooth stones glittered in sunlight as they lay in the shallow water of a stream.

"Of course, Beth," Jan Pretre said, "If you were released, then for your own good, your husband and I, as your doctor, would have to arrange for a sanity hearing. You've had a psychotic episode. You might have harmed yourself or someone else. You'll be found

275

incapable of making your own decisions and . . ."

His words were a droning blur. She couldn't stand to look at him. She studied her calves. They were stubbly; she hadn't shaved her legs in . . . how long? *God, how long would she be here?*

"Beth?"

She didn't raise her eyes but she nodded to let him know she heard him.

"Let me help you. Cooperate with me."

She had no choice. She would *pretend* to cooperate. She nodded.

"Good, Beth. That's better. Tomorrow we'll schedule you for electroconvulsive therapy."

She forced herself not to give a damn. He could schedule her to be strung up by the thumbs while hot coals were applied to her feet. She would go along with whatever he wished, and get out of this madhouse.

She smiled at him. She made sure the smile was shy and hinting at sadness, that it was acquiescing and, more than anything else, trusting.

"Anything you say, Dr. Pretre," she said.

"That's good, that's just fine." She lay on a heavily cushioned table. To prevent injury during the convulsion she'd undergo, she had been given a muscle relaxant. She was also receiving a daily dose of 1,500 milligrams of Thorazine, a powerful tranquilizer, and she felt as limp as laundry on a line.

She was surrounded by male and female nurses and attendants. It was their job to hold her down. "Open your mouth, please."

She opened her mouth for the rubber bite plate. Whatever they demanded—"Swallow these pills, let me have your arm for this shot, please roll over, turn yourself inside out," she would go along with them. That is, the Beth they *thought* her to be would act as submissive as an abused puppy.

But there was another Beth. That was the one buried deep within her. That Beth knew she was not insane, would not let them make her insane, and would hold onto her sanity no matter what!

Graphite salve was smeared on her temples. She bit into the mouth guard. There were heavy hands on her arms and legs. The electrodes were touched to her head.

Blackness in the shape of a huge rectangular sheet of metal dropped on her. She thought *I am dead!* and then she floated away, rising, buoyant and liberated. She gazed down at the Beth who was writhing, eyes rolling wildly, limbs thrashing despite the efforts of those trying to keep them immobile.

Jan Pretre was below her, watching the convulsing Beth, never realizing that there was *another* Beth. Contemptuously, she mocked him with a line from *Peter Pan,* the book her mother had given her for her seventh birthday; Peter, about to be run through by his arch-enemy, Captain Hook, looked the heartless pirate in the eye and said, *Do your worst, you old codfish!*

In the weeks that followed, Beth Louden's psychotherapy was intensive and eclectic. Dr. Pretre was convinced of the efficacy of shock, and so he had 100 volts sent through her brain three times a week, but hers was an unusual case and there were other potentially beneficial approaches. He experimented with heavier dosages of the tranquilizer Thorazine, then, not pleased with the results, administered a drug with an opposite effect, Tofranil, a psychic energizer. Beth went without sleep for fifty-eight straight hours, then collapsed.

He tried narcoanalysis, sending her into a "twilight sleep" with sodium amytal. During one narcoanalytic session, she—the *real* Beth —almost gave herself away. Calmly, in a drug thick voice, she said, "I'm fooling you, you know."

"What's that?"

"I . . . I don't know."

"How are you fooling me, Beth?"

"I mean I was fooling myself, Dr. Pretre, you know, that Michael was doing horrible things. I even thought you were helping him, that you were part of a plot against me." She began to cry. "Oh, Dr. Pretre, help me so I won't fool myself ever again."

Do your worst, you old codfish!

After that she knew that though she had been careful, she must take still greater precautions not to reveal herself. There had to be a hidden and safe and faraway place to send the real Beth when Jan Pretre tried to ferret her out, to seize her and destroy her.

She created one.

The garden spreads for acres and acres, so great a distance that the flowers blend into the sky at the horizon line. Roses and zinnias

*and peace and tulips and geraniums and love
and the thousands of perfumes coalescing
into one heady aroma, the scent of Beth's
garden*

> *there is no fear
> are no wicked secrets
> is no death*

She had a refuge. She stole away whenever
Dr. Pretre came too close.

The petals of a tulip are as soft as a dream.

Michael came to visit. "Yes, I am feeling so
much better, Michael. Yes, I do want to come
home."

*There is nothing more beautiful than the
purple of my morning glories.*

Sometimes Michael brought the children.
"I'm sorry, girls. I didn't mean to scare you. I
was sick. But I'm going to be better soon and
everything will be fine."

*Quick, come with me. Safe in my garden,
the flowers bloom and you will bloom with
them, safe from harm, safe with me!*

Vern and Laura Engelking came to see her.
"I'm blessed to have such wonderful friends.
Thank you. Thank you."

> *I am in
> my garden and in
> my garden I live and am safe
> I live I live I live
> I LIVE!!!*

"Beth won't be any more trouble,
Michael," Jan Pretre said.

279

"Trouble? She's so spaced out she's a god-damned robot," Michael said. He and Jan Pretre sat in a consultation room off the main lobby of Prairie Hills Sanitarium.

"She's docile enough," Jan Pretre agreed. "Her will is virtually destroyed. We've given her what amounts to a prefrontal lobotomy except that we didn't have to do the actual cutting. Tell her to stand up and she'll stand up, but be sure you remember to tell her to sit down or she'll keep on standing until her feet rot off at the knees."

"I don't think she'll have to wait that long, will she, Jan?" Michael said.

Quietly, Jan said, "Not many days from now, we'll be in a new year, Michael. A *new* year . . . for everyone."

"Jan . . ."

"There's nothing to talk about now," Jan said, cutting off the conversation with a brusque wave. "You take Beth home. Remember, though, she isn't always in contact with reality. She drifts away."

Michael nodded. The only reality Beth had to be in contact with would be the reality of death when he killed her.

As he drove to Park Estates, he thought he heard Beth quietly say, "Codfish."

It was Wednesday afternoon, December 21.

NINETEEN

"DON'T YOU think it's a good idea for you to give the kids a call?" Michael asked. It was 11:30 Thursday morning. Wearing a green and white checked flannel shirt and corduroy slacks, Michael sat across the butcher block table from Beth. She was in a simple light blue housecoat that, he thought, seemed about ninety-eight sizes too large for her. Beneath her vacuous eyes, there were crater-like black circles. Her face was pinched and drawn, so pale that her freckles looked like punctures.

"What's that?" she said.

"Marcy and Kim," Michael said. "You do remember the precious little tykes, don't you? I'll bet they're just dying to hear from their dear mommykins right now."

Yesterday, before going to Prairie Hills Sanitarium to get Beth, he had taken the children to the Engelkings. That was Laura's idea. *You could always count on Laura for helpful ideas; when it was time for Vern to kill her, she'd probably suggest a practical way to keep the mess to a minimum.* The kids were on Christmas vacation and so, with no school to worry about, it might be better for everyone if Beth had a quiet few days at home with Michael to get back to her old self.

Shit, if you wanted to find Wonderful Wifey's "old self," you could start looking somewhere past the rings of Saturn. Tack a sign on her forehead: CLOSED FOR THE DURATION.

"Yes, I should call the children," Beth said. Her voice was throaty and autistically flat. She rose like a marionette manipulated by a spastic puppeteer. She shuffled to the telephone on the kitchen counter. There was a slipper on her right foot; her left was bare.

Beth picked up the phone. She said, "The children . . . Where did they go?"

He told her.

She said, "I forget the number."

"Well," Michael said, "try to recall it. Let's see you think as hard as you can."

Beth gripped the receiver with both hands. She closed her eyes after a few seconds opened them and said with a defeated shrug, "I really can't."

"That's all right, honey," Michael grinned. "You gave it your best shot. Hell, you get ten points for trying." He gave her the number, one digit at a time and, her face tense with concentration, she pushed each button in turn.

"Hello? Hello, Laura. This is Beth . . . I'm all right. Yes. I want to talk to . . . I want to talk to Marcy and Kim."

Michael decided she really didn't have all that much to say to the girls. A couple of "yesses," a single "no." "Oh, I want to see you soon," and "I love you" and that was damned near Beth's conversation with the kids, verbatim. He imagined it probably used up what remained of her vocabulary.

"All right," Beth said, "I'll put him on."

She stiffly held out the telephone toward him.

Sure, he was the "perfect pop" so the kids wanted a word with him. That is, Kim was going to remind him that she had her heart set on roller-skates for Christmas and her own Atari, and what about a dog? And Marcy was going on, "Oh, Daddy, I miss you" to him.

He took the telephone. "Hello?"

"Michael?"

"Yes, Jan," Michael said. *Surprise, surprise —another Jan and Vern bit of business that didn't include him? Aw, c'mon, pallys, he knew the secret handshake and everything!*

"Laura asked me to drop over here, didn't you, Larua?"

So Laura was within earshot. That meant Jan would be watching what he said.

"Laura suggested I have a chat with Marcy and Kim, to explain about Beth," Jan continued. His voice was professional, a blend of Leo Buscaglia and Mr. Rogers. "It could help make their adjustment to the situation somewhat easier. But you're their father and I didn't want to do that until I'd spoken to you about it."

Beside him, Beth stood like a droopy mannequin. He pointed to the table. *Sit!* She obeyed the unspoken command.

"By all means," Michael said. "Anything we can do to help those terrific kids get used to their new, improved, whacked-out mom is okay with me. You have a heart to heart talk with them, Jan."

"I will," Jan Pretre said. "They're bright. I'm sure they'll understand. And how is Beth?"

At the table, Beth was staring at the refrigerator.

"Couldn't be better," Michael said. "Not more than five minutes ago, we were discussing the Theory of Relativity. See, she figured out a few mistakes Einstein had in there and she's got them corrected. She's worried about what she should wear when she's awarded the goddamned Nobel Prize."

"Michael"—Jan paused, then said seriously—"keep a close eye on her."

Another warning from Jan Pretre? Orders from headquarters: No more goofs, Michael. Mind those p's and q's. Do not fuck up.

"I'm doing exactly that, Jan," Michael said. "No problem. It's about as interesting as watching a frozen dinner thaw."

"Very well then, Michael," Jan Pretre said. "I'll be in touch soon"—this time, a second's pause—"*very* soon. Goodbye."

Michael put down the telephone. Oh yeah, say it twice and you're right both times—he was *ready* for "very soon."

"Beth!"

Her head turned with the slow movement of a windup toy. He could nearly hear the gears grinding.

"Hey, hey, hey!" He clapped his hands. "It's about lunch time, Bethy babes. And what's the happy homemaker have on today's menu? Something plenty yum-yum, I'll bet!"

"You want me to fix lunch," Beth said.

"Whoo! You got it! Let's hear it for the lady with one shoe off and one shoe on!"

"I can't, Michael."

"No, no," he said, shaking his head. "That's

negative thinking, sweetie-pie, and negative thinking is exactly what we don't need in the Louden household. You remember you're an American, and American ends in 'I can.'" He smiled and savored the threat of it. "Now you get off your ass and let's hear those pots banging!"

Beth did not move.

"Get up, goddamnit!"

She rose. He crooked a finger, summoning her. "Beth," he said sternly, "here's how it works. See, I go to work every day, and I bring home the bacon, yessireebob! That's my job because I'm the husband. Now *your* job is to be the wife and to fry up that bacon for the family. I said your *job*, goddamnit, and that means you have got to do it. Are you starting to get the message? You knock off this walking corpse bullshit. You don't, it's right back to the nuthouse so they can plug your head into the electrical outlet a few more times. This time around, you'll be tuning in shortwave radio on your molars. Is that what you want?"

"Michael," Beth said, "why do you hate me?"

The anger was sudden and total. It seared his flesh from within. *This* nothing, *the nothing who'd someday sensed the truth of his Stranger-self, who'd even tried to deceive him with her 'housewife on a horny holiday affair,' now dared to ask him why he was . . . what he was!*

His hand flew up to grab her throat but he caught himself. He slapped her.

"No questions! None! Not another

goddamned word! Now"—he took a deep breath, held it until he was certain he'd regained control—"it's lunchtime." The lines of his fingers flared red from her ear to her mouth.

He pushed her toward the refrigerator. "Beth no cook, Beth no eat." That wasn't much of a threat, he realized as soon as he'd said it. Beth's appetite had gone on a journey with her mind. The only thing she regularly consumed was her pills, and she would keep doing that if he had to ram them down her throat with his foot.

But he was determined she would prepare a meal, and right the hell now! "Something light. Grilled cheese sandwiches. Yeah, that would be nice."

The task had to be broken down into each of its separate steps: butter the bread. Slice the cheese. Take out the frying pan . . . Arms folded, he was the overseer to an automaton. He wasn't certain if he were gratified or furious in the role.

With the sandwiches grilling (he made sure the fire wasn't too high) he told Beth to pay attention, to turn them over in a minute, and he left to go to the bathroom.

When he got back to the kitchen, the sandwiches were carbonized blocks of dough oozing yellow goo, black smoke rising, and Beth was gone.

Her single slipper had come off, so she walked barefoot through the half inch of powdery snow that had fallen in the early hours of the morning. The temperature was twenty-eight degrees, the sky dismally overcast, the wind fiercely gusting from the north.

The sun shone on her face. It was the golden, world-embracing light one knows only in childhood, the rarified glow that has a clean scent, its warm memory surfacing later in dreams of contentment and color.

She moved down the driveway. The wind blew her hair, flapped the hem of her housecoat against her calves. Around her ankles were miniature whirlwinds of snow.

It was good to feel the grass beneath her bare feet. The grass was an emerald-green; she could feel it quivering with life, the steady life-pulse of the earth. She heard windchimes, delicate "tings" of sound and a distant, smoke-like flute.

She walked to the side of the garage.

She was going to her garden.

> *no fear*
> *no wicked secrets*
> *no death*
> *no death*
> *no death*

She stood in the center of the desolate snow covered plot that had been her spring and summer time pride.

The beauty that surrounded her was such a sweet pinch in her chest that her eyes stung with tears. She was in an endless ocean of flowers. Gladiola were a riot of flaming reds, shimmering purples, the cushion mums blazing bronze and pink, and the lilies, the lilies—the "imperial silver", as formal as a Chinese empress, the trumpet lilies, all golden and blasting a silent fanfare to the heavens, and the "pink perfection"—yes, perfect, oh, perfect! The profusion of color, colors that had not been named because they could not be described. The garden promised infinity and eternity . . .

no death
not death

"Beth! Beth . . . There you are!"
Suddenly, there was something wrong here in her garden. Weeds sprouted, instantaneous and horrid, bursting from black soil to entwine about the flowers, to choke their life-loveliness. The weeds were tendrilled malig-nancies. They attacked her! They wound about her ankles, trying to bring her down . . .
"Beth!"
No!

no death!!!

She had to fight the weeds. She needed weapons. The weeds lashed her calves, wrapped around her feet. She jerked free of them.

Beth went to the side door of the garage. It was unlocked. She walked inside, cold light from the doorway trailing her as the stepped past the rear end of the LTD and Chevette Scooter.

There were her garden tools in a box on the workbench: a three-pronged weeder, a trowel, a cultivator, a ratchet pruner . . . They were too small. She needed a more powerful weapon. There in the corner were the lawn tools, a rake, an edger, a shovel—*a shovel!* She could uproot the weeds, dozens at a time . . .

Kill the weeds!

The pegboard over the workbench caught her eye. Something was missing. Something was not where it belonged. There was an empty hook.

She tried to remember what it was that had hung there, that was meant to be there. She could not, but she knew that something was gone and that left her with a sense of loss. It —oh, whatever it was—was gone and everything was gone, gone or vanishing, vanishing . . .

Her strength drained away. Futility overwhelmed her.

"Okay," Michael said. He stood at the garage door. "Come here."

Walking to him, she struck her shin on the Ford's back bumper. "Just what do you think you're doing, going outside like that in this weather?" Michael said. "If any of the neighbors saw you, they'd think you were crazy!" He smiled, "Hey, you wouldn't want them to think that, would you?"

Beth said, "I went to the garden."

"Your garden?" Michael cocked his head. "Your garden?" He held out a hand. "Okay, let's both of us pay a visit to your garden!"

He dragged her from the garage. Then with a backhanded wave, he said, "And here you have it. Really something, isn't it?"

She no longer saw the weeds. She no longer

saw her flowers.

"Bethy's garden has gone beddy-bye for the winter. Everything's dead, kiddo. Crapped out. *El Zero Ultimato.*"

"No," Beth said.

no . . .
death . . .

" . . . No."

"Yep, and that's all she wrote."

"Michael," she said, "I'm very cold. Can we go back to the house?"

"Congratulations," Michael said. "You just had a real idea." Arm around her, he took her inside.

Michael was grinning; he couldn't stop grinning. "Look what we've got here!" He snatched one of the ruined sandwiches from the frying pan. It was still warm and scratchy to the touch.

As he advanced on her, he felt a dizzying euphoria. It was not the sublime sensation that was his when he killed, but the feeling that preceded that moment, that time when his power was at its peak and his victim was utterly powerless.

"Children in Europe and China are starving and you burn our fucking sandwiches!"

Head hanging, Beth looked at him through lashes. Shit, he saw *nothing* in her eyes! He doubted she had any more idea of what he was yelling about than if he were shouting in Arabic!

All right then, all right and all right! He'd meet her submissive challenge. Beth was going to fucking *hurt*, and she would feel that hurting and beg him to make it stop.

And then he would kill her!

Not yet, no, and not now—but soon!

He calmed himself, relaxing but not letting the glowing energy inside him dissipate altogether. Just some fun and games right now, a pinch and a poke and a twist . . .

But soon . . .

Winter was a dying time for the nothing people. And winter was the killing time, a time to *truly live* and kill and kill and kill . . . for the Strangers! He believed that the way a priest trusted in the surety of kingdom of God.

That was Jan Pretre's promise.

With his left hand, he seized the back of Beth's neck. She didn't struggle. Slowly, he scraped the black sandwich back and forth across her mouth, then her cheeks. It sounded like a worn-out razor blade on a two-day growth of unlathered whiskers. He said, "That doesn't taste very good, does it? It's too well done."

She was rigid and quivering, eyes squeezing shut. He dropped the sandwich on the floor. Her face looked sun-burned, dotted with tiny specks of black.

He paced in front of her like a drill sergeant chewing out a slouch of a recruit. "You were bad to burn the food, Beth," he said. "Bad girl! That's why I had to punish you. And now I have to punish you for running away from home."

Pivoting, he swung, arm at waist level. He didn't put all his force into the blow, but there was power and speed behind the fist that slammed into her stomach.

Beth clasped her arms over her belly and doubled over, whuffing for air and then wretching with a dry, hacking noise. Okay! he thought. That got through to her! One in the old labonza!

"Don't throw up, Beth," he warned. "You throw up, I'll wipe your face in it."

He yanked the hair at the top of her head and forced her to stand erect, jerking her up on tip-toe. With a tone of "reasonable explanation," he said. "You had to be punished, Beth, because you were a bad girl. I'm sure you understand that."

He cranked her head up and down in a "Yes" gesture.

"So now you've had your punishment and I can forgive you, but first, and this is the catch, baby, you have to tell me you're sorry for being such a bad girl."

Her eyes were huge and glazed, the whites shot through with streaks of red. Her mouth was open, tongue stabbing between her teeth as she panted. She did not answer.

"Say 'I am sorry,' bitch," he ordered, punctuating each word by jerking her head.

Her taut throat worked. In a dry, whispered scream, she said it.

"That's better," Michael said. He turned her hair loose. He thought she might collapse but she remained on her feet. "You know," he said, "I hate these little arguments we get into, Beth. I don't like to get upset with you, sweetheart. I love you so very much."

Then, grinning—*Smile at the birdbrain*—he

said, "And I know you love me, too. Tell me, snookums. Let me hear you say, 'I love you.' "

He was ready for a spark of defiance to snap at him. He hoped for it, for the chance to extinguish it.

Sounding like a tape on a telephone answering machine with worn-down batteries, Beth said, "I . . . love you."

All right, pack up the pieces of that game and break out a new board and cards and dice! Fun, fun fun!

"Aw, that's great to hear. That's wonderful! Shit, hearing those magic words gets me right where I live." He tipped his head to the side. "You've got me all romantic, you irresistible sex goddess you!"

He gripped her nose between his first and second fingers, a "Three Stooges" come-a-long. "We're going to make love, cuddles."

The peeping "ooh" she whimpered every step of the way pleased him immensely. In the living room, he drew the picture window's drapes. "Don't want to give the neighbors a cheap thrill," he said.

"Now let's get into the holiday mood!" He plugged in the lights of the aluminum Christmas tree in the corner. An artificial tree . . . He'd never yielded to Beth's wanting the genuine article. He too much liked the secret irony: an artificial tree for his artificial celebration of the holiday. Beneath the tree were decoratively wrapped gifts.

Of course! Michael Louden, father, and Michael Louden, husband, wouldn't neglect any of the members of his dear family. He was one generous guy!

"Now, Beth," he said, "I know you're itching for it. After all, you haven't had it for a long time"—*Not since that Kevin asshole gave it to you. And wasn't he the "last of the red hot lovers?"*—"but I'm no blue-collared redneck who doesn't give a shit about his lady's pleasure. We've got to have some foreplay!"

With both hands, he grabbed the collar of her housecoat and ripped her clothing off her.

"So much for foreplay," he said. He threw her on the couch and with the heel of his hand on her forehead, shoved her down on her back. He unbuckled his belt, opened his button and fly, and pushed his slacks and shorts down to his calves.

He stroked himself quickly, then dropped upon her. He forced himself into her, thrusting hard, making sure every lunge hurt. "Let's get some action going," he demanded. "Necrophilia isn't my speed."

Beth gasped each time he drove his hips down. That was the only sound she made. Her movements were not his own, merely her body's involuntary mirroring of his actions.

He hit his climax, hit it as hard as he could, and stiff-armed, frozen above her, clenched his teeth and then slowly exhaled.

He got off her, pulling up his clothing. "Well, was it good for you, honey?" he said.

Beth's eyes did not shift toward him; she looked at the ceiling. Only the rise and fall of her breasts showed that she lived.

"I mean, did you feel the earth move? Did you have the 'Big O'?"

Beth said nothing, did nothing.

Michael walked to the Christmas tree, stopped, and picked up the small package marked "Beth." "You know, after a wonderful moment like that, I can't help myself. I just have to give you an early Christmas gift."

Going back to her, he tore off the wrappings. He took out the one ounce, cut glass *flacon*. "I know you'll be wild about this," he said, "Oscar de La Renta. This shit is so classy it's not perfume, it's *parfum*. Cost an arm and a leg."

He opened the bottle. He poured the perfume on Beth's face.

The rich scent stung his eyes and made him cough.

Beth did not even blink.

WIth a casual toss, he threw the bottle on the carpet.

"You know something, Beth?" he said. "You're no fun anymore."

TWENTY

"RISE AND shine! Up and at 'em!" Michael hit the light switch. "Hey, hey! Things to do and people to see!"

Only her head showing, Beth lay unmoving beneath a mound of blankets. He had not slept in the same bed with her since Wednesday night. He couldn't tolerate her sick-crazy smell. He did not mind sleeping on the sofa or in a chair; he no longer required much rest or even food. He was running on frenetic energy, racing through the minutes of the day, knowing that each instant's passing brough him closer to the new year and Jan Pretre's implicit promise—The Time of The Strangers.

Besides, the bedroom belonged to Beth and Micheal Louden—to *them*, not him.

He shook Beth.

She groaned. "No. Sleep."

He heaved the covers from her, pulled her up to a sitting position. "Company's coming," he said. "You want to look and feel your very best for our visitors, I'm sure."

Her head lolled to the left. Her mouth was crooked. "Company . . . What's today, Michael?"

"Saturday," he said. "Tonight's Christmas Eve. Very festive occasion, you know. A time to celebrate. Too bad your mother won't be with us this year but she's busy being dead."

Beth did not react.

Michael said, "The Engelkings are bringing the kids back home in an hour or so."

Beth swayed from side to side. "No," she said tonelessly. "Shouldn't come here . . . Don't want them here."

"That's a fine thing for a mother to say!" Michael laughed.

Late that morning, Laura Engelking had telephoned. Was Beth up to having the children? If so, they'd come by in the afternoon. Oh, certainly the girls could stay with Vern and her, but they missed their parents —Marcy especially, such a sensitive child— and it was the "togetherness" season . . .

Why sure, Laura, you're absolutely right! In fact, he was just about to call you with the same idea and here you went and took the words right out of his mouth! Maybe he'd set the self-timer on the Canon Sure-Shot *and tonight they'd all gather around the Christmas tree for a family portrait. Beth might not show up in it, though; he didn't have the right film to photograph a ghost!*

Michael hauled Beth out of bed. She was unsteady. "You shower and get dressed. Pronto!"

"Michael?" she said. She unexpectedly smiled. For a split-second, he thought she had regained her senses. Then the smile became what it was meant to be, a lip-quivering helpless pout, and she childishly murmured, "Don't hurt anyone, okay? Don't hurt anyone anymore."

"Come on!" He sank his fingers into her upper arm and quick-marched her down the hall to the bathroom. She managed to shower on her own. He had to help her get dressed—he chose a blue velour jumper and an ivory blouse—and brush her hair.

"Just as pretty as can be," he said, when he had her seated on the living room sofa. Next to her on the end table was the remaining crystal lamp. What if he snatched it up and hurled it to the floor at her feet, smashing it as he had the other?

No, that wouldn't affect her. Beth was G-O-N-E. All that electroshock, a bushel basket of tranqs, whatever other mind-scramblers that had been pumped into her, and of course that heavy hit of LSD that he'd given her to first zap her off to la-la land, and *voila!* A waxwork figure, one that had not yet had the paint applied to its face.

"Now remember," he said, wagging his finger, "behave yourself. Don't say the wrong thing to our guests. We don't want them to worry. You don't want me to punish you for being bad."

He wondered if he were getting through to her. There was something else that might get the idea across. "The kids are coming home, Beth. It sure would be a shame if something bad happened to them. I'm sure nothing will, if you act right." Maybe that was still too subtle. Raising his voice, he added, "You do anything out of line, anything at all, and I'll break both their necks."

She nodded almost imperceptibly. Message received, he decided.

When the children and Laura and Vern arrived at three o'clock, Beth, hollow-voiced, said "Hello" to everyone. "Hello" and that was it. Then as she was kissed on the cheek by Marcy—"Oh, Mom, I'm so happy you're home and that we're all home and everything!"—and Kim, who needed a push, hanging back, obviously confused and shocked by what she saw, hugged and kissed by both Vern and Laura, Michael saw the desperate, begging glance she gave him: *Am I being good? Please don't hurt them!*

He nodded approval. He sat by her on the sofa and sent the kids up to their room to unpack. Laura took a seat and Vern said, "Whoops! Almost forgot!" He didn't bother to retrieve his coat from the hall closet. He dashed outside and, a moment later, returned with gift-wrapped boxes under both arms.

"Indeed, good friends, it's not the thought, it's the gift that counts!" He cocked his head and smiled broadly. "Hmm, perchance I've not got that particular platitude quite right!"

Michael chuckled and Laura erupted into laughter. *You're going overboard on the hilarity, Laura,* Michael thought. She was straining for cheerfulness, but she hadn't once taken her eyes off Beth.

"Oh, Vern," Laura said, "you're the funniest man in the world. Beth, don't you think he's funny?"

"Yes," Beth said.

Michael said, "Vern's going to need a sense of humor when he sees what we got him."

There was another round of laughter—*Tis the season to be jolly,* Michael thought. The children tromped back down for present

opening. In the midst of paper-tearing—
There was a suede purse for Marcy, "Uncle
Vern and Aunt Laura, it's so stylish!"—"Did
you hear what she said—'So stylish' "—a
cube "weather info" desk radio for Vern—
"Now I can learn about the great out of doors
while I happily stay indoors!"—Michael
caught Laura's head bobbing, hand waving
gesture; it meant, *I want to talk to you.* He
couldn't pretend he didn't pick up on it when
she repeated it even more broadly.

"Why don't you open yours, Beth?" Vern
said, and as Beth listlessly worked the ribbon
off the package, Michael rose and said, "I'll
put us together a drink. Laura, feel like
giving me a hand?"

As soon as they were in the kitchen, Laura
said, "God Almighty, Michael, Beth is . . ."

"Don't you think I know it?" he said. *Now
that was the heartbroken husband for
damned sure! That catch in the throat, the
way the words trailed off into an abyss of
sorrow.* "She's slipping away from me, from
everyone, minute by minute."

He turned his back to Laura. His shoulders
heaved. He bowed his head and put his face
in his hands.

He congratulated himself for a refined
dramatic touch. When Laura placed a sympa-
thetic hand on his shoulder, he took a step
away from her, as though compassion would
make him break down completely. He had to
maintain control, and that was no lie,
because if he didn't, he might slice Laura
Engelking's goddamned interfering nose off
and hand it to her for her charm bracelet!

He turned back to her, blew air through pursed lips. *See what a gutsy trooper he was? Stiff upper lip and no tear in the eye.* "I'm hoping that Christmas with all of us will start to bring her around. If not, we'll have to put her back into the sanitarium. I just don't know what else to do."

"Michael, this has been so hard on you . . ."

"Say, there's one other thing we could try," he said. "Maybe if we gave her some chicken soup." *What the hell was he doing? Laura was gaping at him like he had fewer marbles rolling around in his skull than Beth did.*

"I'm sorry," he said, shaking his head. "Hell, I'm trying to find *something* to laugh about while the only woman I've ever loved . . ."

Booming "Whaddaya gotta do to get a drink around here already?" Vern stepped into the kitchen to be silenced by Laura's snapping eyes. "*You,*" she said, nodding at him, "have to go down to the bar with Michael and help him while *I* go back to the living room and make sure the kids' 'Don't open till Christmas packages' don't get opened."

At the rec room bar, Michael poured whiskey into a shot glass. He tipped it back, emptying it. "Laura is a pain in the ass," he said.

"Fundamentally, I agree," Vern Engelking said.

Michael poured himself another drink. "Want one?"

"Yes," Vern said. "Relax, I'm sure Laura will assume we're having a *mano a mano* discussion."

Pouring Vern's drink, Michael nodded reflectively and said, "Are we?"

"Somewhat keyed-up, Michael? Tense? A bit anxious?"

"Yes, yes, and yes," Michael said.

"Don't be," Vern said. "The future comes quickly for the cunning and the patient and the strong."

Michael said, "Then the future is ours."

Vern Engelking raised the shot glass and drained it.

From the time the Engelkings departed, the day dragged for him. He popped another pill into Beth, hauled her upstairs—"Mom needs her rest now, kids"—and dumped her into bed; she was still dressed. He needed her out of the way. Beth's continued existence had become a moment-to-moment insult and he did not trust himself to hold back.

In winter's early twilight, it started to snow. He gazed out the living room picture window at the big, lazily falling flakes, their airy meandering taunting him with suggestions of timelessness.

At six o'clock, he had a pizza delivered. Kim bluntly expressed her opinion: "Pizza on Christmas Eve? That sucks."

Marcy said, "It's all right, Daddy. I like pizza anytime."

Flip a coin to determine which child he found more loathsome. Hell, the coin would probably stand on edge, and that would be exactly right.

Maybe pizza on Christmas Eve sucked, but

Kim ate like she'd just been rescued after three foodless days on the high seas. She made slurp-chomping noises. She didn't always remember to close her mouth when she chewed, usually when she chose to say something to him.

He got up from the table, telling the girls to clean up after they'd finished. He went to his upstairs office and closed the door. He was out of synchronization, as though he were internally moving at seventy-eight revolutions per minute while the Earth sedately rotated at thirty-three.

He picked up the framed picture on the desk, the one taken at the lake last summer—*No, it was the summer before. Time sure does fly when you're having fun!*—the shot of the four of them, the Louden family. He tightly held between his thumb and forefinger, slammed it face down against the corner of the desk. The non-glare glass didn't shatter; it snapped, and he dropped the photo on the floor.

There was a knock on the door. "Daddy, it's Marcy. Can I come in?"

Sure, Patient Papa always had time for the kids . . . Shit!

Hesitantly, Marcy stepped into the office. "Daddy, are you mad at me? Or Kim?"

"Should I be?"

"No, I don't think so, anyway. It's, well, you seem to be mad or something."

Slow it down, slow it way, way down! he told himself. For a little while longer, *a little while and no more than that*, he had to be Michael Louden. And then Michael Louden, that vapid blob who never had truly lived, would be forever dead, killed like the others that The Stranger would claim as his rightful victims.

"No," he said. "I'm not mad at you or your sister. There's a lot on my mind, that's all."

"About Mom, you mean."

He nodded.

"Is Mom ever going to be better, Daddy?"

"I'm sure she will," he said. "A few weeks from now, you won't even know anything was wrong with her."

"I hope you're right," Marcy said. "I really love Mom." She gave him a half-smile. "And I really love you, too."

"Okay," he said, and then he flashed his "dear daddy" smile. *A little while longer . . .* "Hey, I'm sorry I've been such a grouchy-bear, snapping-gator, cruddy-crocodile. Let's have some fun!"

"What will we do, Daddy?"

"What every red-blooded, right-thinking, all-American family does for Christmas Eve good times! We'll"—he gave her an "are you ready for this" wink—"watch television!"

Marcy giggled. "Sometimes you're even funnier than Uncle Vern!"

"Wow! We'll have a fine old time, you'd better believe it. I'll even make popcorn. I just hope you kids can handle all this big-time excitement." He held out his hand. Grinning, Marcy took it.

He did make popcorn and they did watch television. At ten o'clock the Christmas classic *Miracle on 34th Street* came on channel 32. By the time Edmund Gwenn revealed that he, the real Santa Claus, always slept with his whiskers outside the blankets, Kim was asleep on the carpet and Marcy lay on her side, her head on the cushioned armrest of the sofa, eyes closed.

Michael stood up. Another day was about at an end. Then there'd be another—the thump-galumph of little feet down the stairs for the early morning race to open gifts— and a day after that a day . . . But not so many days now and . . .

A new year and at last, at last, at last!

He tried waking Kim first but all she did was gurgle in unconscious protest. He picked her up. He'd probably have to carry Marcy to bed, too. Once a kid went zonkers, a kid stayed zonked.

Beth also made the zonked list. He checked on her after he had Kim in bed. He went downstairs. When he stepped into the kitchen, the telephone rang.

He had it before the ringing ended. "Hello?"

He heard one word. It was the word. It was Jan Pretre's voice that said it: *"Now!"* Then there was the click of disconnection.

Now! Yes *Now! Not New Year's, with its midnight party-horns blasting and alcohol-charged geniality and its televised Times Square celebration with thousands of faceless nothing people goggling and waving as the camera panned them for their instant of celebrity when they could pretend they mattered.*

No, not a week from now, not another day, not another hour. Now! He loved the perfection of it:

It came upon a midnight clear
God rest ye, merry gentlemen
Silent night, holy night
Peace on Earth, good will toward men

Yes, Now. Tonight. The world turned upside down!

His waiting and enduring and falsity were at an end! He peered out the window above the sink. The great feathers of snow gleamed against the night.

It was so beautiful, so cold. He shivered and felt the flimsy shell that was Michael Louden fall away.

Goodbye and to hell with you, Mr. Nice Guy Down The Block, Mr. Hello and How's It Going, Mr. I Always Give To The Heart Fund! The fake and the fraud and the counterfeit—GONE!!!

He wanted to tear off his clothing, strip himself of these garments worn by Michael Louden, to feel only his flesh and his wondrous freedom, but he could not. Soon he would go into the cold night . . . The Stranger into the Night of Death.

But now—*NOW*—was Death in this house. *In Michael Louden's house . . .*

The Stranger opened the drawer by the sink and took out the butcher knife. Where to begin? Which one? *(NOW this silent night yes this holy night NOW!!!)*

The Stranger knew. Kim Louden—and then the mother, Beth Louden—and then, yes, that for last, Marcy, "Daddy's girl," that uncomprehending bleat of "Oh Daddy" as she tried to understand why her father *who was not her father* had the knife and was killing her!

The Stranger went upstairs.

The steps did not creak.

"Wake up. It's time for you to wake up."

Beth twisted free of the bonds of thick sleep. She sat up. The overhead light glared.

He stood at the side of the bed. He gripped the knife in his right hand, holding it hip-high, the point toward the floor.

"Michael?" she said.

"No," he said, "Michael is dead."

She thought he sounded patient, almost kindly, as though he were trying to help her see it all clearly. She knew he was not Michael. She said, "There never was a Michael."

He did not answer.

"Are you going to kill me now?" she asked.

"Soon," he said. "There's something I want you to see first. Will you come with me, please?"

She stepped down the hall with him. She knew she was not dreaming; she no longer dreamed.

They went into the children's bedroom. She stood with her back to the dresser at the foot of Kim's bed. He was at her right.

The room was lit by the lamp on the night-table between the beds. In the aquarium-cage on the stand by the window, Chopper, the brown and white guinea pig, ran furiously in circles, pinewood chips flying. From the poster above the headboard, ET gazed down at Kim.

All the blood, she thought. *Such a small*

child and so much blood. "You killed her."

"Yes."

"Did you kill Marcy."

"No, not yet. First you and then the other child."

The thoughts streamed through her mind with such speed that they were a single sheet of thought: *Kim was dead could not be saved and Marcy lived and would live had to live had to live live live . . .*

Almost inaudibly, she whispered, "I want to tell you something."

He leaned down, a stranger's face close to hers, striving to hear.

The scream shot out, a scream of all the hurt and rage that she had buried within her, and as she was screaming she transformed her hand into a weapon—*Curved sharp prongs of the garden weeder! Kill the weeds!* —and clawed at his left eye. She felt the thin resistance of the membrane of his eyeball, the pressure of the liquid beneath, but he was turning, pulling away, saving his eye as she ripped deep into the flesh of his face, the bloody skin slimy under her nails.

He turned away from her like a figure on a revolving music-box, bending, shoulders hunched, hand to his face, grunting, "You hurt me." She whirled, picking up the portable television on the dresser, palms pressed on either side of the plastic cabinet. It was no heavier than a beach ball. The plug popped out of the socket as she lifted it, then smashed it, screen down, against the curve of his spine directly beneath his shoulderblades.

His yell and the glassy-banging *whump* of

the imploding picture were simultaneous. The set tumbled off his back.

He was on his knees, feet touching the base of the dresser, head and arms draped over the foot of Kim's bed. A ragged circle was blasted in his shirt and the flesh of his back looked like ground red meat, dotted with bits of gristle, and stringy yellow cords.

But then he raised his head, glared at her, the corner of his mouth twisting up into the bloody streamers she had carved into his face —and he still held the knife.

She jumped over his legs and the wrecked television. She screamed, "Marcy!" and ran.

The stairway was dark. She sped down it but she was careful. She could not afford a misstep.

Marcy would live!

As soon as she reached the foyer, she heard him. He was on the steps, coming after her. She needed a new weapon.

She dashed into the dark living room. She felt her way along the couch to the end table, traced the crystal lamp's cord to the outlet and unplugged it. Holding the lamp by its base, she pressed back against the wall.

"Beth?"

He was in the foyer.

"Beth?"

He was in the living room.

She squinted. She saw nothing.

And then he was there, his smile nightmarish white, an arm's length in front of her. She swung the lamp, felt it hit his upper arm or shoulder, saw the prisms hang in the air between them like too perfect hailstones and then she felt a fiercely cold instrument right below her breastbone.

She dropped the lamp. She rose up on tip-toe as the blade of the knife worked higher within her. They were united now, she thought, for the first time, she and the one who had masqueraded as husbandlover-friend. They were joined by the knife that tore through every pretense and every barrier between them.

I tried, Marcy, she thought. *Live, Marcy!* She looked at her murderer, saw a stranger, said, "You old codfish," and died.

The Stranger rested on the living room sofa. *Now* was his time, The Time of The Stranger, yet things had not gone as they should have. The child died much too easily and quickly. Her eyes not even open and, like that! she was dead. After the suffocating years in the bodily prison of Michael Louden, the first glorious rush of freedom had over-whelmed him; he had not been able to restrain himself.

And the woman! She, an insignificant, meaningless nothing had *hurt* him.

Oh, he was in pain, but he was almost glad for it. Severe pain was a unique sensation, one he had never expected to experience. He knew now what his victims felt, what his victims-to-be would feel, and that gave him new appreciation for his birthright, his killing gift.

The Stranger rose. A victim awaited him, awaited his pleasure! He breathed deeply, filling his lungs with blood-death scent. He felt his strength surge omnipotent within him.

Would she yet be asleep downstairs, now, after all the noise? It was possible. Children slept through hurricanes, earthquakes, volcanic eruptions. And if she were not asleep—perhaps huddled terrified but in an agony of imaginations, oh, better still! A game of hide and seek. Come out, come out, wherever you are!

He went into the dark kitchen and opened the door leading downstairs.

" . . . Enroll now at DeLand School of electronics for the sake of your future." He heard the television commercial. Quietly, clenching the butcher knife handle, he walked down the steps.

The television was the room's only lighting. He went to the sofa.

She was not there!

"MERRY CHRISTMAS!"

The soprano shout behind him sent him jumping six inches into the air, whirling. Another commercial filled the TV screen, an animated advertisement for orange juice, splashing the room with garish, pulsing light, turning her into a psychedelic blur as she ran at him.

She was stiff-armed. It seemed as though she were being pulled like a water-skier gripping a tow-rope, but she held the wooden handles of the hedge-clippers.

With all her weight and speed driving them, the closed blades punched into him an inch above the belt-line, piercing cloth and flesh.

He shrieked and, no strength in his arm, no strength in him at all, dropped the butcher knife. She drove him back and he plopped down onto the sofa. She was on him, straddling his thigh, working the handles of the clippers, twisting and tearing.

He threw back his head and tried to scream again. He could not. The scream was not in his throat. It was white-hot and echoing in the huge, gut-torn crater from his navel to his ribs.

"Guess I'm a naughty girl, huh, Daddy?" she said, with a giggle. She pulled the handles of the clippers fully apart.

Everything inside him was torn loose, uprooted, and spilling out onto his lap. All that remained was the excruciating pain.

"I know you'll have to give me a good spanking for this!" she said. Then she jumped off him, leaving the hedge-clippers rooted in his body. She stepped backward a pace, then another.

"Oh, Daddy, sweet daddy, nice daddy, smart, smart daddy. Is this one of those times when Daddy could just kill his little girl?"

Kill her! He had no strength but the power of the thought itself brought him to his feet. The hedge-clippers tore loose of his massive wound and fell on his foot.

It hurt. He was amazed that he could feel such a tiny hurt while being consumed by a total, great hurt.

Kill her! Kill her!

He managed a half step and his intestines and blood spewed onto his legs and shoes.

"Come on, fall down and die, you dumb bastard."

Kill her!

A foot slid forward into the stinking, slippery mound. He fell down and he died.

EPILOGUE

In Chicago, Eddie Markell was tired and he wanted a drink. He was always tired and he always wanted a drink. He went into a sleaze-hustle bar on Rush Street. First came his drink and then came the B-girl with the hustle. After all, a guy shouldn't be lonely on Christmas Eve.

Eddie Markell said, "You know, I don't give a shit." That summed it up for him. It was The Time of The Strangers and he had waited too long. He shattered the rim of the glass on the table, rammed the jagged edges into her face, and twisted.

She screamed, spraying blood all over and by then Eddie was on his feet, the .357 out. He fired at the bar and the heavy slug literally atomized a three square foot section of it.

By no coincidence at all, Joe Rimaldi was at the tavern. He was a vice-cop come to collect his Christmas bonus from the management for not doing his job. But when push came to shove, the fat was in the fire, Joe Rimaldi was, by God, a cop and that nut with the monster pistol was . . . a nut with a monster pistol.

Joe Rimaldi pulled his Police Positive. His first shot went wild and the second smacked Eddie Markell in the chest.

"I don't give a shit," Eddie Markell said.

When the .357 slug hit him, Joe Rimaldi died instantly and, dead, did a double back flip over a table.

Eddie Markell emptied his pistol, killing three people. He left the bar and got halfway down the block before he collapsed and died.

It was "hot Dr. Pepper" time for the Rasmussens. At Christmas time, their drink of choice was heated Dr. Pepper with floating slices of orange and lemon. A Dr. Pepper punch bowl was on the table in the center of all the cookies and brownies and fudge bars and peanut butter balls Grandma and Mom had made.

Karl Rasmussen, Jr. was sipping his third cup of hot Dr. Pepper, an orange slice tapping his front teeth. Ask anyone, the finest young man in Monroe, Wisconsin was Karl Rasmussen, Jr. The blond high school senior maintained a B plus average in the college prep program, played football and basketball, was president of the First Lutheran Church's youth group, participated in Future Farmers of America and 4-H, and was, along with his father, a full dues-paying, voting member of the county dairy cooperative.

Karl Rasmussen, Jr. said, "I've got a surprise for all of you"—all being his father, Karl, Sr., and mother, Anne Marie, his nine year old sister, Lynn, Grandma and Grandpa Rasmussen, and Judy Stelter, his steady girl friend. Karl went to his bedroom.

Like virtually every country boy, Karl liked hunting and for his fourteenth birthday, his parents had given him a Hi-Standard Supermatic Deluxe, a twelve gauge, five shot, auto-loading shotgun. It was the surprise he returned with.

"Let's all get together, real close together, right there in front of the fireplace."

"Karl, Jr.," his mother said, "this is not funny."

Karl, Jr. shrugged. "Depends on how you look at it. I've always had a quiet sense of humor."

Karl, Sr. realized the seriousness of the situation. He said, "Son, I want you to put down that gun so we can talk, father and son, okay? You tell me now, are you taking drugs?"

Karl, Jr. smiled in the winning way he had for his yearbook photo. "Yes, Dad, I am. I have overdosed on hot Dr. Pepper."

"I'm sorry no one came to see you, Dr. Prescott," Miss Williams said. She had drawn Christmas Eve duty at the small nursing home in Lebanon, Missouri. "It must make you feel terrible that nobody cares if you live or die. Well, I care—and I want you to die."

Miss Williams had an ice-pick. Twice in the chest and once in the throat and then Miss Williams left Mr. Prescott's room. There were six other patients on the floor.

"Laura," Vern Engelking said, "let's exchange gifts." They sat at the kitchen table.

"Now? Don't you want to wait until tomorrow?"

"Ah, tomorrow and tomorrow and tomorrow creeps into your pretty pants from day to day."

Laura giggled. "You sly old fox! You're feeling all romantic, aren't you?"

Vern said, "Ah, love of my life, believe me you cannot know the depths of my feeling for you at this very point in time."

"Do you want your gift now?" Laura said. "I mean, the one I *bought* you? The other gift you're hinting for we'll arrange when we get to bed."

"No-no-no," Vern said. "I wish to bestow my special gift upon you first, my dear."

"I'll bet I know what it is," Laura said. "I've certainly dropped enough hints about that diamond necklace."

"Close your eyes, my dear."

"You're being so silly, Vern!"

"If you don't close your eyes, you won't get your fine surprise," he said in a sing-song.

She closed her eyes. He stepped behind her, took a nylon cord from his pocket, looped it around her neck and drew it tight.

"Gaah!" Laura's head shot forward. Vern pulled her back. Her face turned red and then blue. Her eyes bulged and the veins at her temples writhed. Her tongue shot far out of her mouth.

Slowly, slowly, Vern Engelking increased the pressure.

There is a "New South" where whites and blacks go to the same schools, work in the same places, and even socialize together, but in Beau Bien, Mississippi remains "Old South," and the white people there maintain their tradition of "Keeping the colored in their place." That's why Lee Charles Deveraux, the manager of the Beau Bien Holiday Inn, always addressed thirty-year-old Willie Jones, a custodian, as "boy."

It wasn't that he was fed up with being called "boy" that made Willie Jones go to Lee Charles Deveraux's office and kill him, slashing his throat with a pearl-handled straight razor that had been his father's. Willie Jones did that because it was Christmas Eve and it was *his* time.

Then Willie Jones took the master key to all the Holiday Inn rooms. There weren't many guests at the motel but Willie and his razor were busy for well over two hours.

The emergency room staff at New York's Bellvue Mental Hospital were ready for an overflow crowd. The holiday season was not a universal time of gladness and joy. For many people, it was time for a crack-up, time to blow their tops, to blast off into the ozone. Christmas was a time for crazies.

Nobody thought Dr. Juan Castillo was going to go crazy. In addition to Spanish and English, the middle-aged psychiatrist spoke passable Yiddish and Italian. He was the one who could usually calm down a psycho, get him responding in a more or less rational way. Dr. Juan Castillo was the heart-of-gold staffer others at Bellevue went to see when the job pressures were squeezing them because he was one easy guy to talk to.

Dr. Juan Castillo didn't have the clipboard he usually carried when he came into the emergency room. He had a machete and he

317

started swinging it.

Caroline Lynch had lived in Indianapolis all her life and was happy about the prospect of going somewhere else, even though she did not know where that would be. She was fifteen, mature and responsible, and, because tonight was Christmas Eve, the Hansens were paying her two dollars and fifty cents an hour to baby-sit their three year old Eric. She was, of course, free to raid the refrigerator, to take anything she wanted.

She didn't bother with the refrigerator. She went to Mr. Hansen's tool box and took out a hammer and pounded Eric Hansen's head to a pulp.

The Hansens had told her she might use the telephone just as long as she didn't tie it up too long. Her call to another Stranger took only a minute and he came and got her and they drove west, away from Indiana.

His last name was Friday but he was not a sergeant, just a uniformed patrolman with the Los Angeles Police Department, and his first name was Emil, and not Joe, but that didn't lessen at all the amount of bullshit he had to put up with:

"Dum-de-dum-dum," when he stepped into the locker-room, a gang of idiots with the theme from *Dragnet*.

Or stopping a motorist for speeding and, "Is your badge number 714?"

Tonight, though Emil Friday had more on his mind than the grief he had because of his name. It was Christmas Eve and, in his